RULES OF THE GAME

Joanna could hardly believe she was hearing Nicholas declare, "Rest assured that I shall do the honorable thing. I will take you to my sister's house, not far from Bath, where we shall be married by special license within the week."

True, Joanna realized that Nicholas's proposal came from duty rather than desire. She knew that he could easily have any one of the most enticing enchantresses in the ton. She could not deny that she would be taking most unfair advantage of him to trap him into wedlock.

On the other hand, as both a soldier and man of the world, Nicholas would be the first to admit that all was fair in love as in war. . . .

CHARLOTTE LOUISE DOLAN attended Eastern Illinois University and earned a master's degree in German from Middlebury College. She has lived throughout the United States and in Canada, Taiwan, Germany, and the Soviet Union. She is the mother of three children and currently makes her home in Idaho Falls, Idaho.

The Resolute Runaway

Charlotte Louise Dolan

SIGNET
Published by the Penguin Group
Penguin Books USA Inc., 375 Hudson Street,
New York, New York, 10014, U.S.A.
Penguin Books Ltd, 27 Wrights Lane, London W8 5TZ, England
Penguin Books Australia Ltd, Ringwood, Victoria, Australia
Penguin Books Canada Ltd, 10 Alcorn Avenue, Toronto, Ontario, Canada M4V 3B2
Penguin Books (N.Z.) Ltd, 182-190 Wairau Road,
Auckland 10, New Zealand

Penguin Books Ltd, Registered Offices:
Harmondsworth, Middlesex, England

First published by Signet, an imprint of New American Library,
a division of Penguin Books USA Inc.

First Printing, February, 1992

10 9 8 7 6 5 4 3 2 1

PRINTED IN THE UNITED STATES OF AMERICA

This book is dedicated to
my aunt,
Marjorie Enid Walker Mason,
who introduced me to my ancestors,
who in turn gave me a love for history
on a personal level.

I wish to thank Joyce Ziegler and Mary Jo Rodgers for their advice about colors for my heroine. I also wish to thank fellow writers Karen Finnigan and Dee Hendrickson for their contributions of time and information.

1

Joanna Pettigrew set down the heavily laden basket, which had surely doubled its weight in the mile she had trudged from the village. It was such a relief to straighten her back and flex her arms that she yielded to the temptation to sit down and rest for a moment on the grassy verge in the shade provided by a single oak tree.

She sighed tiredly. It was all Napoleon's fault.

If it were not for Bonaparte and his dreams of glory for France, her father would not have been killed at the Battle of Trafalgar, and her family would not have been forced to accept the charity of Uncle Nehemiah Alderthorpe, whose parsimonious ways had contributed directly to her mother's death from pneumonia two years later.

Joanna's thoughts followed a familiar path, which over the years had become a veritable litany of condemnation for the little corporal who had crowned himself Emperor of France.

If Napoleon had not invaded Spain, her older brother would have kept his promise to her that the two of them would set up their own household. But instead, on his eighteenth birthday, Mark had thought it best to spend every penny of their meager inheritance to purchase a commission, and he had immediately been posted to Portugal.

As soon as Napoleon was defeated, Mark had assured her over and over in each of his infrequent letters, he would make a home for her in London, where his friendships with fellow officers would guarantee him a plum of a civil-service position. He would, he had promised, definitely be home in time for her eighteenth birthday, which was in October last.

But thanks to Napoleon's gluttony in swallowing up large chunks of Europe, even in defeat the Corsican upstart, as her uncle always referred to him, had continued to ruin her life. Instead of Mark coming home as promised, he had gone to Vienna as part of the English delegation—a very minor part, to be sure, but still it had been too good an opportunity to miss, since his experience there would give him a head start in his career.

She had hoped to see him before Christmas, but the peace talks in Vienna had dragged on and the yuletide season had come and gone, and nothing had arrived from Vienna but a letter from Mark, giving his word as an officer in His Majesty's service, that he would be home by Easter. As a consolation he had offered her the unbelievable news that having met Lord This and Lady That, it was not outside the bounds of possibility that he would be able to procure several invitations for the two of them to attend some of the more modest entertainments during the London Season.

Joanna leaned back against the trunk of the tree and stared out across the valley. It was a beautiful day in early May, the sky was blue, the clouds were white and fluffy, and with only a little imagination she could see castles and dragons and giants floating above the rolling hills in a constantly changing panorama.

None of the cloud fantasies were more impossible than the dreams that letter had inspired: dreams of being in London with her brother tall and straight beside her, handsome in his scarlet regimentals; dreams of herself wearing a beautiful silver dress, dancing the night away in the arms of a handsome lord who would cast his heart at her feet. Such foolish dreams.

She had not, of course, related her brother's plans to her aunt and uncle, whose Christian charity was but a thin veneer over their greedy desire to utilize her services as an unpaid servant, at their beck and call from first cock's crow until long after the sun had set.

Joanna had told no one about London except Belinda Dillon, her best and indeed her only friend. Belinda had been so enraptured with the idea of having a companion that she had coaxed her parents into formally inviting Mark and Joanna to stay with them in the elegant town house they had hired for the Season.

But it was not to be. In Austria the diplomats had continued to intrigue and argue and bargain and debate endlessly, while one month of winter followed another, and Joanna had received no further word from her brother until the end of February, when a letter had come from Vienna explaining that as much as he hated disappointing her once again, he could not leave his position until the peace talks were concluded, or he would lose all his chance of patronage.

So Belinda and her parents had departed for London and Joanna had been left behind, with nothing to look forward to except, perhaps, the Little Season in the fall, which might be more auspicious anyway, because that would give her brother all summer to become established in London, or so Mark assured her.

She had scarcely repaired and rearranged her dreams, when in March Napoleon had once again interfered with her plans by escaping from the island of Elba. To Joanna's amazement and horror, not only had the French foot soldiers flocked to him once again, but even the generals had thrown down the fleur-de-lis of the Bourbons and picked up the tricolor of their emperor.

After six months of delay and postponements, Mark had finally left Vienna, but not to come home. He was now in Belgium, where the allied armies were gathering under the supreme command of the Duke of Wellington. Surely this time, with all of Europe united against him, Napoleon would be destroyed and her brother could finally redeem all the promises he had made her.

Joanna's eyes drifted shut and she slid effortlessly into dreams of her brother's homecoming . . . .

Something tickled her nose, and she woke up with a sneeze. Opening her eyes, she decided she must still be dreaming, because beside her a dainty mare shifted its feet, and leaning down from its back was Belinda. She was dressed in a beautiful gold velvet riding habit, and her chestnut tresses exactly matched the flowing mane and tail of her mount. In her hand was her riding crop, which had evidently been the cause of the sneeze. Joanna blinked several times, but the vision refused to dissolve.

"I vow, I do not know how you can sleep at such a time. I have the most exciting news. You will never imagine."

"You are getting married. Oh, Belinda, who is he? An earl? A duke?"

"Do not be a goose. I have no intention of tying myself down to one man, not for many years and years. It is ever so much more fun to have suitors by the score. No, what I have to tell you is even better than marriage. My parents have agreed to take me to the Continent. London is almost devoid of company now. All the really important people are gathering in Brussels, where they are having elegant parties every evening and where I am sure dozens of handsome young officers are just waiting to fall at my feet." She giggled mischievously.

Rising quickly to her feet, Joanna reached up to clasp her friend's hand. "Oh, please, you must take a message to my brother for me."

To her surprise, Belinda shook her head and pouted. "No, I absolutely refuse to do that." Her sulky look lasted only a moment before delightful dimples once more peeked out. "Because the best part I have not even old you yet. My parents have agreed you should come with us. There, what do you think of that? I was just on my way to your uncle's house to invite you when I spotted you sleeping here by the side of the road like a veritable Gypsy. Really, my dear, it is not at all the thing to do."

Joanna's heart, which had leapt at the idea of seeing her brother again after all the lonely years, plummeted at the mention of her uncle.

"What is wrong? Do you not wish to go to Brussels with us? I thought it would be a treat for you."

"Of course I want to go with you, but my uncle will never give his permission."

"Oh, pooh, as if that mattered. The worst he can do is say no. After all, he cannot very well *beat* you just for asking."

Belinda laughed merrily, but it was all Joanna could do to force a smile. Her uncle *could* beat her, and very well indeed. Much more efficiently than Aunt Zerelda, whose arm usually tired after only a few strokes of the birch.

"Your problem, Joanna, is that you are not resolute. Simply tell the old grouch you are going; do not even ask him if you may. Run away if you have to. I need only inform my parents that your uncle has given his permission, and by the time they find out otherwise, if indeed they ever do, we shall be together in Belgium, and they cannot possibly send you back to England alone. So you see, there is nothing at all to stop you. Do say you will come. You do want to, do you not? We are leaving this very afternoon, so you must hurry and make up your mind. There is no time for shilly-shallying."

"I am a-f-fraid"—Joanna stumbled over the words but forced herself to say what she knew had to be said—"that it would be b-better for me to remain here. If there were time to write and get my brother's permission, it would be different, but—"

Belinda's mood, which was always rather volatile, shifted immediately when she realized she was not going to get her own way, and it was with a very cross voice that she had the last word. "I dislike arguing. If you wish to go with us, then be at my house by two of the clock, or I shall simply go without you. And if you do not come with me, I do not think I will even speak to your brother when I am in Brussels because I will be very angry with you for being such a coward."

With that threat she struck the mare sharply with her riding crop and galloped away, leaving Joanna choking in the cloud of dust raised by the horse's hooves.

It was indeed fortunate that her dress was dun-colored, she thought, else she would earn a scold from her aunt for being so disheveled.

Wearily she picked up the heavy basket and trudged on down the lane, her thoughts determinedly toying with the possibility of seeing her brother again.

The *impossibility*, she tried to insist to herself, but no

matter what stratagems she employed, she could not dispel the image of her brother's face, his smile welcoming her, his arms holding her safely . . .

Safe . . . ah, that was the problem. It was all very well for Belinda to go careening off to Brussels on the shortest of notice, because she would be in the company of a fond mother and a doting father. But for Joanna to do such a thing would be foolhardy in the extreme. Anything might go wrong, and then where would she be?

She might arrive in the Belgian capital only to find her brother had been posted back to Vienna. Even worse, knowing Mark's opinion of officers who let their womenfolk follow the drum, he might be angry with her for not waiting patiently in England for his return.

And there was no deluding herself that her aunt and uncle would give her permission to go off on a pleasure trip, much less welcome her back with open arms should something go amiss.

Joanna turned through the gate and paused to stare up the short drive that led to her uncle's residence. Somber and still, it did nothing to welcome her, nor would a stranded traveler see anything about the smallish manor house that would induce him to believe he might find aid and assistance within its walls.

No, if she left her uncle's protection, she could never return, and she was too much the coward to take such an enormous risk.

For a moment she wished with all her heart that she had just the tiniest portion of her friend's courage, but she had not, and that was that.

Skirting the main entrance, Joanna lugged the basket directly to the side door and into the kitchen. With an effort she hoisted it up onto the plank table, then realized with dismay that she was the center of attention.

Mr. Hagers, the butler, was staring at her, his gaze shuttered; Polly and Patsy, the two maids, were slyly watching her out of the corners of their eyes; and Joseph, the groom, who never missed an opportunity to brush up against her, snickered out loud. She felt heat flood her face, but she could do nothing to lessen her embarrassment.

Only Nan, the scullery maid, showed any sign of compassion when Mrs. Hagers, the cook, said in a rough voice, "You're two hours late, my girl. They've been wanting you in the parlor this hour or more."

Two hours! She could not have slept that long. She had paused on her return from the village only for a minute to rest her arms. Surely . . .

With startling clarity Joanna remembered that the cool shade she had sat down in had entirely vanished by the time Belinda found her. She was, indeed, very late, and she could only regret that her uncle was presently in residence and not off on one of his innumerable business trips. It was not that Aunt Zerelda was kinder, just that she was lazier and less inclined to exert herself, not even to chastise her niece properly.

But nothing would be gained by waiting. Even the slightest attempt to postpone the confrontation would merely increase her punishment. Her knees threatening to buckle under her and her stomach in revolt, Joanna made her way through the maze of dark hallways to the room preferred by her aunt. Scratching softly on the door, she received permission to enter.

Aunt Zerelda reached out one plump hand and selected a bonbon. "So, you have decided to return. I was sure that you had taken it into your head to run away with the butcher's brat." After inspecting the sweet carefully, she popped it into her mouth, then fastidiously wiped her fingers on a lace handkerchief.

"I must say, you look as if you have been dragged through a hedge backward," Uncle Nehemiah said crossly, and it seemed to Joanna as if she were already feeling the sting of his cane across her back.

"I . . . I was tired," she stammered without thinking. "The basket was heavy—"

"Silence," her uncle said without raising his voice. "What have we come to, that you dare attempt to excuse your errant behavior, you ungrateful gel?"

Remembering too late that meekness was her only defense, Joanna folded her hands tightly together and bent her head in submission.

"Come here and sit down, my child," her aunt said calmly.

Joanna looked up in amazement. This was totally out of character for her aunt, who usually delayed only until the exact number of lashes had been mutually decided upon before excusing herself.

"Are you waiting for a second invitation?" There was a touch of frost in her aunt's voice this time, and Joanna hurried to do as she was bidden.

"A letter has come for you, my dear," her aunt said, pulling an envelope out from between the cushions of the settee.

With a burst of joy, Joanna recognized the scrawling handwriting. "Oh, it's from Mark. He has written at last," she blurted out, forgetting entirely that she was in disgrace.

Instead of handing the missive to Joanna, Aunt Zerelda held it out of reach, then with a sly smile passed it to her husband, who turned it over and back, inspecting it as carefully as he would a counterfeit five-pound note.

"I fail to see any reason to reward unpunctuality," he finally announced dispassionately, and before Joanna could react, he cast her letter onto the small fire that her aunt kept burning year-round in the grate.

"No!" Joanna wailed, springing to her feet. "Oh, no—please, no!" Struggling past her uncle, she reached for the envelope, but just before she could touch it, the paper burst into flames, and she barely had time to jerk her hand away.

"I do not believe my ears," her uncle said, and for the first time in her life Joanna heard him raise his voice. "Do you have the impertinence to correct me? The audacity to tell me what I may and may not do in my own house?"

"Oh, you are wicked—wicked!" Whirling away from his hands, which were reaching out to catch her, Joanna raced out of the room and down the hallway to the massive front door.

"Stop!"

Her uncle's voice boomed behind her, and automatically she paused, her hand resting on the door latch.

"If you set one foot outside this house without my permission, which you do not have, then you will never be permitted entrance again. Do you understand?"

"I understand." Defiantly she opened the door, and an errant breeze slipped in to tug gently at her skirt.

"If you do not come back into the parlor this instant, then you are no longer part of my family, is that quite clear?" His voice echoed behind her back.

Joanna turned to look at him, but the light from the doorway did not quite reach where he stood in the shadowed hallway. It didn't matter. She knew what the expression on his face would be, but she no longer cared. She was angrier than she had ever been in her life, and her voice shook with the strength of her feelings. "Yes, you have made yourself perfectly clear." With no more hesitation, she turned away from him and stepped through the doorway.

Her anger carried her half the way to her friend's house, but then her footsteps lagged as the enormity of what she had done hit her. She had rushed away from the only place she could legitimately call home, taking not so much as a spare handkerchief with her, leaving all her possessions, meager as they were, behind her, where they would doubtless end their days on the rubbish heap behind the stables.

And she could not even blame her present predicament on Napoleon—she had gotten into this deplorable situation all by herself.

Suppose Belinda had exaggerated slightly, and her parents had not yet actually invited Joanna to accompany them? Suppose Belinda was still angry and had changed her mind about wanting a companion? Suppose the Dillons had already made their departure?

Joanna felt tears gather in the back of her eyes—tears caused not only by the cruel loss of her brother's letter but also by the knowledge that she was now completely alone in the world. And as everyone knew, the world showed no mercy to young female orphans such as herself.

She tried to console herself that at least she had one friend, but she failed to find comfort in the thought. Belinda was beautiful, Belinda was carelessly kind, Belinda was spoiled, but—most important—Belinda was fickle.

Shortly after Mr. Dillon had purchased Riverside Manor, only a year and a half previously, the two girls had met accidentally in the village, and Belinda had instantly decided that she and Joanna were destined to be the best of friends. And so it had turned out.

For Joanna it had been like a miracle, but in spite of her pleasure in having someone to talk to, she could not keep from noticing over the months that Belinda's passions, intense while they lasted, seldom were of long duration.

Her eyes blinded with tears at her own folly, Joanna could scarcely see where she was putting her feet, so when someone touched her arm, she leapt sideways with a shriek.

"I didn't mean to scare you, Miss Joanna, but I heard what happened. We all heard what happened. Such a to-do after you left, you can't imagine. Mr. Alderthorpe threw a bottle of his best brandy at old Hagers and almost beaned him on his noggin, and your aunt—Mrs. Alderthorpe, I should say—was taken with convulsions, and it took Hagers and Joseph and John Coachman to carry her up to her room. It was more entertaining than a raree-show, and I sorely hated to miss out on it, but I couldn't waste my chance to sneak away whilst no one was watching me. I packed up all your things and brung them to you."

"Oh, Nan, you are a true friend." Joanna flung her arms around the scullery maid's shoulders and gave her a hug.

"Oh, no, miss, I couldn't never be a friend to someone as fine as you, but I'm not one to forget a kindness done, neither, and you've been the only one in that house what had a kind word and a smile for me, so I thought it only fitting that I should fetch your things for you. It ain't proper that you shouldn't have your papa's medals and the picture of your beautiful mama." Nan thrust a shawl-wrapped parcel into Joanna's hands. "But I'd best be getting back now, afore I'm missed. You're going to Riverside, I s'pose."

"Yes, but we are leaving at once for Belgium. My brother is in Brussels, and I will be joining him there."

"Ah, well, and that's probably all for the best, then." Nan turned away and hurried down the road, and though Joanna watched, the other girl did not look back and wave good-bye.

Once again Joanna was alone, but at least she had her nightshift and a change of clothing with her. In a more cheerful frame of mind, she walked as quickly as possible, reminding herself that she'd had years of practice at being agreeable, and Belinda could not possibly be as hard to suit as Aunt Zerelda was.

"Joanna! I have asked you three times now what you think of this gold shawl. I wish you would pay better attention, or we will never get finished with our shopping."

"I am truly sorry, Belinda. I was thinking about my brother. Do you suppose we could stop by his quarters on our way back to the hotel? I have learned his direction."

Belinda grimaced, then adjusted her smile. "I am afraid we could not possibly do that today, else I shall not have time to rest for the ball the Craigmonts are giving this evening. Now, pray tell me what you think of this shawl. It is such a bargain, barely half what one would expect to pay in London. I declare, my idea for us to come to Brussels has turned out even better than I had anticipated."

With difficulty Joanna focused her attention on the article her friend was displaying for her inspection. "It looks exactly like the gold one you already have," she said finally, having long ago run out of flattering compliments for Belinda's superb taste in folderols.

"No, no, mine has fringe that is rather too short, whereas this one has quite a long fringe, which is tied in the most cunning manner." Belinda draped the shawl about her shoulders and turned this way and that, impatiently awaiting Joanna's approval.

Joanna dutifully managed to work up a proper admiration for the shawl. "It does look most becoming on you." At least she was not expected to carry the parcels Belinda had spent the last three hours acquiring. A footman following at a respectful distance did that.

And Belinda was not the least bit mean, Joanna had to give

her that credit. No one could deny that Belinda was generous—but only when it was convenient to her. She was not one to put herself out to help another, and in her own way, Belinda was proving to be as inflexible as Aunt Zerelda. They had been in Brussels three days now—three whole days. And Belinda had still not found the time to accompany her to see Mark, nor had Belinda been willing to let her go by herself.

No, Joanna must rest when Belinda was tired, eat when Belinda was hungry, and most of all, spend hours each day dancing attendance on Belinda—admiring each outfit she tried on when she was deciding what to wear, praising each of Belinda's choices when they went shopping . . . and shopping . . . and shopping.

The only time Joanna had to herself was when Belinda and her parents were out for the evening, and Joanna could not—she simply could *not*—wander around Brussels alone at night trying to find her brother.

"Perhaps we could send a footman with a note?" she said out loud.

"Whatever are you talking about?"

Joanna realized Belinda was staring at her in complete astonishment. "My brother. Perhaps we could send a footman with a note to let him know I am here, and then he could visit me in our hotel."

Belinda broke into a peal of laughter, which had the heads of various young officers turning in her direction, a fact which Joanna knew her friend was well aware of. "Oh, my dear, you are too droll. I asked you if you thought these ribbons would do for my copper sarcenet, and you started talking about your brother again. Really, my dear, you are becoming too tedious."

Her smile should have taken the sting out of her words, but there had been so many little cutting remarks, and the smiles were no longer enough to prevent Joanna from feeling the sharp edge of Belinda's tongue.

* * *

"She is beautiful, I will give you that. But what chance do you have with the chit? Her father is rich as Croesus, and her mother is connected to all the best families. Every officer I know is already scrambling to get an introduction to her."

Nicholas Goldsborough clapped his hand on his friend's shoulder, but his attention stayed focused on the vision of delight who had just emerged from the milliner's shop. "Ah, but I have succeeded where others have failed. The Craigmonts introduced me to her last evening, and I even secured a waltz with the young lady. She dances like a dream, by the way, but be warned, if you attempt to cut me out, I shall definitely send my seconds to call on yours."

"Does this mean you refuse to introduce me?"

"No, no, I shall be happy to do the honors, but kindly keep in mind that your job is to distract the companion so that I may have a few minutes to converse alone with the beautiful Belinda."

"Her companion? I had not noticed . . . Good God!"

Nicholas pulled his gaze away from his adored one long enough to see his friend was white as a sheet. "What's wrong?"

But Mark was already moving toward the two young ladies. To Nicholas's surprise, he ignored the incomparable Miss Dillon and went directly to the dowdy little miss standing behind her.

She was not at all in his friend's usual style, Nicholas thought as he followed. Several inches shorter than the incomparable Miss Dillon, the girl had black hair, which was scraped back into a knot at her nape, her dress was a faded brown and obviously designed for someone considerably larger, and her complexion was sallow, almost jaundiced. All in all, Nicholas could see nothing about her to attract his friend's discerning eye, but there was no doubt that Mark was so overcome he could not even speak.

As inexplicable as his friend's behavior was, Nicholas was not prepared to waste this opportunity. "Good afternoon, Miss Dillon. I am pleased to have this opportunity to renew my acquaintance."

"Captain . . . Captain . . ."

"Goldsborough," he said smoothly. "A friend of the Craigmonts'."

"Ah, yes, we danced the waltz. How could I have forgotten?" Belinda smiled at him, and her dimples peeked out, and Nicholas felt himself falling deeper under her spell.

Joanna was ready to die of embarrassment, and all Belinda could do was flirt with the flaxen-haired officer. Why could she not also bat her eyelashes in the direction of the black-haired captain who was staring at Joanna as if she had grown a second head? She could feel herself blushing at the unexpected and unwelcome attention.

"Joanna?"

The stranger's low voice caused her to look up directly at his face for the first time. His shoulders had broadened, and he wore a dashing mustache, but his eyes—his eyes were exactly as she remembered them.

"Mark . . . oh, Mark . . ." She cast herself into her brother's arms and felt herself safe for the first time since she had run away from her uncle's house.

2

Joanna could not understand Belinda's delight in having scores of suitors. Not that there was actually a score of men clustering around Belinda, nor even a round dozen. Today Joanna could count only nine men vying for her friend's attention and impeding what should have been a pleasant promenade along the ramparts above the park.

The fact that they were all treating Joanna as if she were invisible bothered her not a whit. Standing a few feet away from the circle of men at present surrounding her friend, Joanna used the opportunity to evaluate them with a critical eye, which would doubtless have amazed them, had they been able to read her mind.

Eight of them were not worth passing the time of day with. One had a laugh like a horse, the second had a protuberant nose and a receding chin, another was incredibly handsome but had not two thoughts to rub together, and the rest vied with each other for the honor of being most nondescript. None of them added to Belinda's consequence, at least not in Joanna's opinion. Even the fancy uniforms on six of them were not enough to start young girls' hearts fluttering.

Only the ninth man, Captain Nicholas Goldsborough, had not a single flaw. He was handsome without being pretty, intelligent without being prosy, witty without being cruel—in every way he was perfection. A score of suitors like Captain Goldsborough—now, that would be something to see!

Given his lack of true competition, Joanna was all the more puzzled that Belinda did not single him out, that she did not direct all her attention, all her smiles, all her gurgling laughs toward Captain Goldsborough, and allow the rest of her suitors to retire disheartened from the lists.

Joanna, on the other hand, was not that indiscriminate. She was not going to waste her opportunity to savor every moment of the captain's presence. She had no intention of dividing her notice among all of her friend's suitors, nor had she any inclination to admire the view of Brussels laid out so neatly below them.

Instead, she planned to use her time wisely to store up memories of the way Captain Goldsborough's shoulders filled out his uniform to perfection, of the way the sun turned his blond hair to sparkling gold. She would treasure forever the smiles he bestowed so readily on others. She would never forget his blue eyes . . . which were now looking directly at her. Oh, my! For a moment she thought her heart had stopped beating, but then it resumed pounding in her chest.

As if her thoughts had captured his attention, he eased himself out of the group of men and approached her where she was standing a bit apart. With an unfamiliar tightness in her throat, she glanced up, then down, afraid suddenly to meet his eyes.

Out of the corner of her eye she was aware of him drawing nearer, and she felt as if a god had suddenly descended from Mount Olympus—Apollo, the sun god, to be precise. Captain Goldsborough, by his very proximity to her, was sending intense heat through her body, and she could feel it rising to her face, betraying her thoughts.

"Good afternoon, Miss Pettigrew. Your brother asked me to make his excuses. His fluency with languages has made his presence necessary at a meeting between the Prince of Orange and one of the Austrian generals. I believe"—and here he paused, and she looked up to see him smiling down at her—"that Mark has received private instructions to moderate the prince's language in translation. Last week, if the stories circulating in Brussels are correct, the prince managed to offend one Danish general, two Prussian colonels, and even several of his own officers. With Napoleon so close at hand, Wellington is not eager to lose the services of any of his coalition forces at this time."

There was such kindness in the captain's eyes that Joanna felt her shyness melt away, and although she had never before had occasion to converse with an eligible young man, she now found it was the easiest thing imaginable to stand talking with him.

"How is it that the Prince of Orange needs an interpreter? German is so similar to Dutch, one would think he could at least understand the spoken word, even if he cannot converse fluently in the language."

"Ah, there is the rub. Slender Billy was educated in England and can scarcely make himself understood in his mother tongue. But come, there is no point in our standing here like this. Let us seat ourselves in comfort on that bench, since it would appear that your companion is well-occupied."

He took her arm to lead her to the stone bench, which was but a few steps away. He was only being polite, she reminded herself, but still she could not control the way her heart skipped a beat and her blood began to heat at his touch.

"As a friend of your brother's, I hope I may ask you a favor."

For a moment Joanna's mind raced as fast as her heart, casting about for some way she might be able to help such a godlike man, who must surely be able to do anything and everything he chose. What on earth could he want of her?

"Perhaps I presume too much," he added with a rueful smile.

Realizing she had delayed too long in answering him, she hastened to reply, "But of course I shall be happy to help you in any way that lies within my power." She sounded too eager, even to her own ears, so she tried to make her voice more casual when she added, "Since you are, after all, one of my brother's best friends."

Was he going to ask permission to call on her? Or take her driving in the park? Or perhaps he was going to suggest a pleasant outing or an excursion into the surrounding countryside?

"I am hoping you can tell me which ball your friend Miss Dillon will be attending this evening and what color dress she will be wearing."

The years of experience with concealing her thoughts from her aunt and uncle now stood Joanna in good stead, and she carefully hid her disappointment from the captain. It would not do at all for him to discover how foolishly she had been enjoying his attention, and how she had mistakenly thought he had even the slightest interest in her.

For a moment she looked down at her hands, which were twisting her handkerchief into a knot. Then, affixing what she hoped was a casual and friendly smile to her face, she glanced up and gazed directly into the captain's blue eyes.

"I believe the Dillons are planning to attend the rout party given by Lord and Lady Wilberford, and Belinda is intending to wear her orange silk gown with bronze ribbons, although I cannot guarantee that she will not change her mind between now and then and choose to wear another dress."

"A lady's prerogative, to be sure. But I shall take my chances and see if I cannot find a suitable nosegay that will not clash with those colors. And what of the gown you plan to wear this evening? Might I also know its color?"

Even while he asked, his eyes strayed back to Belinda, and Joanna could not pretend he was asking for any other reason than common courtesy. He was a true gentleman . . . but that was not the same thing as a suitor. In any case, he could not be considered one of *her* suitors.

"I . . . I had not planned to attend," she stammered.

"Not attend? Does Miss Dillon then plan to keep you hidden away at home while she enjoys herself at the parties?" The captain looked at her in astonishment, the warmth gone from his blue eyes.

For a moment, Joanna was tempted to destroy forever the captain's high regard for her friend, but almost instantly she retreated from that thought. She was not a petty person who could let him be unjustly critical of Belinda just so that he might turn to . . .

What a ridiculous idea! Even if she destroyed forever his interest in Belinda, he would not transfer his attention to a drab little nobody like her. If he ceased to pay court to her friend, he would also vanish completely out of her own life.

Thus Joanna did not even have the consolation that she

was doing the honorable thing when she hastened to correct him. "Oh, no, you misunderstand. She has, of course, always begged me to accompany her, and has even offered me some of her own gowns to wear, but I . . . I . . ." Joanna hesitated, suddenly realizing that the truth would not do.

She could not explain to Captain Goldsborough, who had shown great bravery when facing French guns, that she was too cowardly to face a ballroom full of strangers. "I have been waiting until my brother has an evening free to escort me," she concluded lamely.

It was not precisely a lie, but it was definitely phrased in a way guaranteed to conceal the whole truth. Not wishing Mark to find her presence in Brussels a handicap to his budding career, she had, in fact, never asked her brother to accompany her to any of the evening festivities, nor even suggested that she was not perfectly content missing out on all the parties that Belinda enjoyed so much.

"If that is the case, it is easily enough remedied. You must allow me to stand in Mark's stead. I have a sister of my own, you know, so I am quite adept at playing the role of brother. You may count on me to see that your dance card is kept filled and that no cads and bounders are allowed to do aught to distress you. So say you will attend this evening."

He was inviting her to a ball, albeit as a surrogate brother, but still she could not hold back a feeling of delightful anticipation. "I promise," she replied, smiling up at him. With his help, she could face the prospect of a ballroom full of strangers, if not with equanimity, then at least without abject fear.

"Oh, I cannot tell you how glad I am you decided to come with us this evening." Belinda reached over and patted Joanna's hand. "I have missed having a friend to talk over the parties with."

The Dillons' carriage rumbled over the cobblestones, and Joanna, who was wearing a hurriedly taken-in olive-green dress of Belinda's, was not at all sure she was glad. With every bump of the wheels her heart lurched, and by the time the coachman pulled up in front of the house rented by Lord and Lady Wilberford, she wanted nothing more than to remain cowering in the dark corner of the carriage where no one could see her.

Only the thought of her promise to Captain Goldsborough enabled her to release her grip on the carriage strap and allow Mr. Dillon to hand her down.

The street in front of the house was jammed with carriages and the sidewalk was overcrowded with people waiting to enter, and Joanna instinctively shrank back. The ladies were so elegant, and the gentlemen loomed so terrifyingly tall above her. Whatever had made her think she belonged here?

Beside her a woman in a shockingly low-cut scarlet gown was clinging to the arm of a man in a German uniform, and ahead of her a party of five young English cavalry officers were loudly discussing the merits of their favorite horses. No one appeared to have noticed Joanna, for which she could only be thankful.

"Oh, look, up ahead, I do believe that is Lord Uxbridge. Do you suppose the duke will be in attendance this evening?"

Joanna was about to confess that she had not the slightest idea what Wellington's plans for the evening were, when Mrs. Dillon answered calmly, "I have heard he is expected to drop in later, after the opera."

Relentlessly propelled by the flow of the crowd, Joanna moved forward, finally entering the residence, then slowly being squeezed up the stairs. Her immediate fear was that she might be trampled in the crush. But even that seemed a preferable fate to the more likely prospect of being separated from the others in her party and left to face the masses of strangers all alone.

Once, when she had been four or five, her father had taken them to a fair, as a special treat. She had loved it, until somehow she had gotten separated from her family. Surrounded by large strangers, she had been terrified for what seemed like an eternity, before her brother had found her and scooped her up in his arms and told her not to be such a baby.

Just such a feeling of terror possessed her now, and she would have given anything to reach out and grab Belinda's hand and cling to it . . . except that Joanna was not a small child, and she could not behave in such a childish way, no matter how comforting it would be.

To add to her distress, the heat on the stairs was formidable, and the mingled scents of hot wax, sweat, and various musky perfumes almost gagged her. It was only after they reached the ballroom that she felt able to take a deep breath.

At once she was awestruck. Never in her life had she seen anything to compare to the view that met her eyes—the monstrous porcelain chandeliers hung with lusters, the colorful uniforms on the men, the diamond- and ruby-encrusted women, the orchestra playing the most beautiful music Joanna had ever heard—it was all overwhelming to her senses. Nothing she had previously experienced had prepared her for this spectacle.

Beside her Mrs. Dillon raised her lorgnette and coolly surveyed the crowded room. "Rather flat, I am afraid. I suspect we would have done better to have gone to the musical at the Sedgwicks', except that German sopranos always give me such a headache."

Pushing her way through the masses of people like a man-of-war, Mrs. Dillon led the way to a bank of gilt chairs where the chaperones were sitting with their young charges. After she and the two girls were duly seated, Mr. Dillon announced his intention of finding the card room and left them to their own devices.

"Are you not excited?" Belinda leaned over and whispered in Joanna's ear. "Your very first dance."

"I must confess that 'terrified' more nearly describes my emotions," Joanna whispered back, trying her best to keep her voice light, as if she were making a joke.

"Coward," Belinda said with a gurgling laugh. "You have nothing to be afraid of. I shall see to it that you have a partner for every dance. Oh, lah, here come my devoted admirers." Releasing Joanna's arm, she began fluttering her fan and looking demure.

In minutes they were surrounded by a growing crowd composed mostly of young officers, all jockeying for position as near as possible to Belinda. One of them stumbled against Joanna's chair, and for a minute she was fearful she might end up with an ensign on her lap.

Then, to her total horror she heard Belinda say in a loud voice, "I have decided that anyone wishing to dance with me this evening must also sign my friend's card."

Dead silence followed Belinda's tactless remark; then everyone—officers, chaperones, and the other young girls in the immediate vicinity—turned to stare at Joanna. It seemed an eternity, but was probably only a few seconds before general conversation resumed, and there was a rush to sign her card.

Her embarrassment at Belinda's public announcement was so great, Joanna was unable to meet the eyes of any of the young men who one after the other were introduced to her. They politely, albeit hurriedly, solicited dances from her, and her mumbled acceptance was apparently adequate response.

In spite of the impressive number of names soon scrawled on her dance card, almost all her pleasure in the evening was gone, destroyed forever by Belinda, who had made it blatantly clear to everyone that Joanna was nothing more than an object of pity—a charity case, too plain to attract the slightest masculine attention.

After such an inauspicious beginning, what other disasters might the evening hold?

Her only consolation was the posy that Captain Goldsborough had sent to her—a mixture of yellow and white blossoms that were unfamiliar to her. Clutching it tightly to her breast, she silently prayed that somehow she might be rescued from the nightmare she now found herself in.

Then, as if her thoughts had conjured him up, a masculine form filled her line of vision, and Joanna looked up to see Captain Goldsborough smiling down at her.

"I hope you have saved a waltz for me."

Instantly her embarrassment and her fears receded. She was safe at last. "I am not sure which dances I have promised and which are still free." Looking down at her card, she saw that Belinda's admirers had written their names primarily beside the country dances, leaving the waltzes for the most part free. She smiled in relief and held out her card to the captain.

"Ah, the first waltz is to be mine. I am honored." He quickly scribbled his name down for the first and last waltzes, then introduced Lieutenant Walrond and Captain Fitzhugh, two other officers in her brother's regiment, who also signed their names. Joanna was well aware that Captain Goldsborough had undoubtedly coerced them into requesting dances, but she could only be glad he had not made it public knowledge the way Belinda had.

"I am happy to see that you are carrying my flowers," Captain Goldsborough said, his eyes straying to Belinda.

Feeling sympathy for his shattered hopes, Joanna was compelled to explain, although it was really not her place to do so, "Belinda received so many nosegays, and she could not wish to hurt anyone's feelings, so in the end she chose to carry the flowers provided by her father."

Captain Goldsborough's expression lightened a bit, and he politely discusssed the sights of Brussels with her until her first partner claimed her for a country dance.

"Sank you for za dance, Fräulein Pettigrew."

Allowing her partner, a rather fat German major who spoke surprisingly good, although heavily accented English, to relinquish her into the care of Mrs. Dillon, Joanna tried to convince herself that she was having a marvelous time. It was surprisingly hard to do.

"I believe this is my waltz, Miss Pettigrew."

Joanna was pulled out of her musings to see a young English officer bowing in front of her. Not remembering his name among so many she had been introduced to, she surreptitiously checked her dance card. "To be sure, Lieutenant Gryndle." She moved out onto the dance floor with him.

It was not that she disliked the dancing—she loved it and had discovered she was able to remember without difficulty the steps of the country dances Belinda had taught her back home in England. Nor did she have the slightest trouble following her partner's lead during the waltzes, although she still found it shocking to be held so close in a man's arms.

Unfortunately, no one appeared to notice how proficient she was. Even while dancing with her, her partners were not able to keep their eyes and their attention off Belinda. None of them so far, except of course for Captain Goldsborough, who was in all ways a perfect gentleman, had made even the slightest effort to engage Joanna in conversation.

Not that she could blame them. Who would not prefer to feast his eyes on her friend, whose brilliant good looks made not only Joanna but also every other young girl in the ballroom look drab in comparison, and whose gay laughter made even the most cynical chaperone smile?

Lost in thought as she was, Joanna was caught completely off-guard when her partner suddenly stopped dancing and pulled her behind some heavy velvet draperies and into his arms.

It happened so quickly, she was able to gasp out only a startled "Oh" before he pressed his lips against hers, squeezing her ribs so tightly he virtually cut off her breath.

Just as Joanna thought she must surely faint, Lieutenant Gryndle released her, and she staggered backward, gasping for breath.

The lieutenant's face seemed to be contorted with pain, and she realized someone was twisting his arm behind his back . . . .

To her dismay, Joanna was able even in the dim lighting of the little alcove to recognize that the man who had rescued her was Captain Goldsborough. What must he think of her, to have found her in such a compromising situation?

In a low voice he muttered something in the lieutenant's ear. Joanna could not make out the words, but whatever the captain said, it caused the blood to drain out of Lieutenant Gryndle's face. He started to reply to the captain, but another jerk on his arm cut off the excuse he was going to offer.

Moments later the captain released him, and without an apology or a backward look, the lieutenant fled through the curtains, leaving Joanna alone with the captain.

His expression was so fierce, for a moment she was almost

frightened of him, but his words immediately made it clear that he did not hold her to blame for what had happened.

"Are you all right?"

She tried to tell him she was, but she was shaking too much to speak, so she only nodded. He cursed under his breath, then put his arm around her shoulder. She leaned her head against his chest and tried desperately to calm the overrapid beating of her heart, which was not caused entirely by Lieutenant Gryndle's attack, but partly by Captain Goldsborough's masterful rescue.

It was, after all, very romantic to be saved by the man she most admired, just as if she were the heroine in a romantic novel.

"It is my fault," he said finally. "I had no idea that Gryndle would single you out for attention. Although he is of good family and is accepted everywhere, he has already acquired a rather unsavory reputation. He will not bother you again, of that you may be sure. And I shall let the others of his ilk know also that if they bother you in any way, they will have to answer to me."

Captain Goldsborough smiled down at her, and her heart, which had begun to slow down, again began to race.

"I promised you I would look after you like a brother, and so I shall do."

Like a brother. All the silly romantic notions fled out of Joanna's mind, and she was able to step away from Captain Goldsborough's arm and say quite matter-of-factly, "Thank you very much for your help, but I believe you had best return me to Mrs. Dillon now, before someone else decides to make use of this alcove and discovers us here."

She was quite proud of the way she projected a calmness she was actually far from feeling. She could only hope that no one would suspect anything was amiss.

There was more to looking after a young lady than seeing to it her dance card was filled, Nicholas realized. He shuddered inwardly at the nearness of the disaster he had just averted. Since he was the one responsible for Miss Pettigrew's presence at the dance, how could he ever have explained to her brother that while under his care her reputation had been sullied, or even completely destroyed?

He could only be thankful he had not had a partner for this dance, and so had happened to notice who Joanna's partner was. As soon as he had recognized Gryndle, Nicholas had started making his way around the ballroom toward the couple, halfway expecting the lieutenant to try something of this sort. He had arrived a scant minute too late, and he would forever regret that Miss Pettigrew had been subjected to such cavalier treatment.

As they reached their destination without further mishap, his companion released his arm and reseated herself at Mrs. Dillon's side. Nicholas searched Miss Pettigrew's face for signs of distress after her ordeal, but her expression was quite calm when she looked up at him and thanked him in a quiet voice.

"If I might borrow your dance card for a moment?" he requested, also keeping his voice low so that Mrs. Dillon and the other chaperones would not hear.

"Oh, yes," she murmured, thrusting it at him as if it burned her fingers.

A quick perusal revealed the name of another man he would never have allowed his own sister to dance with, and two more were questionable. Deciding it was better to err on the side of caution, he crossed off all three names and handed the card back.

"If you will allow me, I shall find you more suitable partners."

"Willingly," she said. "And I thank you again for your assistance."

He did not deserve her trusting smile, but he would see to it that he did not fail her again.

3

The moon was setting when Nicholas strode into the hotel that was doing temporary duty as a makeshift officers' club. As soon as the Dillons had departed the dance, taking Miss Pettigrew along with them, he had determined to seek out her brother and persuade him to take a more active interest in his sister's welfare.

But his friend was not sleeping in his quarters, nor was he engaged in any official duty. By dint of questioning, Nicholas had finally tracked him to this place.

The main room was low-ceilinged and smoke-filled. Those few officers who remained were sunken in half-stupors, the candles were guttering in their sockets, and the soft light filtering around the edges of the heavy curtains at the windows indicated that there remained at best two or three hours for sleep before their attendance would be required on the parade grounds.

Gazing around impatiently, Nicholas finally spotted his friend. In one corner, almost hidden by a keg of French brandy balanced precariously on four gilt chairs, Mark was still playing cards with an Austrian major, who appeared so far gone in his cups, it was unlikely he could even read the spots on the cards.

Just as Nicholas reached them, the major's head fell forward onto the table, and he began to snore loudly. Mark calmly stood up and began clearing the table of coins and banknotes, stuffing them carelessly into his pockets.

"Not a bad evening's work," he said cheerfully, his voice betraying only slight traces of brandy. "The estimable major whom you see before you was suffering from the twin delusions that he understands the intricacies of piquet and that he can hold his liquor. I believe I have corrected his misconceptions on both scores.''

Nicholas did not return the smile. He had intended to make it clear to his friend that his first responsibility ought to be to his sister and that he should be willing to give up his own preferred entertainment to accompany her to dances.

But now that the moment was at hand, Nicholas realized it was not the easiest thing to do, to question another man's way of handling family matters. A great deal of tact would be required.

Mark began buttoning his coat. Looking down at the sleeping major, he asked, ''Do you suppose he will remember how I have fleeced him? Or do you think the brandy has so befuddled his mind that tomorrow evening I can again entice him into playing with me?''

Recognizing his opportunity, Nicholas jumped in with both feet. ''It would be more to the point if you would accompany your sister to the Andervilles' ball tomorrow evening. I am sure she would be overjoyed to have your escort.''

''My sister?'' Mark stared at him in amazement.

''Yes, your sister. You do remember that you have a sister, don't you, and that she is here in Brussels?'' Nicholas's anger spilled over. So much for tact.

He turned to walk away, but Mark caught him by the shoulder and spun him back. ''You think I prefer to spend my time with conceited drunkards like the major rather than with my sister? You think I would not prefer to take Joanna riding in the park than to waste my time translating the fulsome compliments that all and sundry generals feel compelled to exchange? Do you think I wish to see my sister clad in her friend's cast-offs and living off some rich cit's charity?''

Nicholas shook off his friend's hand. ''Then why do you ignore her? Why do you not concern yourself more for her welfare?''

Nicholas was shocked and a little embarrassed by the naked emotion visible in his friend's eyes. Turning his head away, he pretended an interest in the playing cards that were spilled on the table.

"I have no choice," Mark said bitterly. "You have an estate to go home to; your brother-in-law is a duke, you have family, connections, money. I have nothing to fall back on, so I must forgo enjoying the present and look to the future, confound it."

His voice was becoming louder, and Nicholas realized they were in danger of rousing the few remaining officers from their alcoholic stupors. Taking his friend by the elbow, he led him out of the club and into the street.

"I cannot afford to pass up an opportunity, whether 'tis spending an evening fleecing an Austrian major or spending an afternoon running errands for one of our own officers," Pettigrew continued dispassionately as they walked in the direction of their lodging.

Then he stopped walking and turned to face Nicholas. "Do you understand? If it were not for Joanna, I could perhaps stay in the military, but I must provide her with a home, which I cannot do if I am sent from one posting to another or if I am put on half-pay. And I am not so foolish as to pretend she might someday attract a husband."

"Surely you are exaggerating the case. Granted, Joanna is rather plain, but there is nothing about her features which would cause someone to take her in disgust. Besides which, her generous spirit and sweetness of manner are quite appealing. In addition, I have found her pleasant to talk to, and I do not regret the time I have spent in her company."

"Men do not, however, marry women for their conversation, nor does sweetness compensate for lack of dowry. Men marry where they find beauty or wealth or powerful connections."

"On the other hand, consider this: I have a cousin about Joanna's age, who is more like a little sister to me. Dorie is quite pretty, she is an heiress, and now that Elizabeth, my sister, is the Duchess of Colthurst, Dorie can be said to be extremely well-connected. She would thus seem to be a perfect candidate for marriage, but she is such a madcap, she would make a most uncomfortable wife, and I pity the man who ends up with her. Although now that I think on it, if she were a man, I would not hesitate to have her serve in any regiment I commanded."

"That is all very well and good, but let us be realistic. My sister has many good qualities and I love her dearly, and if the world were a logical place, she would marry a man who loves her and raise a houseful of children. But surely you have noticed that men are rarely thinking logically when they propose marriage—or else they are thinking quite logically of land and estates and government consols."

Since his sister had once said virtually the same thing to him, Nicholas could not dispute Mark's analysis of Joanna's chances.

"Your cousin will doubtless receive innumerable offers," Mark continued, "whereas my sister would not attract the least attention, even were I able to finance a Season for her. No, in spite of what you think of me, I have long ago accepted my responsibility where she is concerned. It is unfortunate, really, the way things turned out, because she was a very pretty child when she was younger."

At Nicholas's urging, they started walking again, picking their way carefully along the cobblestoned streets.

"My only chance," Mark said, "since I have no university degree, is to acquire a civil-service position, and to that end I must devote my time here to making contacts. So far I have several promises." He laughed, and Nicholas could hear the self-mockery in his friend's voice. "No, I delude myself. I have received no promises at all, only vague half-promises, which may be remembered or may already be forgotten. And there is so little time. Once Napoleon is defeated and the army is demobilized, there will be hundreds of other half-pay officers, all competing for the few positions available in London."

They walked in silence for a few minutes, and Nicholas cursed himself for having been so blind to his friend's dilemma. "I can speak to my brother-in-law. If Darius knows of any position, I am sure he will be happy to recommend you. After all, it is not as though he would be recommending someone sight unseen. You served as an ensign under him in the peninsular campaign, before he became a duke."

The offer failed to produce even a smile on his friend's face, much less a word of thanks. "Well?" Nicholas asked, feeling a little irate at the lack of response.

"Well, what? Do you know how many times I have gotten my hopes up at a similar remark? If, if, if—that is all I ever hear. *If* something opens up, *if* Lord So-and-so is agreeable, *if* the position is not already filled. Can you guarantee that your brother-in-law will know of an opening? Bah, you are no different from the rest of them." Hunching his shoulders, Mark picked up his pace, as if trying to leave Nicholas behind.

Nicholas easily caught up with him. "No," he corrected, "I am not like all the rest. I will make you a promise that is not conditioned by any ifs."

Mark stopped in his tracks and turned to face him, but did not say a word.

"I give you my word of honor," Nicholas said, "that I will find you a good position when this campaign is over, and I shall not even qualify it by saying *if* we defeat Napoleon."

For the first time since the subject of Joanna had come up, Mark smiled. "Aye, and I've no doubt either on that score. Wellington will send that upstart corporal running back to Paris with his tail between his legs."

Dorinda Donnithorne stood looking out the window of Colthurst Hall. It was raining, raining, raining, and she was bored, bored, bored. If only she could find some way to persuade Cousin Elizabeth to let her go to Brussels, where Nicholas was with Wellington's army.

She heaved a mighty sigh, but there was no response behind her. Turning, she looked at Elizabeth, who was embroidering rosebuds on a tiny dress for her daughter.

"It is no use your standing there sighing, Dorie," Elizabeth said without looking up from her needlework. "You are not going to get my permission to go to Brussels, no matter how bored you are here with us. Your mother would positively expire of the vapors if I let you go there. And even if you persuaded me, there is still my husband, and I doubt even I could convince Darius of the wisdom of such a course of action. I know it is small consolation, but Gorbion says the rain will end by evening and tomorrow will be fair."

"Oh, Beth, 'tis not you who are boring, and it is not the rain that I find so depressing." Dorie hurried to her cousin's side and sank down on her knees. "I love visiting you here at Colthurst Hall and playing with Louisa and the twins. But the days keep going by in the same way, with nothing to look forward to."

"You have only to endure another ten months of our company, and then you will be presented at court and have your Season."

"Oh, pooh, as if I care about that." Dorie stood up and began to pace around the room, feeling as restless as a caged fox. "I don't even *want* a Season in London. Do you think I have any interest in such things? I would gladly trade my entire Season for a chance to go to Belgium this week. Everyone is in Brussels now, simply everyone."

"And everyone will be in London next spring, so I fail to see why you are so set on going to a foreign country just so that you can attend dances and parties, which I am sure are no more exciting than the assemblies in Bath. Your mother has given her permission for you to attend them this fall, you know."

"But that is not the point. Oh, no one understands me. I should have been born a boy so that I could be a soldier like Nicholas. History is being made, perhaps even while we speak. When Wellington comes face-to-face with Napoleon, people will finally learn which one is the better general. And I don't want to be left out of the excitement. I want to be part of it. Oh, Beth, please help me persuade my mother to let me go with the Jamisons. They are leaving for the Continent the day after tomorrow, so there is still time to send them word. Please?"

Elizabeth laid her sewing in her lap and looked up at her. "I had not thought you so callous, that you would look forward with such glee to the slaughter of hundreds of young men. I can only hope you have not expressed such views to Darius, else you will have sunk yourself below reproach in his esteem."

Dorie felt the blood drain from her face. Hurrying across the room to her cousin, she cast herself on the floor, and clasped Elizabeth's hands in hers. "Oh, Beth, do forgive me. You know I am not truly hard-hearted or unfeeling, and I know that war is not the glorious, heroic affair that so many people think it is. I remember too well what it was like when we were fearful of finding Darius's or Nicholas's name on the casualty lists. But the battle will happen, no matter if I am there or here, and I would so much rather be there. Oh, can you not understand? I look at my future and see myself trapped in a marriage with a proper and eminently suitable young man who will doubtless bore me to distraction. I know it is my fate and the fate of all the young ladies of my position in society. But I cannot look forward to it the way they do. Oh, Beth, is it truly wicked of me to want a little adventure before I must settle down as a wife and mother?"

Looking up into her cousin's eyes, Dorie saw understanding and forgiveness, and with relief she laid her head down on Elizabeth's lap. "I should have been a boy," she repeated. "Then I could have been a soldier like Darius and Nicholas."

Elizabeth began to stroke her hair, and in spite of herself, Dorie felt some of the restlessness leave her.

"Someday, my dear, you will meet the right man, and even if he is proper and suitable, you will not find him boring."

"It is not as if I would be all alone with no family in Brussels," Dorie persisted. "Nicholas is there, and he can take care of me."

"Nicholas is too busy being a soldier to waste his time looking after a brainless chit like you," Elizabeth said with laughter in her voice.

"Brainless? Brainless?" Distracted by the insult, Dorie lifted her head. "If I have no brains, then how am I able to best Darius at chess? And piquet? And billiards? And I would be able to beat him at fencing if he would only consent to teach me to handle a foil, I know I could."

"There is nothing to stop you from asking him again. Perhaps you can change his mind. You may tell him I heartily recommend that he give you fencing lessons." Elizabeth prayed her husband would forgive her for suggesting such a thing, but she had reached the point, after two days of listening to the rain and to Dorie's entreaties, that she had to have a little peace and quiet herself. And if Dorie failed to persuade him, maybe she herself could convince her husband that Dorie was never going to fit into the common mold, so they might as well give her an outlet for her excess energy.

After her cousin left the room in search of Darius, Elizabeth did not immediately pick up her embroidery. Two worries had kept her awake on many a night recently. The first was, of course, concern for her brother's safety during the upcoming battle. The second was the question of Dorie's future husband.

What was needed was not only a man who would not bore Dorie to tears, but also one with enough strength and determination to keep her under some degree of control. Unfortunately, it had recently occurred to Elizabeth that if such a man were indeed to be found, he would most likely *not* be found in London, since he would doubtless find drawing rooms no more to his liking than Dorie did.

Alexander Mathers, Baron Glengarry, rolled the wool over the ewe's back and stood the sheep up, switching his attention to its head, where he quickly cleared its neck and right shoulder, then belly. "Wool away," he called a bare minute later. He was not the fastest shearer on the estate, but he was adept enough that his help was welcomed.

Young Jamie darted forward to retrieve the fleece, and the ewe was released to run bleating off to join her shorn sisters, who were huddled together as if embarrassed by their nakedness.

An unexpected hush momentarily settled over the group of men, and Alexander turned his head to see a man in Lowland garb picking his way down the path toward the sheep pen. Recognizing the man as one of his mother's footmen, Alexander swore softly to himself.

Then he deliberately turned his back and grabbed another sheep. Tucking its shoulders between his knees, he began to clear its belly.

"Excuse me," the stranger said, his voice proclaiming him English. "Can anyone here tell me where I might find Lord Glengarry? I have an urgent message for him from his mother."

Alexander did not slow the steady rhythm of his shears, but there was an unnatural stillness from the rest of the men, which should have been enough to arouse the footman's suspicions had he not been as obtuse as all the English.

Finally Walter Robertson replied, "His lordship is no' here at the moment, but if ye give us the message, we will do our best to pass it on."

"I am to tell him that his mother is deathly ill and requires his immediate attendance at her side."

For a moment Alexander felt stricken, and pain twisted deep in his chest, but before he could reveal his presence, a nasty suspicion reared its ugly head. Over the years his mother had become more devious in her attempts to entice him to Edinburgh. . . .

But surely she would not go so far as pretending to be on her deathbed. . . .

On the other hand, with each year that passed, she was becoming more determined to find him an English bride. It was just possible she was that treacherous.

After a long pause, during which he made no effort to respond to the messenger, Robertson spoke again. "Do ye no' have any other message from Edinburgh?"

"Just one from Mrs. McPherson, the cook. She requests that you send a pair of fat geese and three young goslings back with me if you have such to spare."

All the tension went out of Alexander immediately, and he resumed clipping the ewe. So his mother had two friends staying with her, complete with three marriageable daughters. With such an overabundance of candidates for his hand, he could see why she had tried such a desperate gamble. But pretending to be on her deathbed was going too far, and so he would tell her. But only after Mrs. McPherson sent word it was safe to go to Edinburgh.

Bless Mrs. McPherson. She was just as determined to see him wedded as his mother, but only to a proper Scottish lassie. Well, he had no intention of marrying any woman, be she Scottish or English, until he was much, much older.

There were too many salmon waiting to be hooked, too many stags ripe for the chase, too many willing lasses to be bedded. He was not ready at five-and-twenty to give up spending most of his days in the Highlands, not ready to dance attendance on a wife, who would, more than likely, whine and complain if he came home reeking of wool and sheep, or if he vanished for weeks at a time with his cronies.

Perhaps in ten years, when he was thirty-five, he would consider marrying to please his mother . . . or he might even wait fifteen or twenty years. There was no hurry. Granted, he must someday provide an heir, but he could see no reason to get leg-shackled in the near future, especially not to some thin-blooded English miss who would probably be terrified at the mere sight of a proper elkhound.

To be sure, his mother was English, but then, she was an exception.

"Mrs. McPherson says if you cannot send any right away, she can have them fetched in a day or two."

Alexander almost dropped his sheep in surprise. Surely Mrs. McPherson was not trying to tell him his mother was prepared to drag her friends up into the Highlands if he did not present himself on her doorstep?

"Wool away," he said in an unnaturally gruff voice, and Jamie darted forward to peer up at him anxiously. "The Western Isles," Alexander hissed.

The boy had the good sense to wait until he was well away from Alexander before he piped up, "Lord Glengarry has gone on a verrry long trip to the Western Isles."

Robertson immediately picked up his cue. "I am afraid he didna tell us which island he was going to, so it may take us a good while to track him down, but we shall do our best to deliver the message. We can only hope his lordship will arrive in time to bid his mother farewell."

Alexander risked a glance at the messenger and saw such a guilty look on the man's face, he knew for certain his mother was not suffering from anything more than a desire to acquire a daughter-in-law as English as she was.

Not that she would be put off long by a mere fib. With three prospective candidates on hand, he had better make haste to the islands in actuality, before she could come in person and catch him unawares.

Unlike the footman, she would be able to recognize him even when he was dressed in rough work clothes and standing in the middle of a herd of sheep whose bleatings were surprisingly reminiscent of the silly chattering of a gaggle of society misses.

The orchestra was playing a waltz, and Joanna sat beside Mrs. Dillon, watching Belinda dance with Captain Goldsborough.

"Do they not make a handsome couple?" Mrs. Dillon commented for the second time that evening. "He is so personable, so charming, and he has such address. It is too bad Captain Goldsborough has no title and his estate is no more than respectable. He is highly connected, to be sure. His brother-in-law is the Duke of Colthurst, and his cousin is married to Simon Bellgrave, whose wealth is unmatched."

Joanna murmured an automatic response.

Beside her Mrs. Dillon continued. "Sometimes I think we shall never find the perfect combination of title and wealth and good looks for my daughter. Still and all, if Belinda sets her heart on her captain, I am sure Mr. Dillon can arrange for some kind of title to be granted him. One has only to contribute enough to the proper causes, you know, and that kind of thing can be handled discreetly. To be sure, being the first man to bear a title is not as prestigious as being the seventh or the tenth or whatever, but still, I quite have my heart set on my dearest Belinda being the wife of a peer."

Mrs. Dillon continued speaking in much the same vein, until they were interrupted by a commotion at the entrance to the ballroom. Looking over to see what was occurring to attract so much attention, Joanna saw that several officers in uniform had entered and were surveying the crowded room. Something about their expressions made it clear to her that they had not come to dance.

Then, to her surprise, she recognized her brother among them. He spoke to one of the others, who turned and looked at her also; then Mark began to make his way around the room to where she was sitting. The other officers began likewise to move about the room, obviously searching out specific men, who left off their dancing to consult with the newcomers.

Beside her Mrs. Dillon began to complain. "Mercy me, I declare, something important must be afoot. Oh, if only we could have wangled an invitation to the Duke of Richmond's ball, then we would be among the first to know. Joanna," she said sharply, "do be sure to ask your brother for all the details. I do not wish to be the last to hear what is going forward."

Mark arrived at Joanna's side only moments before Captain Goldsborough and Belinda joined them. Ignoring the dictates of propriety, Joanna cast herself in her brother's arms and hugged him with a desperation born of total fear.

He returned her embrace, but did not offer her any false assurances.

"Napoleon?" Captain Goldsborough asked beside her.

"He crossed the River Sambre this morning and has already engaged some of Blücher's outposts and driven them back."

Mrs. Dillon gave a shriek, and Joanna clutched her brother more tightly. He gave her one last hug, then disengaged himself from her arms.

"I must join my regiment," he said, looking down at her. "We are marching out tonight to meet the French."

Although she felt as if she would die from terror, Joanna did her best to hide her fears from her brother. Forcing a smile she did not in the least bit feel, she said, "I know you shall defeat them."

"Defeat them?" He laughed. "Napoleon has said the

French eagles will soon be borne in triumph through the streets of London. Well, he is correct, but it is English soldiers who will be carrying them, not French conquerors."

Moments later he and Captain Goldsborough were gone, as were all the other young men in their smart uniforms. With them went all the gaiety that had marked the evening, and it was not long after that that the other guests began to depart.

Joanna followed Mr. and Mrs. Dillon down the stairs as if in a trance, her mind totally occupied with fears for her brother's safety. As they rumbled along in their coach, she was scarcely aware of Belinda chattering beside her.

"Oh, is this not exciting? After all this waiting, at last the time for battle has come. Oh, look, Joanna, there is a regiment of foot already marching off. Is it not glorious? They are so handsome in their uniforms. I declare, it is positively inspiring to see our brave soldiers going off to fight for us, do you not think so?"

So great were Joanna's anxieties, she totally forgot her place and responded from the heart. "Glorious? They are going off to die, and you find it inspiring? Have you never once considered that many of those handsome young men you have been dancing with this evening will be dead by this time tomorrow?"

Belinda gasped, and Mrs. Dillon rushed to her daughter's defense. "That is quite enough, young lady. You will not mention such morbid subjects again, is that clear?"

Tears filling her eyes, Joanna turned her head away from the others and stared blindly out the window. It was true, no matter what the others called it. War was not a matter of pretty uniforms and gaudy medals. Battles meant death and suffering. There was nothing glorious about young men being blown to pieces by cannonballs or hacked to death by swords or . . .

She could no longer control her tears, but allowed them to stream unchecked down her cheeks. Luckily the three Dillons were too busy discussing Belinda's success at the ball to pay Joanna any further attention on the ride back to their hotel, and soon she was able to escape to her own room, where she cried herself to sleep.

* * *

Joanna stood at the window of the private parlor Mr. Dillon had rented and looked down at the street. Since shortly after noon, a steady stream of wounded soldiers had been pouring into Brussels. Some were still able to walk, but others were carried on litters or trundled along in rude carts.

So much had happened since she had said good-bye to Mark. The regiments had marched away during the night with fifes playing and drums beating. By early morning—was it only yesterday—the town was virtually emptied of men in uniform.

About three o'clock in the afternoon they had heard thunder to the south of the city. Except it had not been thunder, it had been the artillery. Wellington had engaged the French at Quatre Bras, and Napoleon himself had attacked the Prussians under Blücher at Ligny. So far no one knew precisely what the results had been, but the more wounded soldiers poured into Brussels, the less likely it appeared that the English had scored a victory.

Behind her Belinda asked, "How long do you think it will be before we can go to Paris? Oh, *how* I have longed to stroll down the Champs-Élysées. Just think of the dresses, the bonnets, the shoes! And they say the opera has no equal in England."

When Joanna did not reply, Belinda said in an irritable voice, "Oh, do come away from that window, Joanna. I cannot imagine why you wish to see such revolting sights. Really, the sight of blood makes me quite nauseated. I do not understand how a lady can involve herself in such matters."

Joanna clenched her teeth together to keep from uttering the words she wanted to say, words which could easily alienate Belinda forever.

Yet despite her friend's comments, Joanna could not move away from the window. Her attention stayed fixed on the wounded men; her eyes kept scanning the crowds. She could not stop looking for her brother's face, always afraid she would see him.

The door to the sitting room opened, and Mrs. Dillon

bustled in. "Oh, dear . . . oh, dear, the most dreadful thing—your father has discovered someone has stolen all our horses right out of the stable, and the grooms have disappeared to a man." She joined Belinda on the settee and clasped her daughter in her arms.

"The French have utterly defeated Blücher," Mrs. Dillon wailed, "and without the Prussians, there is no chance of Wellington standing up to Napoleon—not with that ragtag army of his. Oh, it is too late—we are doomed, *doomed,* unless your father manages to buy more horses. He is going out into the countryside to see if there might not be some horses available there, and he says we must be ready to flee to Antwerp as soon as he returns. I have given instructions for the maids to start packing. Oh, we should never have come to this wretched foreign country. The landlady here told me that Corsican monster has given his soldiers instructions to assault women and children!"

There was a rap at the door, and Mrs. Dillon gave a little shriek and clutched her daughter even tighter. "Oh, save me, save me, they are here already—do not let them take me!"

It was not the French, however, but only the aforementioned landlady. "There is a man here with a message for Miss Pettigrew," the woman said. Standing aside, she let the stranger in.

Except he wasn't a stranger, at least not to Joanna. Despite the streaks of mud on his face, she recognized Davidson, her brother's batman. She clenched her fists until her fingernails dug into her palms, but the pain in her hands could not compete with the pain in her heart.

"Your brother sent me to fetch you, Miss Pettigrew. He has been wounded and is asking for you."

He was alive. Thank God, Mark was alive. Joanna let out the breath she had been holding, then moved quickly toward the door.

"Where are you going?" Belinda's question confused Joanna for a moment. Where was she going? Was it not obvious? "I am going to find my brother."

"Oh, but you cannot possibly go out there in the streets.

It is too dangerous." Mrs. Dillon did not hesitate to voice her objections. "Have you not been listening to a word I have said? No, no, you must stay here where you are safe, and we will send one of the footmen to inquire how your brother goes on."

Joanna did not even pause to consider other possible options. She could not. Her brother was wounded and was asking for her. She must go to him, she must.

Belinda caught up with her in the corridor and detained her with a hand on the arm. "Joanna, this is madness. You have to stay with us. The French army is coming, and we must be ready to depart at a moment's notice."

"My brother is wounded—how can you wish me to abandon him?"

Belinda scowled, and her voice took on the petulant tone Joanna had grown quite used to in the last few weeks. "Well, it is not as though you could do anything to help him. You have no training in caring for the sick, and there are surgeons to take care of the wounded officers, after all."

Joanna shook off her friend's hand and ran after the batman, who did not bother slowing his stride to allow for her shorter legs. Even as she caught up with him, thunder crashed overhead, and the first drops of rain began to fall.

4

Captain Pettigrew was not going to live to see another sunrise. Davidson had figured that much out before he had gone, as commanded, to fetch the sister. Already, in the hour it had taken for that task, the captain had become feverish and was no longer lucid. But then, very few soldiers survived abdominal wounds.

The batman touched his own abdomen, where his master's money belt now resided. Who'd have suspected the captain would have had so many pieces of gold hidden away? It was sheer good fortune on the batman's part that he had found the hoard when he was binding up the captain's wound.

He felt a twinge of pity as he watched the girl weeping over her dying brother, but not enough sympathy to change his plans. Never again would the circumstances be so agreeable to his purpose. Not only was a small fortune in his grasp, a fortune that he doubted anyone else was even aware of, but the general confusion and panic in Brussels would make it well nigh impossible for a search to be successful, even if someone did discover the theft.

Slipping out of the crowded tent, he found the captain's horses where they were tied. Mounting the one and leading the other, Davidson turned their heads toward the coast, where a new life beckoned him—a life of prosperity, thanks to the captain's unknowing generosity.

The tent erected on the outskirts of Brussels offered protection from the pouring rain, but no respite from the nightmare in which Joanna found herself. All around her, wounded men were moaning, begging for help, and crying out for water, but to Joanna's dismay, her brother uttered not a sound as he tossed fitfully on his rude pallet.

Why did no one come to help him? Why was he left to suffer so? Where were the surgeons who were supposed to tend to the officers?

There seemed to be no organization, no planning, no orderly system of care being given. Wounded men were carried in and laid down in rows, and the bodies of the dead carried out only when more room was needed. A few women moved about among the rows of injured soldiers, bandaging their wounds, soothing them, bringing water, or spooning broth into their mouths. No one paid the slightest attention to her brother except Joanna.

"Wake up, Mark, do wake up! Oh, please don't die!" Joanna clutched her brother's hand. His skin was dry and brittle, so hot it felt as if it were scorching her own hands.

She had to find a surgeon, she had to, even though it meant leaving her brother unattended for a short while. Maybe one of the other women would know where she could find help for Mark?

Moving to block the way of one whose arms were filled with bottles of water, Joanna asked timidly, "Excuse me, ma'am, but—"

Without letting her finish the question, the woman shouldered her aside and continued on her way through the tent.

Her slight store of courage used up, Joanna was ready to burst into tears and abandon her search, but she could not afford that luxury. Her brother had no one else to help him, his batman having unaccountably disappeared.

"If 'tis water you need, miss, you'll find a chemist's shop about two hundred feet down the lane to the right. Giving us all the bottles of water we can carry, he is."

The soft Irish voice came from behind Joanna, and she turned to see a tall heavy-boned woman with a kindly face. "Oh, thank you, thank you. It is not water I need, but a surgeon to help my brother. Do you know where I might find one?"

The woman did not answer directly. She paused, then

asked in a voice full of pity. "Where is your brother now?"

"Over here. Oh, please, for the love of God, you must help me find someone who can make him well again." Clutching the woman's arm, Joanna tugged her over to where Mark lay, the pallor of his skin in marked contrast to his flushed cheeks.

"Ah, the saints preserve us, 'tis Captain Pettigrew. Such a fine young man. My husband served as sergeant under him for many a campaign in Spain." Kneeling down beside him, the woman pulled back the thin blanket covering him.

Joanna had one glimpse of bloody bandages before the woman quickly replaced the blanket.

"You must help me find a surgeon, you must. Please, I beg of you."

The sergeant's wife rose to her feet and her eyes were sad.

"No, no, it can't be." Joanna's voice was no more than a whisper.

The Irishwoman pulled Joanna into her arms and held her, rocking her back and forth as if she were a small child. "Ah, but there's nothing the surgeon can do. In the hands of God, your brother is now."

"No, I cannot simply give up and let him die," Joanna clung to the older woman and fought desperately against the tears that were demanding release. "I must find a surgeon, I must."

"Ah, colleen, the surgeons have no time for the dying. They must do what they can to save those who still have a chance," the reply came, its harshness mitigated by the soft Irish brogue. "With such wounds as the captain has, there is naught anyone can do but pray that he does not suffer long."

Joanna took a shuddering breath, struggling to maintain control. With every fiber of her being, she wanted to deny what was happening. She wanted to make time retrace its steps—she wanted to go back to the evening before, when her brother had been well and whole . . .

Someone tugged at her skirt, and she looked down to see a young boy whose left arm ended in a bandaged stump. His eyes were glazed with fever, but he was conscious. "Water, for the love of God, bring me water." His voice was an almost unintelligible croak.

No! He did not know what he was asking. She could not leave her brother's side, not when Mark was dying. She could not!

"The choice is yours," was all the Irishwoman said, but Joanna heard the unspoken reproach.

Grieving at her brother's side was a luxury that would be paid for by the suffering of others. "Where is the chemist's shop?" she asked, her voice devoid of emotion.

" 'Twill be easier if I show you how to get there," the Irishwoman replied.

"Belinda, oh, my dearest Belinda, you must wake up!"

"Really, Mother, must you shout so? 'Tis the middle of the night." Belinda rolled over in bed and pulled the blanket up over her head, but her mother snatched it away.

"Get up, get up! Oh, do not delay! Every moment you dally brings the French soldiers that much nearer." Her mother continued to shriek and flutter about the room, picking up one object after another, only to drop each one so that she could pick up something else. "Your father has finally returned with a pair of horses, and we must flee for our lives. Oh, if only we might have left yesterday, when there was ample time."

Wide-awake now, Belinda scrambled out of bed and rang for her maid, but no one came.

"The servants have all run away during the night," her mother wailed. "We have been abandoned to our fate."

"Papa?" Belinda asked.

"He is obliged to harness the horses himself," her mother explained. "Oh, do hurry and get dressed."

"I cannot dress myself," Belinda said, shocked to the core that her mother would even suggest such a thing.

"Then have Joanna help you, but hurry! Oh, dear, this is terrible. We shall all be killed—or worse!" Wringing her hands, Belinda's mother scurried out of the room.

A quick check of Joanna's cot in the dressing room adjoining the bedroom revealed that her bed had not been slept in. For a moment Belinda was puzzled, before she remembered Joanna had gone dashing off to see her brother.

It was the outside of enough, Belinda thought, struggling to take off her nightgown by herself and then pulling on the only dress she owned that fastened down the front. Talk about ingratitude! After all that Belinda had done for her, the least Joanna could have done was be at hand when she was needed. Such thoughtlessness, such selfishness on Joanna's part was truly unconscionable.

Mary Katherine O'Flannagan watched the sky begin to lighten in the east. It had been a long night of almost constant rain, but then, she was used to such, having followed the drum for fifteen years, ever since she had married Patrick O'Flannagan.

For the moment, the city was still, and most of the wounded men in the tent behind her were sleeping quietly. Even while she savored the beauty of the morning, Mary Kate knew this day that was dawning so beautifully would bring a storm even more terrible than the one they had just endured during the night.

Instead of thunder, their ears would be assaulted by the boom of artillery; instead of raindrops, the brave English soldiers would be exposed to showers of bullets and shot.

From talking to the wounded stragglers who had trickled in during the night, she knew Wellington had halted his retreat at Mont St. John, near the little town of Waterloo. Where the Prussians under Blücher had taken themselves off to was anybody's guess. As for the Belgian and Dutch soldiers, as fast as they were deserting, it would be a wonder if any of them were left to fire a shot at the French.

No, in spite of the fancy talk of coalition armies, a victory this day would depend upon Wellington and the English foot soldiers. If the English squares could hold against the French cavalry, Old Douro would win the day. She thought of her husband, who would be in one of those squares, and she automatically made the sign of the cross.

You form lines when the infantry attack, he had explained to her a long time ago. But when the cavalry attack, a line is a death trap. A soon as a man goes down, or two men or ten, there is a gap in the line, and the horses go through, and once the line is broken—once the cavalry are behind you—all is lost.

Luckily, horses cannot be made to charge directly at a square, Patrick had told her. No more than you can get a horse to run straight at a wall. No, the silly beasts always veer off to the side and run between the squares. But unlike a line, it matters not if the cavalry get between and behind the squares. From whatever direction they approach, they still face a row of bayonets in front with two rows of guns behind. And no matter how many of your men go down, there are no gaps for the horses to break through, because you simply close ranks, and the square shrinks in upon itself.

Her husband had explained it with such confidence, as if squares could not be beaten. But they could be, especially when half of them were composed of Belgian and Dutch foot soldiers, who had a marked tendency to throw down their arms and run like scared rabbits the first time they heard a shot fired.

And even if by some miracle the squares held today, what price would be paid? How many men would be standing by the end of the day, and how many would be lying dead or wounded within the squares?

Ah, her husband would be scolding her for such gloomy thoughts if he were here.

Mary Kate stepped back inside the tent and moved to where the poor English girl was sleeping on the ground beside her brother's pallet. Miss Pettigrew deserved her rest. She had worked as hard as any seasoned campaigner throughout the night, pausing only briefly now and then to check on her brother, who had not regained consciousness.

She had proved surprisingly resilient despite her small size, and her courage had equaled her brother's. Captain Pettigrew was not the only brave English officer who had given his all for his country. The Highlanders had suffered the worst, but their courage had allowed the rest of the English forces to retreat in good order.

Many a wife and mother, sister and daughter, would be

heartbroken when they received news of Quatre Bras. And even more after the fighting today at Mont St. John.

Somewhere a cock crowed, and Miss Pettigrew stirred, then sat up, looking around in bewilderment, as if not remembering where she was. Then her eyes fell on her brother, and she gasped. Bending over him, she began to weep. The reason was readily apparent: Captain Pettigrew's sufferings were at an end.

"Come, colleen." Mary Kate put her hand on the girl's shoulder. "There is nothing more for you to do here. I'll walk along with you and see you back safe and sound in your lodgings. Doubtless your friends will be wondering what has become of you."

Although still racked by deep sobs, Miss Pettigrew allowed herself to be helped to her feet, and then Mary Kate led the way through the streets of Brussels, which were again thronged with desperate civilians. Yesterday it had been only the English and other foreigners who were in a panic to escape the French army. Today even the Bruxelloises were running around like chickens with their heads twisted off.

It was not a safe city for a young girl to walk through alone, but Mary Kate was large enough to handle any drunken lout or thieving deserter they might encounter.

Joanna had a feeling of disorientation when she and Mary Kate stepped inside the foyer of the hotel where she was staying with the Dillons. It was so familiar, so normal, as if her whole world had not been wrenched apart, as if there had been no battle, as if she had not spent the night tending wounded soldiers and watching them die . . . as if even now her brother was not being buried with the others in a common grave.

In a trance, she led the way toward the stairs, but to her amazement, the landlady blocked their way.

"And just where do you think you are going?" the woman demanded in a harsh voice.

For a moment Joanna was too surprised to answer, but then she replied calmly, "My friend and I are going to my room."

"You do not have a room here."

The anger Joanna felt at the world in general for allowing her brother to die now had a focus. "I am staying with the Dillons, as well you know, so stand aside," she said sharply, trying to push past.

The woman, who outweighed her by at least three stone, easily resisted her efforts. "The Dillons left for Antwerp hours ago."

Bewildered, her tired mind unable to grasp the significance of what the woman was saying, Joanna ceased her efforts to gain the sanctuary of her room.

"So we've no place for the likes of you in my house," the woman went on. "We run a respectable establishment here. I must ask you to leave at once."

"Just a minute, my good woman." Mary Kate's soft Irish voice had a hint of steel. "We are not leaving without Miss Pettigrew's belongings."

"The Englishwomen took everything with them. They left nothing behind for this one," the landlady said.

Mary Kate moved past Joanna and, grasping the landlady by the arms, easily lifted her off her feet. Holding her suspended in midair, the sergeant's wife said angrily, "You will fetch out the young lady's baggage at once, do I make my meaning clear? Any delay will cost you dearly."

"But I cannot give you what I do not have, and 'tis gone—everything is gone," the woman protested.

Mary Kate did not bother to answer; she just shook the woman the way a dog shakes a rat.

"Stop, stop," the landlady began to shriek. "I'll get it if you will just put me down."

She was dropped the few inches to the floor, and she instantly darted into a room to the left of the stairs. She tried to shut the door behind her, but Mary Kate could move fast for a woman her size, and she easily held the door open.

The landlady glared at her large adversary, as if estimating her chances of outwitting the Irishwoman. Then, apparently accepting the inevitable, she vanished into her room and reappeared a few minutes later, producing the portmanteau

Belinda had given Joanna to use. Instead of picking it up, Mary Kate opened it.

"Come and check it, miss," she called to Joanna. "This thieving woman may have already stolen something."

The landlady puffed up like an enraged hen. "I am not a thief; I am an honest citizen."

"We have already had a sample of your honesty," Mary Kate replied bluntly. "You are a liar and a thief, and a very bad one at that."

The landlady was not about to let the insult pass, and she began to screech at Mary Kate.

Although she could not bring herself to care about such trivial things, Joanna checked her belongings. As near as she could remember, they were all there—her father's medals and her mother's miniature, and the numerous dresses, ribbons, and shoes that Belinda had given her.

Closing her portmanteau again, she picked it up and moved blindly toward the door. Behind her Mary Kate and the landlady continued to berate one another.

Joanna paused on the steps and looked at the city of Brussels, which was spread out around her. In all the thousands of houses, large and small, elegant and shabby, there was no place she could call home—no relative she could turn to, no big brother to take care of her.

In her memory she saw Captain Goldsborough's face, heard him say he would be like another brother. Was he still alive somewhere out there? Or did he lie dead like Mark?

She should never have left her uncle's house, never . . . but then, if she had not, her brother would have died alone, with no one beside him who loved him . . . .

Dry-eyed, she stood there reliving her few precious moments with her brother—the morning of their first reunion . . . the afternoon he had taken her to watch his regiment on parade . . . the evening he had danced with her . . .

So few memories, yet so precious.

The angry voices behind her ceased with a crashing of doors, and then Mary Kate emerged from the hotel. Taking the portmanteau from Joanna's hand, she said, "Come along with me. There's always room for one more at my lodgings if you don't mind sharing a bed."

Despite her fierce efforts to maintain control of her emotions, Joanna now began to tremble all over in reaction to the events of the past few hours, and she suddenly felt too weak to put one foot in front of the other.

Mary Kate put one arm around Joanna's shoulders and gave her a squeeze. "I don't snore, so that you can be thankful for. My mother always said no matter how dark it seems, if you think hard enough, sure and you'll find something to be thankful for."

It seemed very dark to Joanna. Indeed, it was the darkest day of her life, darker even than when her mother had died, because then at least she had still had Mark. But with Mary Kate's strong arm to lean on, Joanna managed a fragile smile.

Nicholas stood with his batman at the edge of the regimental encampment, looking out across the plain at the white buildings of Paris. For twelve days the regiment, with the rest of the allied army, had made their way unopposed through the French countryside. Then on the first of July, the Prussian guns had commenced firing, but no orders had come down for them to join the battle.

Finally, yesterday, the fourth day of July, the guns had remained silent, and instead of artillery shells, rumors had been flying—rumors that the French were suing for peace.

"Did you ever expect, Elston, that they would allow us to chase them right up to the very gates of their capital?"

His batman spat on the ground. "Them frogs are a difficult folk to understand. Lettin' us march through their villages, and 'stead of tryin' to stop us, they just waves their little flags and cries out, 'Welcome, welcome, thank you for invadin' our country.' Like to turn my stomach, it does. A nation of cowards and turncoats, they are." He laughed. "Can you picture such a thing happenin' in England? A French army marchin' right up to the gates of London 'thout a shot being fired? I think not."

Nicholas laughed, but there was more bitterness than humor in his laughter. Too many of his friends lay buried in Spain and now in Belgium also. And too many of those still living would carry the wounds of battle to their dying day. And all because of that egotistical maniac who had twice set out to conquer the world. "You are right. It is as inconceivable as imagining the Duke of Wellington deposing the Prince Regent and crowning himself Emperor of All Britain."

Beside him Elston chuckled, then added, "And settin' his brother up as King of Scotland, and another brother King of Ireland, and proclaimin' his son King of the Channel Isles."

They were interrupted by a messenger, who brought not only a packet of letters that had been following them from Brussels but also the welcome news that the campaign was indeed over, the first of the treaties having already been signed.

Nicholas was reading a letter from his sister, full of news of little Louisa and the twins, Catherine and Edward, when Sergeant O'Flannagan approached him. "You'd better read this, sir."

Taking the note, Nicholas read:

> mondaye the 19th my dere paddy—i hope this Letr fines you welle i Looke forwarde to Seeing you agine please tell captn golsboro that captn petrigrus Sistr is with me he is ded an her frens wente off and Lefte her aske him what he thinks is best done yore Loving wife mary kate.

Unable to believe what he was reading, Nicholas scanned the short note a second and third time, but the message did not change. As inconceivable as it was, the Dillons had apparently left Brussels without taking Joanna. How could a man calling himself a gentleman have done such a despicable thing—abandon a young girl after having once assumed responsibility for her?

Nicholas cursed Belinda's father. Despite his social standing, the man still had the soul of a tradesman and was apparently less concerned with doing the honorable thing than with saving his own skin and his moneybags.

As great as was Nicholas's rage, it was nothing compared to his fears. Mark's sister had already been alone for two and a half weeks, and it would be more days—perhaps even weeks—before he could resign his commission and return to Brussels. He could not begin to imagine how terrifying it must be for her.

"My Mary Kate will be taking good care of the child," O'Flannagan said in a gruff voice. "You need have no worries on that score. But still and all, it would be best if we knew how to get her back to her kinfolk."

Nicholas remembered the promise he had made Mark—a promise he could no longer redeem since Mark was dead. But on the other hand, he could still carry out the spirit of the promise—he could not find Mark a position that would enable Mark to provide his sister with a home, but Nicholas could escort Miss Pettigrew back to her uncle in England. At the very least, he owed his friend that much.

Again the sergeant spoke up. "If you could think on the problem and let me know what might be best?"

"I shall handle the problem personally," Nicholas said harshly, his mind already turning to practical matters, such as deciding whom he would need to speak to first about obtaining permission to sell out. Elston had already told him that he had no interest in returning to civilian life, so Nicholas would also have to ask around and see if he could find another officer who might be needing a batman.

As for himself, he did not regret for a moment leaving the army. Unlike his brother-in-law, who had not wished to resign his commission and take up the title of Duke of Colthurst, Nicholas had long ago lost whatever taste he'd had in the beginning for the military life, and he would be quite content if he never saw a uniform again or heard another shot fired in anger.

Darius might find honor on the battlefield, but all Nicholas could see in war was needless death and destruction.

The skirl of the bagpipes crowded the cottage and spilled

out into the night. As if competing with the storm outside, the music became ever wilder, the tempo ever quicker. One by one the other dancers were forced to retire to the edges of the room, until Alexander had the center of the floor to himself, the only one able to keep his feet moving nimbly enough to follow where the wailing melody led.

Abruptly the music stopped, and in the resulting silence he heard an unexpected voice. Turning toward the door, he saw the familiar figure of his estate manager, the shoulders of his coat soaked through from the rain.

"Lads," he called out, a smile of welcome on his face, "I make known to you Walter Robertson. He is a bit dour, but then, he's from the south, born in Glasgow. Walter, what brings you here to Barra?"

Robertson did not return his smile. "I've a message from your mother. She has need of you in Edinburgh."

"Ach, no, she has not found herself another young lady trying her best to catch a braw Highlander, has she? Well, tell her I am still not available."

" 'Tis not a trick this time. Wellington has defeated Napoleon at a little town in Belgium."

Immediately a wild cheer went up from the assembled party, but when Robertson remained looking grim, they gradually quieted down. "They say we lost a full third of our troops," he continued when the room was still enough that he could again be heard.

At his words, the mood of the room became somber, and there were no cheers or smiles when he continued, "The Highland regiments were almost wiped out. Your cousins Ian and Hugh are both gone, as well as Jamie McDowell and Neil Buchanan. And young John McBoyle has lost a leg." Robertson reached inside his coat and produced a packet wrapped in oilskin. "I've brought an account of the fighting."

Several hours later, after the dispatches had been read and discussed, and the other islanders had one by one left for their own cottages, Alexander sat with his host, an old man upward of eighty.

"My four sons were all lost at sea in a storm thirty-eight

years ago last April, and my wife died seventeen years ago this November," he said, then fell silent for a long while before he finally spoke again. "I am old and I have grown accustomed to living alone, but there are times like this when I long to have a grandchild beside me. Someone to take care of my croft when I am gone. Someone to live here in this cottage where my father and grandfather and great-grandfather lived. Someone to fish the waters where I have fished for sixty-seven years."

Alexander stared into the fire, and in its flickering depths he could see the faces of his cousins and friends, so young, so vigorous, so full of life.

So young . . . and now they would never grow old, never marry, never have children. Alexander began to rethink his decision not to marry and settle down. "Life is uncertain," he said. His statement sounded so simple, and yet it was actually quite profound, he realized for the first time. There were no promises, no guarantees that the tomorrows would keep turning into todays.

"Aye, life is a fragile gift. That is a lesson all fishermen learn early on," replied the old man. " 'Tis not given to us to know the span of our lifetime until we come to the end, when that knowledge is of little advantage. My father always told me we must live each day as if it is our last, never letting the sun set on an injustice or a quarrel, lest we be taken during the night."

Laying his hand on the old man's shoulder, Alexander said, "I thank you for the hospitality you have shown me, and regret that I must leave you on the morrow. But my mother has need of me now." To himself he added: And 'tis time I stopped delaying and set about the necessary business of finding myself a wife.

Joanna lifted the lid of the soup pot, in which an old rooster had been stewing all day. The bird, as tough as it was, represented half the sum of money she had received for the last of the dresses Belinda had given her. By selling them, she had managed to contribute a little toward the expenses for the meals and lodging she and Mary Kate shared.

When this money was gone, she would be forced to sell her father's medals and her mother's miniature. And when that money was also gone, she had no idea how she would proceed. For hours on end she had racked her brain to think of some way to support herself, but she had no skills, no particular talents, nor was she strong enough to work as a laborer in the fields. She did not even know French or Flemish or Dutch, and so could not even attempt to find a position in a shop.

To be sure, the sergeant's wife would not throw her out on the streets. Mary Kate had made that quite clear. But Joanna could not accept endless charity, either.

She lifted a spoonful of the broth, blew on it to cool it, then tasted it. Something was still lacking, but she did not have enough experience with cooking to tell what it was.

Behind her the door opened, and without turning to see who was there, she said, "Come and taste this and see if you think it needs more basil or more pepper."

A man's voice answered her. "From the delectable aroma, I would say that the only thing that stew is still lacking is a loaf of fresh bread to eat it with."

Even when she turned and saw Captain Goldsborough standing in the doorway smiling at her, she could not believe he was really there. She had hoped too long in vain to accept easily that her unspoken wish, her deepest longing, had come true.

5

Miss Pettigrew was even thinner than Nicholas remembered, and her eyes looked bruised in her gaunt face. In the interval since he had said good-bye to her, she seemed to have aged years rather than weeks, and it was obvious life had not been treating her gently. He could only thank a merciful providence that Mrs. O'Flannagan had chanced upon her. Again he cursed the Dillons for the callous way they had abandoned a defenseless young girl. Such cowardly behavior demanded retribution, but for now, Miss Pettigrew's welfare must come first.

"You are welcome to share our meal," she announced, looking as solemn as a little barn owl. "There is enough for all of us, and Mary Kate will not mind, I am sure."

"Thank you for your hospitality," he replied with the same formality, not sure how he should broach the subject of escorting her back to England.

"Will you be staying in Brussels long?"

Seizing the opportunity she had given him, he said more bluntly than he had intended, "I am on my way home to England, so I have come to escort you back to your relatives."

She blanched, as if he had struck her, and he silently cursed his heavy-handedness. Would he never learn to be tactful? To consider his words before he spoke? "I promised your brother."

"My brother commended me into your care?" she asked, her voice so soft he could hardly make out her words.

"Not exactly that. But I did make him a promise, which

I can no longer redeem, so I feel an obligation to see you safely returned to your Uncle Nehemiah."

Her eyes opened even wider, and he realized with a jolt that they were now glazed with fear. He bit back a curse. What had happened to her in the last few weeks to make her afraid of him, when she was accustomed to treating him like a brother? Who had so mistreated her that she was now backing into a corner, as if trying to put as much distance between them as possible?

He resolved to question the Irishwoman when she returned, but for now he would do all he could to act as if he had noticed nothing amiss and hope that he could avoid frightening the child further with some thoughtless remark.

"Can you ride?"

She looked at him blankly, clearly confused by his question.

"At the moment, all I have with me are two riding horses," he explained. "It will be more convenient if we can manage without a carriage until we are across the Channel. I can purchase a vehicle in Harwich for the rest of our journey, but I need to know if you can ride a horse."

She shook her head. "When I was very little, I had a pony, but he was sold after my father died. Since then I have not had any opportunity to ride."

"Would you have any objections to riding pillion?" Watching her face closely, he was resolved to drop the plan if she showed the slightest sign of fear or distress, but she actually looked relieved.

"Whatever is the least trouble for you," she replied. "I do not wish to be a bother."

He smiled in what he hoped was a reassuring manner, and the corners of her mouth turned up slightly. It was a rather tentative smile and obviously cost her a great deal of effort, but at least it was better than the frightened look she had worn earlier.

While sharing the stew, which tasted as good as it smelled, Nicholas mentally cursed the entire French nation—all those patriotic citizens who had been so quick to support their emperor's grandiose plans.

The price the rest of the world had been forced to pay for Napoleon's ambitions had been too high, and his final defeat had been bought not only with men's lives but also with the lives of women like Miss Pettigrew. Compared to what her future would have been had her brother lived, her prospects were now quite bleak, and Nicholas could only regret that he was not married so that he might be able to offer her a comfortable position as companion to his wife. In his own household he would also be able to ensure that she was looked after properly.

But at least she had relatives who would take her in. Some of the women whose husbands and brothers and fathers had been killed did not have even that much.

Nicholas lay in his bunk and moaned. To Joanna he looked as pale as death—and more than once on this long journey across the Channel he had said he would sooner stick his spoon in the wall than endure another hour of being tossed about in such a manner. Since he had not yet even cast up his accounts, as so many of the other passengers were doing, she thought there was very little real possibility of that happening. But such opinions she kept to herself.

"One of the sailors mentioned that a cup of hot tea might make your stomach feel better," she said tentatively.

Nicholas responded to her suggestion by ordering her out of the cabin with such force that she was quite reassured as to his ultimate recovery. He might feel as if he were dying, but he was in no real danger of becoming food for the fishes.

Leaving him to suffer in private, which he obviously preferred, she made her way along the swaying corridor to the stairs leading up to the main level. Reaching the deck, she paused for a few minutes and surveyed the scene. Really, Nicholas did not know what he was missing by remaining below.

To be sure, the breeze was a bit brisk, and the sea was rather choppy, which was causing the horizon to rise and fall, and was making the deck beneath her feet not only roll but also pitch. But still, the sky was such an intense blue, and the sea gulls were fascinating to watch as they wheeled overhead in constantly changing patterns. She took a deep breath, and the very air itself was so clean, so fresh, it seemed as if no one had ever used it before.

Putting the constant motion of the ship out of her mind was easier than ignoring the nagging voice of her conscience, however. Her enjoyment of the voyage was marred by the fact that she was willfully deceiving Nicholas. Even though they had been together for several days now, she had never found a good opportunity to confess . . . or at least that was the excuse she had been giving herself.

But there was no real excuse, because the proper time for her to have told him she had run away from her uncle's house was before they left Brussels—before they had taken even the first step on their journey.

She pulled her cloak more tightly about her, but even its warmth could not improve her spirits. If anything, it only made her feel more guilty. Nicholas had bought it for her before they left Brussels, and it was the first brand-new item of clothing she could remember ever owning. Made of a beautiful lime-green wool, it was so fine and soft, at first she had been almost afraid to touch it. Would Nicholas have given it to her if he had known she was deceiving him?

It was not even as if she could gain any advantage by lying. As much as she might wish it, she could not keep the truth from him forever.

How angry would Nicholas be when they arrived at her uncle's house and he discovered she was not welcome there? Very angry, more than likely, and he would also have nothing but contempt for her when he learned that her uncle had actually forbidden her to go to Brussels and that she had deliberately defied his rightful authority.

Yet as much as she dreaded Nicholas's scorn, it was nothing compared to the fear she had felt ever since he had mentioned her uncle's name. She had scarcely given Uncle Nehemiah and Aunt Zerelda a thought since she had left England with the Dillons. They had traveled in luxury and she had enjoyed herself first on the journey and later in Brussels, with no thought of the ultimate price she would be forced someday to pay.

But as soon as Nicholas had told her he was returning her to her family, the folly of her actions had become clear to her. She almost wished her uncle would make good his threat and refuse to take her back. But Uncle Nehemiah was too miserly to pass up the chance to use her again as an unpaid servant.

He would take her back into his household . . . but only after meting out suitable punishment. How many strokes of his cane would she feel before his wrath cooled? Before his sense of injustice was appeased? How many times would he drive her to her knees before he would magnanimously forgive her for rejecting his charity?

Gathering her cloak around her, Joanna made her way along the deck past coils of rope and kegs lashed together, until she reached the prow of the ship. Somewhere out ahead, beyond the hazy horizon, lay England. And with each and every surge of the ship through the waves she was being carried closer to her uncle . . . and to her punishment.

Nor would it end with a beating. Uncle Nehemiah was quite experienced at carrying grudges. Years from now, he would still be using this flagrant disobedience on her part as an excuse to deprive her of the slightest pleasure.

Yet despite the price Uncle Nehemiah would demand, if she had it to do over again, she would make the same decisions she had made. In the empty years to come, she would at least have her memories of Brussels to comfort her—not only the memories of Mark, but also the memories of Nicholas.

In the few days they had been traveling together, she had discovered he was not quite as godlike as he had seemed at first. Although usually even-tempered, he did have a tendency to snap at anyone who spoke to him for the first hour or so after he woke up in the morning. And also, of course, he was not at all a good sailor.

Unfortunately for her heart, the disillusionment had come too late. Riding pillion behind him all the way from Brussels to Antwerp—her arm holding his waist tightly and her face pressed against his back—she had become far too intimately acquainted with his body. There had been no way to refrain from noticing the play of his muscles as he guided the horse, no way to avoid becoming accustomed to his masculine scent, no way to shut her ears to the sound of his heartbeat, no way to keep her own heart from speeding up when he spoke to her.

No longer could she find ample satisfaction in worshiping him from afar. The Nicholas she now yearned for was not a godlike being; he was definitely a man made of flesh and blood.

Even now—even when he was green with seasickness—she wanted nothing more than to be kneeling at his side, soothing his brow, bringing him comfort.

No, if she were to be honest—and she must practice being more truthful, even with herself—what she actually wanted was to be lying on that narrow bunk beside Nicholas, to feel his arms holding her as tightly as she had held him. She wanted once more to hear his heart beating strongly beneath her ear . . . .

She shook her head to clear it of such foolish thoughts. She could never actually behave in such a wanton manner, of course, and her wishes to the contrary, she would have to accept that there would be no more opportunities to be close to him again—no more waltzes with his hand on her waist, no more riding pillion with *her* arm around *his* waist.

And all too soon, she thught wistfully, she would not even be able to look at his face except in her mind's eye. Heart-sick at their inevitable parting, which was coming nearer and nearer with every dip and rise of the ship, she stared straight ahead . . . and gradually realized that the haze on the horizon had resolved itself into land.

That would certainly cheer Nicholas up more than the offer of a cup of tea. Returning a short time later to his cabin, she found him sitting up on the side of his bunk, holding his head in his hands. He did not bid her welcome, and she had to wait until he had cursed the sea and the boat and the weather and the English Channel and the French people who were responsible for his being where he was, before she could tell him her news.

"You mean this torture has an end?" he asked, disbelief in his voice.

"Well, we are not on a trip to China, after all. The captain predicted it would be a fast crossing, and so it is turning out to be. I asked one of the sailors, and he said we should be in the harbor in less than an hour."

"You are an angel to bring me such wonderful news; I could kiss you for that," he said absently.

Just for a moment she thought he meant it, and her heart rejoiced. But then she realized it was only an expression, and she had to turn away, lest he see the disappointment she could not keep completely concealed.

Joanna moved very carefully around the room, knowing that the slightest sound would wake Nicholas, who was sleeping in the adjoining room. The walls were paper thin, and if he discovered what she was up to, he would not only forbid her to do such a thing but also more than likely do it in such a loud voice that he would wake all the other guests staying at the inn.

It was not as if there was anything seriously wrong with her plan, either, but like most men, he would doubtless disapprove of it on principle. Rather than risking an argument, which she knew he could win by sheer volume of voice, she had decided to take the coward's way out and simply leave him a note telling him what she had done. Then he could return to his own home with an easy conscience, relieved of his obligation to her brother.

Really, it was a good plan, and she could not think why it had not occurred to her earlier. They were only ten miles from her uncle's house and only twelve from Riverside, where the Dillons would be. And unlike Uncle Nehemiah, Belinda was not prone to holding a grudge.

Joanna had only to explain why she had stayed away that entire night in Brussels after they had specifically told her their departure was imminent, and she was sure the Dillons would forgive her for any delay and inconvenience she might have caused them and accept her back into their household.

To be sure, it would be little more than a temporary

reprieve from Uncle Nehemiah. She could not, after all, expect to live off the Dillons' charity forever. But there was a possibility, however slight, that if she made herself useful enough, the Dillons might keep her on as an unpaid companion to Mrs. Dillon even after Belinda married, which she was sure to do, so beautiful and charming was she.

And even if her stay with them turned out to be only a matter of weeks or months, every day Joanna could avoid returning to Uncle Nehemiah's household was a blessing not to be cast aside lightly.

It was so obviously the best thing to do under the circumstances that she felt somewhat guilty for not explaining to Nicholas in person. But then she would have to tell him everything, including the fact that she had run away from her uncle's house, and that she could not do. No, she would avoid all arguments and unpleasantness by leaving a note, telling him she had decided to finish the last few miles of the journey to her uncle's house alone.

Luckily, she'd had the foresight the night before to borrow a quill and ink from one of the maids, who had also been able to arrange for Joanna to ride most of the way to Riverside with a neighboring farmer who was taking a cartload of produce to market.

Still feeling very much the coward despite all her rationalizations she seated herself at a little table and began to write.

Nicholas was not in a good humor when he turned into the driveway of the Alderthorpe residence. If pressed, he would have to admit that he was never at his best when he first awoke. In general, however, his temper was even, but not on a day when he was served up an impertinent note with his breakfast.

Thank you for your help, but I no longer need your assistance, was the essence of the message Joanna had left for him. Apparently she expected him to accept her assurance that nothing untoward would happen to her if she wandered unprotected around the English countryside.

His imagination, however, had been working feverishly during the last ten miles, and the pictures it had shown him had done nothing to sweeten his disposition. Descending from his carriage, he hitched the hired horses to a post beside the drive, then pounded on the door of her uncle's house.

After a lengthy interval the butler opened the door and requested he state his business.

"I wish to speak with Miss Pettigrew," Nicholas replied, his tone barely civil.

"I shall inquire," the man said before shutting the door in Nicholas's face.

On top of everything else, this rude reception was too much, and it was all Nicholas could do to refrain from again pounding on the door—or kicking it in.

Taking his own sweet time, the butler eventually re-appeared and wordlessly ushered Nicholas into the house. Leading him through a dark, musty corridor, the servant finally opened a door and stood aside to let Nicholas enter an overheated sitting room.

A quick glance revealed that the only occupant of the room was a stout middle-aged man with a florid complexion. "State your business," the man said with no preamble.

"I have no business with you," Nicholas replied in the same blunt tone. "My business is with your niece, Miss Pettigrew."

"I have no niece," the man replied, his expression now openly hostile.

"When I inquired after the Alderthorpe residence, I was directed to this house," Nicholas said, refusing to be put off so easily.

"I am Nehemiah Alderthorpe," the man finally admitted, his voice cold and emotionless. "But I no longer have a niece. The girl was fully aware of the consequences of her actions when she went running off to Brussels to see that worthless brother of hers."

At these callous words, a red haze filled Nicholas's vision. "Her brother was a brave and loyal officer in His Majesty's service, and he was fatally wounded at Quatre Bras defending his country's flag."

The fat man shrugged. "A not unexpected occurrence, I believe, when someone chooses to be a soldier."

"This is your nephew we are talking about," Nicholas said angrily. "Have you no respect for the dead?"

"My nephew chose not to take my advice, just as his sister chose to flout my authority. Consequently neither of them is my responsibility."

Unable to control his temper any longer, Nicholas moved forward with intent to cause bodily harm. Mr. Alderthorpe's haughty expression wavered slightly, and he took a step backward. "Now, see here," he blustered, apparently realizing he had gone too far.

Before the man could finish whatever feeble excuse he was about to make, the door opened behind Nicholas and a woman spoke in a coy voice.

"Hagers told me we had company. Pray introduce our visitor, my love."

Looking relieved at the interruption, Mr. Alderthorpe carefully skirted Nicholas and joined his wife by the door. She was even fatter than her husband, who now carefully positioned himself behind his wife's skirts.

"This man, whoever he is," Mr. Alderthorpe explained, "has barged in here demanding to see Joanna."

"My name is Goldsborough, Nicholas Goldsborough. I served in the same regiment as your nephew, who died of wounds received during the battle at Quatre Bras."

"I see," the fat woman said mildly. She waddled over to the settee, which groaned as it received her weight. Picking up a box of bonbons, she selected one and bit into it. "So you are saying that my husband's niece has been alone in your company for several days?"

As unobtrusively as possible, her husband sidled past Nicholas until he was again stationed safely behind his wife.

The woman's jaws moved rhythmically, and she masticated two more bonbons before finally speaking again. "I fail to understand why you are here."

Nicholas took a deep breath. How to explain that Joanna had run off, leaving only a note? "I wish to satisfy myself that Miss Pettigrew has arrived home safely."

"She is not here," the woman said flatly. "And this is no longer her home. If she does attempt to return, she will not be admitted. This is a decent Christian household, and we will not allow it to be contaminated by your discarded mistress."

"Mistress! She is not my mistress and never has been."

The woman shrugged. "Whether you have taken advantage of her or not, that is what the world will believe when they learn she has been traveling with you unchaperoned. You may have a blithe disregard of such things, but I shall not allow my reputation nor the reputation of Mr. Alderthorpe to be tarnished by association with such an unregenerate sinner."

Behind his wife, Mr. Alderthorpe smiled in satisfaction, clearly enjoying Nicholas's frustration. Recognizing the pointlessness of any further discussion, Nicholas turned on his heel and found his way back to the front of the house, where the butler wordlessly opened the door for him and shut it behind him.

As he drove away, Nicholas's anger was tempered by his fears for Joanna's safety. Halting his horses at the end of the driveway, he considered which way he should turn, left or right. England might be a small country relatively speaking, but it still contained an impossible number of square miles when one was searching for a lost girl.

"Psst! Over here!"

A girl's voice called from somewhere to his left, and he turned his head toward the sound.

"Oh, sir, don't let them see you talking to me, else I'll get a skinning, I will."

Flicking the reins, Nicholas moved far enough down the lane that his carriage could no longer be seen from the Alderthorpe residence, whereupon a young female servant wearing a stained apron emerged from the bushes.

Looking once over her shoulder, she bobbed a quick curtsy, then said in a rush, "If you are looking for Miss Joanna, she is prob'ly at Riverside with the Dillons." Again checking over her shoulder, she said, "I got to get back now, afore I'm missed."

"Wait—how do I find Riverside?"

She hurriedly gave him directions. "Oh, sir, yer not aimin'

to force Miss Joanna to come back here, are you? He'll beat her somethin' terrible, he will, and lock her in the cellar with the rats, and I won't be able to help her, sir, no matter how I wishes I could."

"No, I would never even consider bringing her back here."

With tears in her eyes, the girl thanked him, and then, before he could give her a coin for her assistance, she was gone.

He did not have to go all the way to Riverside. About a mile down the road he spotted a small figure trudging along tiredly, dragging a portmanteau. Joanna did not even bother to look up until he halted his horses beside her. When she did, the surprise on her face angered him even more. Was her opinion of him so low that she had truly believed he would so easily abandon her?

"Get in the carriage!" he commanded, his voice harsh even to his own ears.

Joanna had never seen Nicholas so angry. "You really did not have to come after me. It is not at all f-far to my uncle's house, and I am quite familiar with this neighborhood. I can w-walk the rest of—"

Before she could finish speaking, Nicholas leapt down and caught her around the waist and virtually tossed her into the carriage. Throwing her bag into the back, he climbed in and took his place beside her. Close up, his ferocious scowl was even more intimidating.

Without saying another word to her, he backed his horses and skillfully turned the carriage around in the narrow lane. Then at a trot they set off in the direction of her uncle's house.

Twice she opened her mouth to say something to him—to explain why she had gone off leaving only a note, to explain that she had found only a caretaker at Riverside, the Dillons having departed three days previous for Paris—but each time, one look at Nicholas's set expression and the words died in her throat. It was only when he drove past her uncle's house without checking his speed that she had to speak up.

"Excuse me, but you have missed the turn. That is my uncle's house back there."

"I know which house it is. I have already made the acquaintance of your esteemed uncle," he said, his voice little more than a low snarl.

"Oh. Then you know I ran away."

"Yes, I know."

Joanna sighed. "I should not have done so, I realize full well. And I suppose Uncle Nehemiah told you he will not take me back?"

"Yes," Nicholas snapped out, his eyes firmly fixed on the road ahead, "he told me."

"Please stop the carriage," she said urgently, and to her relief, he reined in his horses. "You must take me back there. Even though Uncle Nehemiah is angry now, he will forgive me and take me back. I know he will."

"After he beats you?" Nicholas's words were like a slap.

"How did you know?" she said faintly. "I never told anyone, not even Mark."

"One of the kitchen maids saw fit to enlighten me."

Nan, she thought. Oh, Nan, I know you only wanted to help, but you should not have told. "Be that as it may, it is my only home. I have no other relatives to go to."

He picked up the reins and signaled to the horses, which began trotting again, but still in the wrong direction. She put her hand on his sleeve, but he shook it off.

"No, you must turn around and take me back," she insisted firmly. "My uncle will forgive me."

"Your aunt will not," Nicholas replied.

"My aunt? But she always follows my uncle's lead. Why should she object to my coming home if he does not? I fail to understand."

"It is not so difficult to understand. You have been alone in my company for several days now, which means your reputation is in tatters. In a word, I have compromised you."

Reputation? Compromised? Joanna was so stunned she could not think of a thing to say. None of what Nicholas was saying made any sense.

"But you may rest assured that I shall do the honorable thing," Nicholas continued. "I am taking you to my sister's house in Wiltshire, not far from Bath, where we shall be married by special license within the week."

6

Two days of sitting in a carriage beside a man who spoke only when spoken to and then only in monosyllables was enough to make even the almshouse seem an attractive alternative, Joanna thought. Well, if Nicholas was going to continue refusing to speak to her, she, for her part, would not even *look* at him.

He was remarkably willing to shove all the blame for their present predicament off onto her while he played the role of patient, suffering martyr. She had already, numerous times, reminded him that it had been his idea to escort her back to England. But instead of admitting that he was thus equally at fault, he had merely looked pained and muttered something about honor. As if honor were the answer to everything. Bah!

Furthermore, she had pointed out to him that if he had only done what she had suggested in her note and allowed her to finish the last few miles of the journey alone, he would never have met her Uncle Nehemiah, plus her Aunt Zerelda never would have discovered that the two of them had been traveling together unchaperoned. At the mention of Uncle Nehemiah, Nicholas had looked ready to explode, but no matter how red his face had become, nor how much effort it had obviously cost him, he had gritted his teeth and refused to say a word.

Really, he was impossible! With every mile they traveled, Joanna became more determined that never—never!—would she marry this irritable, choleric, ill-humored, provoking, illogical, cranky, narrow-minded *man.*

The devil take him and his precious honor! He could

purchase all the special licenses he wanted—he could drag her bodily before a dozen vicars—but she would absolutely, outright, point-blank refuse to take him as her husband.

She sneaked another peek at the man sitting stony-faced beside her in the carriage, and as usual, the sight of his familiar features caused her heart to soften. No matter how much logic she might have on her side, she could not look at Nicholas and stay angry. If only he were not so handsome . . . If only he were not basically such a kind person . . . If only . . . She sighed. What she really meant was: if only he loved her and truly wished to marry her.

Her throat ached, and she had to blink back the tears that welled up in her eyes. She could no longer delude herself; she would marry Nicholas in an instant if he actually desired her as his wife, rather than merely pitying her. But he did not love her, and because he did not, it was up to her to do something to prevent their nuptials. If she married him, for whatever selfish reason, she would be responsible for a lifetime of unhappiness—Nicholas's unhappiness, which by extension would also mean her unhappiness.

For her part, despite his present ill humor, she would like nothing better than to be near him for the rest of her life. But she could too easily imagine what a disaster it would be if he were forced to marry her when his heart was already given to Belinda.

Joanna bit her lip. Now that she thought on it, her present predicament was all the fault of King Henry the Eighth. If he had not wished to marry an excessive number of wives, England would still be Catholic, and she could simply take herself off to a nunnery, and that would solve all their problems.

Nicholas heard a sniffle beside him and saw Joanna surreptitiously wipe her eyes. Did she have to make it so obvious that she could not bear the prospect of marrying him?

She had been bleating about logic ever since he had told her they would have to get married. Logic? She did not even seem to know what the word meant. *Logically* she should have jumped at the chance to acquire a husband and a home of her own, but from the way she had been reacting, one might almost suppose he was driving her to the guillotine rather than to an appointment with the village vicar.

He glanced down at her where she was sitting crumpled in a pathetic heap beside him. Did she think him so much of an ogre that even Uncle Nehemiah was preferable? Bah, he would never understand women!

Only one thing he was sure of—when he explained the situation to Darius, his brother-in-law at least would understand about honor and duty and responsibility.

Just before noon, Nicholas slowed the horses and turned in between a pair of stone pillars. At the end of the private drive Joanna could see a beautiful house of honey-colored stone. It was grand enough to strike terror into the stoutest of hearts, and Joanna, who was admittedly a coward, was thrown into a state of total panic.

Mrs. Dillon's words, scarcely heard at a dance and then immediately forgotten, now came back to haunt Joanna. "His brother-in-law is the Duke of Colthurst." A duke! This was even worse than Joanna had realized. A duke! Oh, Nicholas's relatives would be so angry that she had trapped him into marriage. A duke! Oh, my, this was dreadful!

She felt faint and instinctively reached out and clung to Nicholas's arm. She wanted nothing more than to hide her face behind his shoulder, but she could not tear her gaze away from the approaching disaster.

"Can't think where everyone has gone off to," Nicholas said in a normal voice. He reined to a stop in front of the imposing steps. "I've never been here when there were not half a dozen gardeners and grooms lurking about. My sister did not mention anything in her letters about taking a trip."

He climbed out of the carriage, then turned to help Joanna down. She kept her eyes carefully lowered so that he would not see the abject fear in them and despise her more than he did already.

Grasping her arm firmly, he virtually dragged her along with him up the steps to the massive front door. He pounded on it vigorously, but no one came.

"Blast," he muttered. Trying the door latch, he found it unlocked, and to Joanna's dismay, he entered without waiting for a proper invitation.

"Where the deuce is Kelso? Not even a footman here to answer the door." Nicholas dropped her arm and began to open one door after another, but the house appeared to be totally deserted.

Then a small door behind the main staircase opened and a beautiful blond girl emerged. Dressed in a buttercup-yellow gown, she was like a ray of sunshine lighting up the large entry hall. Catching sight of Nicholas, she whooped with glee, then ran and threw herself into his arms.

Joanna instinctively shrank back into the shadows.

"Nicholas, you're home! Why did you not warn us you were coming? Have you left the army for good? How long are you staying? Oh, it is so good to see you." She kissed him on the cheek, and Joanna felt her insides twist with jealousy.

"Calm down, Dorie. I'll answer all your questions later, but for now I need to talk to Elizabeth and Darius."

"Oh, Nicholas, the most wonderful thing—Maggie and Munke got married this morning. We are all celebrating down in the servants' hall. I was just going upstairs to relieve Beth, who is up in the nursery minding the children. I'll tell her you're here. She will be delighted—indeed we are all so glad you have come home safely." She started to dart away again, but Nicholas caught her arm.

"Stop! I shall go up there to speak to her. You just find Darius, but don't spread it around that I am home. I want to speak to him and Elizabeth privately before it becomes general knowledge that I am here."

"Secrets, Nick?" the girl asked with an impish smile. "You know I will discover everything sooner or later, so you might as well save the effort and tell me sooner."

"Later, brat. Now, get along and fetch Darius. Tell him I have gone up to the nursery."

Joanna was hoping Nicholas had forgotten all about her, and indeed he had given that impression ever since he had dragged her inside. But he waited only until the door had closed behind the girl before looking around impatiently.

Spotting her where she cowered behind a massive urn filled with fresh flowers, he said curtly, "Come along, now."

When she failed to move, he strode to her side, caught her arm, and she was forced to accompany him, even though her feet wanted nothing more than to be going in the opposite direction. The only thing she could be thankful for was that Nicholas slowed his pace to accommodate her shorter legs, rather than taking the stairs two at a time as he always seemed inclined to do.

"Who was —?" She wanted to say: Who was the girl who kissed you?—but she caught herself in time. "Who was the girl you were speaking to?"

"Hmm?" Nicholas's mind was obviously miles away—which was where Joanna would have preferred to be also. "Oh, that was Dorie. My cousin," he added by way of explanation. "She is a hoyden, but I'm sure you'll like her."

But would Dorie like her? Joanna wondered. It was rather doubtful, she thought, especially when Nicholas's cousin discovered she had trapped him into an unwanted marriage.

The door to the nursery was open, and Nicholas paused before entering. "You make a pretty picture, Elizabeth," he said with a smile.

Peeking around him, Joanna had to agree. The woman seated on the chaise longue was beautiful and as serene as a Madonna, while three toddlers who were clustered around her looked like little cherubs.

Catching sight of Nicholas, the three scrambled down and barreled across the room, hurling themselves against him and clinging to his legs like little limpets.

Somehow he managed to scoop all three of them up. They each gave him wet, smacking kisses, then allowed him to deposit them again on the floor.

The woman waited her turn, then also embraced him and kissed him on the cheek. "Oh, Nicholas, it is so good to see you. Welcome home."

He returned her hug. "I have brought someone to meet you." With his arm still around his sister, Nicholas turned to Joanna, who wanted to sink through the floor. "This is

Joanna Pettigrew, the sister of one of my friends. You may remember my mentioning Captain Mark Pettigrew in some of my letters. He was killed in Belgium, so I have brought Joanna home with me."

"Oh, my dear, I am sorry about your brother." Holding out both her hands to Joanna, the duchess got to her feet. "Come sit here beside me, my dear. You look quite fatigued from your journey. Please believe me when I say you are welcome to stay with us as long as you wish." Efficiently she scooted all three of the toddlers aside so that there was room for Joanna.

"We shall not impose on you long," Nicholas said. Although he still smiled, a coldness had crept into his voice that Joanna could not ignore. "As soon as I can produce a special license, Joanna and I are going to be married."

The beautiful woman's expression did not lose a bit of its serenity. If anything, her smile became wider. Giving Joanna's hand a gentle squeeze, she said, "How wonderful. I have always wanted a sister."

Joanna promptly burst into tears, and one after another the three babies joined in, their wails quickly drowning out her sobs.

Elizabeth looked at the young girl sitting beside her. Joanna Pettigrew was pouring out a disjointed account of all the events that had conspired to place her and Nicholas in their present predicament, and it was all Elizabeth could do not to pull the poor mistreated child onto her lap and hold her and comfort her as if she were as young as Louisa and Edward and Catherine.

But she wasn't a child. Young in years Joanna might be, but her childhood had been left behind in Brussels, her innocence destroyed forever by tents filled with wounded and dying young men. All Elizabeth could do to comfort her was hold Joanna's hand, which felt so cold and frail, it only made it that much harder for Elizabeth not to pull the younger girl into her arms.

That Joanna was head over heels in love with Nicholas was soon obvious. Equally apparent was that he felt a strong sense of responsibility for her. Unfortunately, marriage under these present circumstances would be almost certain disaster.

"I would have thought," Nicholas said impatiently, pacing back and forth in Darius's study, "that you, at least, would understand why I have to make Joanna marry me."

"And why is that?" Darius asked.

"Because of you and Elizabeth, of course. Because you were in the same situation."

"I offered for her, if that is what you are referring—"

"Exactly!" Nicholas interrupted without letting him finish. "You did the honorable thing. Well, now I am in the same kind of situation, and it is my duty to marry Joanna."

"I disagree," Darius said mildly. Nicholas stopped his pacing and glared at him, enough hostility in his expression to make a whole regiment of privates shake in their boots. Darius, however, was not a green recruit, nor was he easily intimidated. "To begin with, I did not force your sister to marry me. I *proposed* marriage, and it was her choice whether to accept or reject my offer. While I will not dispute that it is clearly your duty to offer for Joanna, I cannot agree that honor demands that you coerce her into accepting your offer."

"But she must agree. It is not as if she has any other options. I told you what I found out about her uncle, and her aunt, I suspect, is undoubtedly just as cruel in her own way."

"Then," Darius said, rising to his feet and clapping his brother-in-law on the shoulder, "it is up to us to provide Joanna with other options, so that she may have the freedom to choose her own future."

"So you see, your grace, now Nicholas says we must be married at once, but I cannot bear to ruin his life."

Before the duchess could answer, there was a tap at the door, and the duke entered, followed closely by Nicholas, who looked even angrier than the last time Joanna had seen him. The duchess gave her hand a gentle squeeze, and Joanna felt as if some of the other woman's courage were flowing into her through their conjoined hands.

The duke placed a chair conveniently near to the chaise longue and seated himself calmly, but Nicholas stalked over to the window, and with hands clasped behind his ramrod-straight back, stared out at the gardens.

"Well, my dear," the duke said, smiling at his wife, "what have you to suggest?"

"There is really only one thing to do," the duchess replied, and Joanna's heart sank at the thought of a lifetime of unending misery. "Since Miss Pettigrew does not wish to be forced into a marriage of convenience, the obvious answer is for her to stay here with us for the next few months. Then in the spring she can have her Season in London with Dorie."

Instead of rejecting such a preposterous scheme, the duke smiled and said, "Exactly the thing, my dear. I knew I could count on you to find the perfect solution."

"B-but . . ." Joanna was horrified at the duchess's suggestion. "But I c-could not p-possibly accept such charity," she finally managed to say.

By the window Nicholas muttered something under his breath, but the duke and duchess both ignored him, focusing all their attention instead on Joanna, who huddled miserably in her place and wished once again that she were anywhere but here.

"While I respect your scruples, it would not, in fact, be charity," the duke replied calmly. "I would merely be paying back a debt of honor that I owe your brother."

"A debt? Surely you cannot have borrowed . . ." Joanna stopped, horrified at her own presumption in speaking so to a duke.

"Your brother saved my life once in Spain," the duke said smoothly, as if she had not interrupted him. "The debt I owe him is too great ever to be completely repaid, but you must allow me to do this one small thing in return."

He smiled at her, and Joanna almost forgot herself so much she started to smile back, before remembering he was a duke.

"This is ridiculous," Nicholas said, turning to face the three of them. "We have been traveling together alone with no chaperone for almost a week, and Joanna's reputation is now in tatters. I have compromised her, and the only way to avoid a scandal is for her to marry me."

Joanna gasped, but the duchess gave her hand another squeeze, then said calmly. "Fortunately, I doubt that anyone who matters knows about your journey and your lack of a chaperone. We can only be grateful the servants here were otherwise occupied, so that even they are not yet aware of your arrival. We shall merely concoct a fictitious widow in whose company Joanna traveled here, and the matter is resolved without the slightest hint of scandal."

"A widow." Nicholas snorted in disgust, but Joanna could see that his resolve was weakening.

"To be sure, it might be wise for you to take yourself off for a while before you make your official appearance on the scene," his sister suggested. "Some of the servants are clever enough that they might remark the unusual coincidence of two people traveling separately from Brussels, who contrive to arrive precisely at the same hour."

"Is that what you prefer, Joanna?" Nicholas glared at her.

She nodded her head, then managed to squeak out a reply. "Yes."

"Very well." Nicholas stalked over to the doorway, then turned back to face them. "I was planning to visit a friend near Oxford anyway, so I may not be back for several days. Expect me when you see me."

Then he was gone, taking Joanna's heart with him.

That night Elizabeth lay in bed with her head on her husband's shoulder, her mind too filled with worries to allow her to sleep.

"What is troubling you, my dear?" Darius asked, his hand coming up to stroke her hair.

"You never told me about almost losing your life in Spain. I had thought you were no longer keeping secrets from me."

Laughter rumbled up from his chest. "Well, if you insist on knowing all the horrifying details of war, I shall be happy to oblige you. The occasion, if I remember correctly, occurred in the summer of 1810, when our supply trains had gone astray and we had had nothing to eat for five days except hardtack. Pettigrew managed to trap a pair of rabbits, and he 'saved my life' by sharing the resulting stew with me."

With a chuckle, Elizabeth snuggled up closer against him. "If you were a man of lesser appetites, I might think you were exaggerating the incident, but having become accustomed to the quantities you can devour at one meal, I agree we do indeed owe an immeasurable debt to the Pettigrews."

"I wish I could do something for all the widows and orphans who have been left destitute by this wretched war."

"You are already doing more than most landowners. You hire veterans of the peninsular campaign whenever you can do so, and you are planning to speak out in Parliament on the question of pension reform," she said soothingly.

"But will anyone in the government listen?" he asked, and she could not find an answer to that question. At least not an answer that would please either of them.

Dorie waited impatiently for her cousin to stride the last few yards up the little hill behind Colthurst Hall where she had asked him to meet her. Nicholas was still several feet away when she said angrily, "You are the greatest beast imaginable."

His face darkened into a scowl. "What has Joanna been saying about me?"

"Ha! Ha! I knew you had some connection with her. She has not said one word about you, because she has scarcely left her bed since she arrived. No, I am mad at you because you appeared three days ago quite unexpectedly and told me to fetch Darius but not to let anyone else know you were here."

"So?"

"So?" she said, her eyes narrowing. "You dare to ask me *so*? In case it has slipped your mind, Nick, you also said you would explain everything later. Do you recall? But then you vanished for three days without speaking to me again, and now you ask me *so*? So I have been dying of curiosity for three days, but I, at least, have not failed *you*. I have not told anyone—not anyone at all—that you were here that day."

"You should have asked Elizabeth."

"Your sister has spread a Banbury tale around about some patently fictitious widow escorting Joanna home from Brussels. When I question Elizabeth about this widow, she just smiles serenely and changes the subject."

Nicholas gave her an enigmatic smile also, and Dorie immediately felt her temper rise another notch.

"Smiling won't work for you, Nick, because you have already promised to explain everything, so start talking."

"I am not sure I should. It might be better to let Joanna tell as much as she wishes you to know."

"I told you, she has done almost nothing but sleep the whole time she has been here. Hepden has scarcely been able to rouse her long enough to spoon broth into her mouth. Really, Nick, if you were taking care of her, I think you made a wretched job of it. The poor girl was on the point of collapse when she arrived."

Nicholas cursed under his breath. "I was only taking care of her on the journey back to England. Before that no one was taking care of her for weeks. In fact, she was working herself to the point of exhaustion every day helping take care of the wounded soldiers in Brussels, so I don't want you pestering her with a lot of questions when she does wake up."

"I have no intention of pestering her, and I am glad you brought her to us, because it will be quite fun to have a friend here my age, but everything you say only adds to my curiosity. *Someone* has to tell me the whole story, Nick, because I cannot bear to know part of a secret and yet not know the whole thing. You know curiosity is my one besetting sin."

Nicholas smiled at her, and this time it was a genuine smile, not a mask to hide behind. "I would agree that you have more curiosity than a cat, but that it is your *one* sin is still open to debate."

"Nick, ple-e-e-ase . . ."

"Very well, brat, but you might as well sit down and be comfortable if I am to spare you no detail."

"Good." With blithe disregard for what Hepden would say about stains, Dorie sat down on the grass, then crossed her legs in a manner that would have scandalized her mother, had she been there to see it. "And when you are done telling me about Joanna, you can tell me every little detail about the battle of Waterloo."

Groaning, Nicholas lowered himself to the ground beside her. "You are a cheeky brat, and I pity the poor man who marries you."

"I do not intend ever to get married," Dorie replied. "I have decided to wait until I am twenty-one and come into my inheritance, and then I am going to be the first woman to circumnavigate the world."

"I think that has already been done," her cousin pointed out.

Dorie shrugged. "If so, I am sure I can find something else to explore."

"Equally outrageous?"

"Equally *exciting*," Dorie corrected.

Joanna stood in the center of the lovely bedroom she had been given. Clad in nothing but her shift, she felt horribly exposed and embarrassed, but she was under strict orders to stand up straight and not fidget.

Miss Hepden, who for the last ten days had appeared in the guise of a ministering angel, had abruptly transformed herself into a totally unrecognizable person. She was presently subjecting Joanna to the most thorough scrutiny she had ever had to endure.

Miss Hepden, Dorie had informed Joanna, was a dresser with unmatched qualifications. Not an abigail—Dorie had corrected her on that—but a dresser, whose ministrations could add immeasurable consequence to any lady she served, no matter what that lady's rank.

Joanna, lacking as she did the slightest consequence, was more than overawed. She felt downright guilty that such an august personage would deign to waste her time on such an insignificant nobody as herself, and reminding herself that Miss Hepden was a servant did nothing to help. The only way Joanna could stand still under the present eagle-eyed inspection was by remembering how kindly Miss Hepden had treated her earlier.

"Well, the bones are good," Miss Hepden finally pronounced. "They need only a little meat on them, which task can safely be left for Mrs. Mackey to deal with. The hair must be cropped, which will allow the natural curl to come out. As for colors, nothing will do but the clearest blues and reds—"

"Oh, but I am in mourning," Joanna blurted out.

At once Dorie objected. "You cannot mean to wear black. Surely your brother would not have wished you to deck yourself out like an old crow."

"Black will be a wonderful color for you," Miss Hepden said sternly, looking down her nose at Dorie as if daring the young girl to contradict her. But Dorie was not so foolish as to argue. She immediately pretended to have developed a fascination with the carpet under her feet.

Turning back to Joanna, Miss Hepden continued speaking as if the interruption had not occurred. "Very few people can wear black successfully. You are one of the fortunate ones, however. Black will make your skin look like porcelain. But you must never wear green or gold or brown or orange. Never."

Dorie bounced over to the nearly empty wardrobe and inspected the few dresses Joanna had hanging there. "Oh, dear, these are all the wrong colors."

"Dispose of them immediately," Hepden ordered. "Now that Miss Pettigrew has been officially placed in my charge, she is not to leave this room again until she is properly attired."

Joanna was not the least bit sorry to part with the dresses, which were little more than rags. But then, to her dismay, she realized Dorie was also removing the beautiful cloak Nicholas had bought for her in Brussels. "No, oh, no, you cannot take my cloak away."

Disregarding her orders to stand still, Joanna darted across the room and snatched the lime-green garment out of the other girl's arms.

"But the color is all wrong for you," Dorie protested. "Surely you are not thinking of disregarding Hepden's advice?"

"Th-then I shan't wear it, but I shall keep it forever. Never will I part with it. There are sentimental reasons," Joanna added when both Hepden and Dorie stared at her as if she had been out in the sun too long and addled her brains. "It was a present."

The other two exchanged looks, then smiled at her and told her of course she must keep it in that case. She suspected they were now under the erroneous impression that it had been a present from her brother, but she said nothing to correct their mistake.

The cloak was all she had of Nicholas, who had been deliberately avoiding her company for the last week and who had departed for his own estate in Somerset just that morning.

Tears came to her eyes at the thought of not seeing him again for months—indeed, perhaps never again—and she hugged the cloak to herself in abject misery. She was only vaguely aware of the other two women tiptoeing out of the room, leaving her to grieve in private.

7

Turning in at the gates, Nicholas pulled his team to a halt. Beside him, Richards, his groom, was suitably impressed.

"Blimey, so that's where our own Miss Elizabeth lives. Done us right proud, she has."

Nicholas had to agree Colthurst Hall was an imposing sight, although no country residence could be expected to show to best advantage at this time of year. Four months earlier the sun had been bright, the breeze balmy, and the grounds had been green and lush. In August it had been only his own thoughts that were desolate.

Urging his horses forward once again, Nicholas realized with mild surprise that his memories of battles and dying friends had faded enough that even though the landscape beside the drive leading up to the house was bleak, the sky leaden, the trees and shrubs brown and sere, and the wind as sharp as any butcher's knife, he himself was feeling quite cheerful at the prospect of Christmas with his sister's family.

The harvest had been good at Oakhaven, but more important, it had been most beneficial for him to work in the fields like a common farm laborer. The hard physical effort had exhausted his body and the undemanding companionship of the other workers had brought him a peace of mind that had allowed him to sleep undisturbed through the night for the first time since Quatre Bras.

In a word, he was not only ready but also eager to be with his family once again—with Elizabeth and Darius, little Louisa and the twins, even his cousin Dorie, who, according to reports, remained ever the hoyden. Elizabeth had written that Joanna was proving to have a calming influence on

Dorie, and that to everyone's relief, Dorie had not been able to induce Joanna into actively participating in any of her mad starts.

Which did not surprise Nicholas in the slightest. Joanna do something rash? Such a timid little mouse as she was, the mere thought of her engaged in any kind of outrageous behavior was so ludicrous, it brought a smile to his lips, and he realized he was quite looking forward to seeing her again also.

In the last few months he had scarcely spared her a thought, once his sister had reassured him that Miss Pettigrew was thoroughly recovered from her ordeal in Belgium. He must be sure, however, to single Joanna out for some special attention during the holidays, so she would not feel neglected. After all, had he not promised her he would be like a brother?

Coming to a stop in front of the house, Nicholas flipped the reins to Richards, leapt down from his carriage, and went bounding up the broad, low steps. This time Kelso was properly on hand to open the door for him.

"Ah, good afternoon, Captain Goldsborough."

"Not captain anymore, Kelso, I am once again just plain mister. So where has my sister got herself off to? The nursery as usual, I suppose."

"No, today she is entertaining some of the neighbors in the blue salon."

By the time the butler finished this pronouncement, Nicholas was already halfway up the stairs. "You needn't bother to announce me, Kelso. I'll just pop in on her for a few minutes before I dress for dinner."

Doubtless the old biddies sipping tea with his sister would be horrified when he appeared without bothering to change out of his traveling clothes, but he didn't especially care what their opinion of him was.

The door to the blue salon was open, and as he approached he could hear the strains of a Viennese waltz being pounded out with a heavy hand on the pianoforte. His Aunt Theo must have already arrived for the holidays, because no one else he knew managed to make every piece that was played sound like a military march.

As he stepped into the room, the sight that met his eyes had nothing to do with tea or dowagers. There seemed, instead, to be an extraordinary number of young bucks gathered in this one room. Nicholas recognized one young man who lived on a small estate in the neighborhood, but beyond that they were all strangers to him.

The furniture had been pushed to the edges of the room, the rugs rolled back, and at his entrance Aunt Theo continued punishing the keys in her merciless way. All other eyes were focused on the three couples dipping and turning in the center of the cleared area. No one, in fact, took the slightest notice of the new arrival.

Without difficulty Nicholas recognized the tallest young lady as his sister. Not looking the least bit matronly, she was waltzing in the arms of a young man obviously several years her junior. The lad was decked out in an outlandish costume, which he undoubtedly considered all the crack. His extravagantly high collar and his shockingly flamboyant waistcoat, however, only made it extremely difficult for Nicholas to suppress a grin.

To his delight—and very much to his amazement—the second young miss being twirled around the room was none other than his hoydenish cousin, Dorie, who had put up her hair and who was looking quite elegant. Nicholas hadn't known she could clean up to such advantage—a compliment he'd better keep to himself, since Dorie could not be expected to have given up all her pugnacious behavior just because she had let down her skirts.

Nicholas shifted his attention to the third young lady, who was waltzing with a most handsome partner, whose attire was only slightly inclined toward dandyism. The young man had a most fatuous expression on his face, which was easily understood, for his partner was the most enchanting little thing Nicholas had seen in an age. With black curls framing a heart-shaped little face and skin like alabaster, she was delicately built, but with such an exquisite figure, she, more than any woman he had ever encountered before, truly deserved the encomium "Pocket Venus."

However had he missed making the acquaintance of such an incomparable on his previous visits to Wiltshire?

While he was staring at her in fascination, the dance came to an end, the couples separated, and there was a surge of laughing young men jockeying for position and importuning the three ladies for a chance to be their next partners.

The thought of anyone else but himself dancing with the lovely black-haired miss sent Nicholas shouldering his way through the throng.

"Nicholas! You're back!" Dorie launched herself at him, and he caught her in a bear hug. Despite her grown-up looks, she was still apparently a sad romp.

Setting his cousin back on her feet, Nicholas embraced his sister, then turned toward the third young lady, expecting an introduction.

No one, however, seemed to think it necessary, and he was about to demand that they not forget the standard courtesies when he realized that he knew those large violet eyes now gazing up at him. Joanna!

She held out her hand to him, and he took it automatically. At her touch, his heart began to do strange things in his breast.

"I am so glad you have come to share Christmas with us, Nicholas."

There was a chorus of protests at her use of his given name, but she merely turned and smiled at them all. "Oh, but of course Nicholas must dance the next waltz with me. You see, he has promised to be like a brother to me." She looked back at Nicholas and smiled.

Although he managed to keep his smile firmly fixed on his face, and thus avoided disgracing himself, Nicholas was no longer feeling the least bit cheerful when he put his hand on Joanna's tiny waist and began to dance in time to the music Aunt Theo was again banging out on the pianoforte.

Her brother! She thought of him as a brother! Even while the smile grew wooden on his face, Nicholas realized this was not even the worst of it. That poor little dab of a thing who had, while his back was turned, grown up to be the most enchanting young lady he had ever met, had only four months previously become positively hysterical at the mere thought of marriage to him.

Why, oh why, had she ever said the word "brother?" Joanna berated herself for even bringing up the past. It was obviously distasteful to Nicholas, because his smile had immediately frozen on his face, and his eyes were now shuttered.

Undoubtedly he assumed she was criticizing him for acting in a less-than-honorable way after compromising her reputation. She wished there were some way she could reassure him that she held him in the highest regard and did not think his actions had been the least bit dishonorable. Fortunately, she realized before the words were out of her mouth that any additional mention of the events of last August would only worsen the situation.

She would give anything to bring the smile back to his eyes, to dispel the brooding look he was not even attempting to conceal.

Despite everything, Joanna could not long resist the pleasure of being back in Nicholas's arms, and she felt a deep disappointment when the piece was concluded and the dance came to an end.

To her chagrin, Nicholas did not even stay to ask her for a second dance. Even while the others crowded around her, he vanished through the doorway without a backward glance.

Although she had earlier enjoyed dancing with each of the young men, who were all quite pleasant and totally innocuous, Joanna found herself now strangely reluctant to feel any other man's hand on her waist where Nicholas's hand had so recently rested.

Over the vociferous protests of all the young men, she suggested that they had been waltzing long enough, and now they should really practice some of the country dances. Dorie also protested that she was eager to continue waltzing, but with Elizabeth supporting Joanna, the matter was soon arranged.

Which was fortunate, because she was feeling so fragile,

she strongly suspected that if any of the young men tried to hold her in his arms, she would break down in tears and be forced to flee from the room. Never would she be able to live down such a disgraceful display of emotion.

As it was, her mind was so filled with the vision of Nicholas—so much more compelling in the flesh than in her memories—that she could not concentrate on the steps of the country dance, which she had long ago mastered, and after she thrice stepped on her partner's toes, he cheerfully began counting out the steps for her and reminding her when she should turn and when advance and when retreat.

It was all very embarrassing, and she could not be sorry when Elizabeth announced it was time for a little refreshment. She could only wish Nicholas would see fit to rejoin them for tea.

Hearing someone enter his study, Darius looked up from the accounts he was working on. "Ah, Nicholas, I am glad to see you have arrived already. Elizabeth was worried that you might have had carriage trouble along the way."

"How could she worry? I am here a full day ahead of when I said I would arrive."

Darius smiled. "When you have been married for a few years, you will understand that logic has very little to do with a woman's capacity for fretting."

Nicholas did not return the smile. Instead he frowned—no, thought Darius, if one would be honest, one would have to call it a scowl.

"Speaking of logic, what is Elizabeth about, to let such a cursed assortment of caper-merchants and fribbles and Bond Street beaux into the house? I have never seen such a misbegotten crew, and I do not approve of them hanging around and dancing attendance on Joanna. Nor on Dorie either," he added in what was obviously an afterthought.

"Admittedly they are all rather young and still somewhat foolish," Darius replied calmly, "but I have known their fathers and older brothers for years, and I cannot, after all, forbid our neighbors' sons admittance into our house without causing grave offense. But rest assured that however outlandish their choice of costume, there is nothing wrong with any of the lads that a few more years of experience will not correct."

Nicholas began to pace around the room, and Darius recognized in his brother-in-law the same restlessness he himself had often felt before his marriage had brought him an inner peace. It would appear that Elizabeth had the right of it when she had told him her brother was already caught, though it was equally obvious Nicholas was unaware of how deeply he cared for Joanna.

"I have promised her I would take care of her like a brother," Nicholas blurted out. "So I feel it is my duty to see that no undesirable types are lurking around her."

And that, thought Darius, is undoubtedly the real reason you now have your nose out of joint. Joanna has apparently done or said something to indicate she still thinks of you as a brother, and you are not at all happy to be cast in such a role. Would that I could tell you she actually dreams of you as a husband, but that, my boy, you must discover for yourself.

To Nicholas he only said, "Would you wish to ride out with me for a bit before dinner?"

And Nicholas, who had spent the entire day on the road, immediately expressed his eagerness for a good gallop.

Alexander's mother handed him a cup of tea, her friends asked him if he was looking forward to seeing England, and their daughters all coyly expressed the hope that he should not forget them when he was introduced to all the beautiful young ladies he would doubtless meet in London.

He obediently sipped his tea, mendaciously replied that he was indeed looking forward to becoming acquainted with his English heritage, and with a great deal of effort even managed to produce the requisite assurances that no matter how charming the ladies might be in London, he would never find anyone there who was prettier than the present company.

But behind his glib compliments he felt real consternation. If Edinburgh were this confining, however would he survive four months trapped in London? Why, oh why had he let his mother persuade him—no, trick him—into agreeing to spend the entire Season visiting his English uncle? And now she was even insisting that he go a month early, so that he could acquire the proper wardrobe. His kilts, she had informed him, would not be leaving Scotland.

The sense of his own mortality, which last summer had seemed quite inescapable, completely inevitable, and dangerously imminent, had entirely faded, but not, to his everlasting regret, before he had made the unfortunate promise to his mother.

Considered rationally, there was no legitimate reason for him to have panicked. He still had more than enough Scottish cousins left to inherit the title and carry on the family name, should something disastrous happen to him. And right now London itself was the only major disaster looming on his horizon.

Nor could he even hope that his mother might be persuaded to release him from his promise, no matter how rash and ill-conceived it had been. He had already tried that route, and she had remained totally adamant.

Four wasted months—it did not bear thinking about. Four months when he could not wet a fly in a stream or sail across a loch or even—here he suppressed a smile, lest the young ladies now present should notice it and misinterpret it as interest in them—shear a sheep.

And once lost, those days could never be regained. Indeed, now that he thought about it logically, that was all the more reason not to fritter his time away in London. The old fisherman's words came back to him, that one must treat each day as if it were one's last. Did he truly wish to spend his last days in London, of all places? No, he did not, and so he would inform his mother.

In fact, the more he thought about marriage in general, the more he realized that even when he was thirty-five or forty-five, he would not be ready to settle down. He was undoubtedly meant to remain a bachelor all his days, as brief or as long as those days might be.

But, he thought glumly, such an argument would only make his mother more insistent that he have a London

Season, just as if he himself were some silly chit who needed to be "popped off." It was downright embarrassing, and an insult to his manhood.

"Another cup of tea, dear?" His mother smiled at him, a sly, treacherous smile, as innocent as a fox's, and he had the lowering feeling she knew everything he had been thinking and that she was one step ahead of him all the way.

Christmas dinner, and the table had groaned with such an abundance of food, that they had all stuffed themselves to the point of moaning, or at least Joanna felt that way. Except she could not feel the least inclined to moan with Nicholas as her dinner partner. Darius and Elizabeth were seated at the ends of the table, and Dorie and her mother on one side, which left Joanna to share the other side of the table with Nicholas.

She had basked in his undivided attention throughout the entire meal, and they had talked of a multitude of subjects, including lastly a thorough description of his estate, which to her way of thinking did indeed sound like the perfect place to live.

"So I think you will agree that Somerset is vastly superior to Wiltshire, and it is not merely my own partiality that prejudices me in its favor."

Nicholas smiled when he said it, and Joanna felt such an upwelling of happiness in her heart, she would have agreed with him if he had said Somerset had just risen on gigantic wings and flown off to the moon.

"Attention, please!" Darius rapped on his wineglass, and the various conversations ceased. "We have an announcement to make. My dear, do you wish to do the honors?"

"I shall leave them to you," Elizabeth replied with a quiet smile.

"Then I wish to inform you all that Elizabeth intends to present me with another pledge of her affection."

"Oh, Beth, that's wonderful." Dorie leapt up so quickly, she almost tipped over her chair. Hugging her cousin, she asked, "When is the baby due?"

"The middle of July."

"Oh, then you cannot—" Dorie stopped in mid-sentence.

"No, I shall not be able to chaperone you and Joanna in London."

"That's all right," Dorie assured her. "My mother can manage."

Mrs. Donnithorne immediately asserted that of course she was fully capable of launching two young ladies into society, but whatever Elizabeth's opinion may havc been, Joanna felt herself not the least bit reassured. Something was bothering her, and with a feeling of dismay she realized it was the smile that Dorie could not quite repress.

Joanna had grown to know and dread that particular smile. It invariably meant that Dorie was plotting some outrageous scheme. London, which Joanna had almost started to look forward to, now began to take on a sinister aspect, and it was with a sinking feeling of impending disaster that she rose to follow the other ladies out of the room, leaving the men to their brandy.

"I don't know how you can sit there so complacently," Nicholas said to Darius, who persisted in taking the whole matter much too lightly. "You know perfectly well that Aunt Theo is no match for Dorie. And if that scamp is not firmly suppressed, then heaven only knows what kind of scrapes she will drag Joanna into."

"Well," Darius replied, "if you feel that strongly about it, the only thing I can suggest is that you yourself spend the Season in London, where you can keep an eye on Dorie . . . and Joanna, of course."

Nicholas threw himself down in the chair next to his brother-in-law and considered all angles of the situation. The plan had much to recommend it. Of a certainty, he could not be expected to stay at Oakhaven, where he would doubtless waste all his days in pointless worrying.

"I think I shall do exactly that," Nicholas said finally. "After all, Joanna has had very little experience, and London is full of cads and bounders waiting to prey on green, unsuspecting girls. Yes, I feel it is nothing less than my duty to accompany them.'' He raised his glass in a toast. ''Let us drink to London.''

''To London!'' Darius paused with the glass almost to his lips; then a wicked imp of mischief made him add, ''Do you know, the most marvelous thing has just occurred to me. If you are there in person, it will be very easy for you to help Joanna find the proper husband.''

Nicholas choked on his brandy.

''Oh, we are going to have such adventures!''

Joanna sat on Dorie's bed and contemplated her companion, who had been giving off sparks of suppressed excitement ever since the duke had made his announcement.

''But, Dorie—''

''No, no, I shall not listen to any of your prophecies of doom and gloom, Joanna.'' Dorie spun around in circles until she became so dizzy she collapsed backward into a chair. ''Everything is falling out perfectly. You know very well I have been dreading the tedium and the boredom we shall be forced to endure. Well, my mother is a dear, but she is so flighty and absentminded, a regular flibbertigibbet, that she cannot begin to match wits with me. Once we are in London, we can do whatever we want without her discovering it until it is too late.''

''Too late? Do you hear what you are saying? The course you are proposing is nothing but a path leading directly to social ruin.''

''Exactly! I am so glad you are not slow-witted. Once I have put myself beyond the pale, everyone will stop trying to marry me off, and I shall be allowed to lead my own life. Have I told you I plan to travel all around the world?''

''Yes,'' Joanna said despairingly, ''you have told me.''

''Oh, I see what is bothering you.'' Dorie leapt to her feet. ''You are worried that your reputation will likewise be ruined.''

''If that happened, I must tell you it would be more than unfortunate, it would be the end of everything. For you should realize it is already very difficult for me to live off the duke's generosity, freely given though it is. I cannot expect, however, to continue accepting his charity for the rest of my life."

"Do you mean you actually *want* to find a husband in London?"

Dorie looked at her in amazement, and Joanna realized with a sinking heart that the thought of marriage to anyone except Nicholas was anathema to her. But she could not tell Dorie that. Dorie would immediately tell Nicholas, and he would again feel honor-bound to marry her. "No," she admitted finally, "I do not wish to find a husband in London." Which was not a total lie, since she had already found the husband she wanted.

"Then there is no problem," Dorie said, rushing over to hug her. "When I am twenty-one, I shall come into my inheritance from my grandfather, and then you shall live with me, and we shall both be as merry as grigs."

A lifetime of putting up with Dorie's fits and starts—with trying to keep her out of the worst of the scrapes she seemed always to be wanting to throw herself into—the idea was so appalling, Joanna was almost tempted to demand that Nicholas do his duty and marry her.

Dorie again began to dance around the room. "You can come with me around the world, and we shall become famous as the intrepid lady explorers."

"But, Dorie, have you considered that I am not really very intrepid?"

"Of course you are. You even ran away from home, which is more than I have done . . . yet."

"Surely you are not seriously contemplating running away! Dorie, I must make you understand that it is not at all comfortable to be on your own in a foreign country. Please believe me when I say that although adventures may sound exciting when one talks about them afterward, they are not at all enjoyable when one is living through them. Nothing on earth would persuade me to set forth all alone on a journey again."

"But you would not be all alone—I would be with you. And I guarantee neither of us would be bored, which is a fate much worse than any other disaster that might befall us."

Dorie gave her a smile of triumph, but Joanna felt not the least bit reassured.

"But . . . but . . ." What could she say that would make Dorie understand that blindly courting danger was not a viable option?

Before she could try once more to persuade her friend to abandon her outrageous plans, there was a tap at the door, and Dorie opened it to admit Nicholas.

At once Dorie's look of glee was wiped from her face, and she deliberately assumed the expression of a properly demure young lady. "Ah, Nick, dear, how solemn you look. But you should not be wearing such a long face on Christmas Day. Put away your cares and be merry—enjoy the holidays! 'Tis the season to be jolly, you know."

"I have been giving the matter of *your* Season much thought, brat, and I have decided your mother will need some assistance with you. So you will be happy to hear that I have arranged to live with the three of you for the entire duration of your stay in London."

Dorie grimaced, but was unable even to fake any enthusiasm for Nicholas's plan. Joanna, however, could not manage to hold back a smile of pleasure. Nicholas was going to be living with them in Mrs. Donnithorne's London residence. Why, that would mean she would more than likely see him every single day.

"And before you get any ideas of avoiding me, brat, I shall be accompanying you to every single dance and musical evening and Venetian breakfast and whatever other ridiculous affairs the hostesses dream up."

At Nicholas's words, Dorie actually stuck her lower lip out in a pout, but Joanna rejoiced inwardly. To think, she would have a chance to dance with Nicholas again, to sit beside him—

"Moreover, do not expect to go driving in the park or attend the theater or the opera or Vauxhall Gardens without me—"

"You go too far," Dorie interrupted. It was obvious even to an untutored eye that she had passed the point of being able to disguise her rage. "I shall never allow you to become my watchdog."

Joanna was in alt, all her earlier misgivings about a London Season forgotten. In her wildest dreams, she had never thought she would have such an opportunity to be with Nicholas . . .

"Accept what cannot be changed, my dear little cousin, and abandon all your plans to scandalize London society." His voice held a note of command, as if he were addressing a recalcitrant private. "There will be no scandals, and you will do nothing to make yourself the object of gossip. You and Joanna are now my responsibility, and you will both be under my watchful eye until I find you each a suitable husband. And do not delude yourself that I am looking forward to that chore. I am, in fact, eagerly longing for the day when I can give you into the care of some besotted fool, who will doubtless have his hands full keeping you out of mischief."

With those words he turned on his heel and quitted the room, leaving Joanna every bit as incensed as Dorie—and every bit as determined not to let Nicholas pick out a husband for her.

8

As soon as Nicholas was gone, Dorie began to pace back and forth on the Aubusson carpet. "Now we are indeed in a coil. Nicholas will be a much stricter chaperone than ever Elizabeth would have been. Whatever are we going to do about him? We cannot allow him to force us into marriages not of our own choosing."

"Well," Joanna said fiercely, unable to hold back her feelings any longer, "I do not know what you are going to do, but I fully intend to marry Nicholas."

Dorie looked at her in amazement, and Joanna would have given anything to call back her intemperate words, which had surprised her fully as much as they amazed Dorie.

"Marry Nicholas? Whatever for?"

Screwing up her courage, Joanna looked her friend right in the eye and admitted the truth she had been trying for too long to deny. "Because I love him," she said simply.

Dorie came over and plopped herself down on the bed beside Joanna. "Well, this is quite an unexpected turn of events. But now that I think it over, I can see that you will suit each other to perfection. And I, for one, will be quite happy to call you cousin."

"But it is not quite that easy," Joanna protested. "Unfortunately, he does not love me. You heard what he said—he intends to find me a suitable husband. He is looking forward to getting rid of the both of us."

"Oh, pooh, that is nothing but talk."

"And you must admit that with his estate and his family connections, he can look much higher than me when he decides to marry."

But Dorie was no longer paying attention. She had that faraway look in her eyes that meant she was concocting an impossible scheme. She was, in fact, so deeply engrossed in her thoughts, she appeared not to notice even when Joanna gave up on her and left the room.

It was the middle of January, and Aunt Theo, as she had instructed Joanna to call her, had departed the previous week to visit her other daughter, Florie Bellgrave. Today their last remaining guest was likewise departing. Joanna stood disconsolately at the window of her room, once again watching Nicholas drive out of her life. This time, at least, it would not be so terribly long until she saw him again—a mere six weeks, in fact, before he returned at the beginning of March to escort them to London.

Belinda would doubtless also be in London by then, which was a rather depressing thought. If she decided to crook her little finger, Joanna had no doubt but that Belinda could reanimate Nicholas's infatuation for her. If indeed it was infatuation and not enduring love.

Behind her the door opened, and a few moments later Dorie stood beside her. "I have been thinking, and what we need is for you to be abducted. Then Nicholas can ride *ventre à terre* to your rescue, which will make him realize how much he loves you."

"And I *think* that you have not been *thinking* at all, you have been reading more of those silly romances by Mrs. Radcliffe. Despite your fantasies as to what it would be like, I can imagine nothing more horrible than to have a strange man make off with me. And besides, Nicholas doesn't love me to begin with, so how can he realize he loves me if in fact he does not? I am afraid he is more likely just to bawl me out."

"Just because there are a few drawbacks to my plan does not mean it will not be feasible."

"No," Joanna said firmly. "Absolutely not. I refuse to allow myself to be abducted, and that is that."

"Well, then I suppose I shall have to come up with another scheme to help you, because the way you have been mooning over Nicholas, I think you would be very poor company traveling with me around the world."

Joanna looked at Dorie in dismay. "Mooning over Nicholas? Surely I have not made my feelings for him so obvious that everyone has remarked it?"

"No, no," Dorie hastened to reassure her. "If anything, you have made it quite apparent that you do not wish to be left alone with him. If I had not heard you say with my own ears that you love him, I would be much more inclined to think you held him in disgust."

"I have merely been trying to avoid any compromising situations," Joanna said, "and I do hope he has not gotten the wrong impression."

"Well, you would do better to cast yourself at his feet and beg him to marry you," Dorie said impatiently. "If I were in love with a man, I should certainly not hesitate to tell him exactly that."

"But you are in a completely different position than I am."

"If you are referring again to your lack of dowry, then you are slandering my cousin. Nicholas would never let such mercenary factors enter into consideration."

Stung by the criticism, Joanna replied rather tartly, "I was referring to my lack of courage. Not everyone has your intrepid spirit."

With a grin, Dorie linked arms with her. "But I do believe the Lady Catherine does, so let us ignore all men and go up to the nursery and play with the babies awhile."

"Are you forgetting that Lord Edward is a member of the male half of the population? And he is not at all willing to be ignored."

"We may easily exempt any male under five from exclusion," Dorie said cheerfully. "Unless, of course, he also decides to start telling us what to do."

Three weeks after he returned home, Nicholas received a long letter from his sister, in which she enumerated with quite unnecessary enthusiasm all of Joanna's current beaux. His recently acquired little sister, or so Elizabeth wrote to him, was becoming quite the belle of Bath, and there was no doubt in anyone's mind that even without a dowry, there would be no difficulty at all in finding her a suitable husband.

With an oath, Nicholas crumped up the letter and pitched it into the fire. Despite her intelligence, Elizabeth sounded like a total lack-wit, prattling on about Joanna's suitors. Nicholas had met the majority of them during the holidays, and they were all suffering from severe deficiencies—major drawbacks that rendered them totally unsuitable as potential husbands for Joanna.

Blast it all, if he were in Wiltshire now, he would take a horsewhip to the lot of them! But he wasn't there, and Darius, who had earlier seemed a right enough sort of fellow, persisted in letting those callow youths run tame around Colthurst Hall. It did not bear thinking of!

Feeling too angry to write a civil response to his sister's letter, Nicholas strode out to the stable, where he ordered his favorite horse to be saddled.

"Begging your pardon, sir, but a storm do be coming up—"

One fierce look from Nicholas, and Richards jumped to obey the command, with no further attempt to dispute Nicholas's right to ride his own horse on his own land whenever he might choose.

During his long ride through the wind and then the rain, it gradually became clear to Nicholas just why he was so angry. He did not feel antipathy for Joanna's suitors because of their own deficiencies, but because the mere idea of her married to anyone but himself was absolutely, positively, totally unthinkable!

Why had it taken him so long to know his own heart? He had not been blind to Joanna's good qualities—he had even prattled on to her brother about what a good wife she would make. And yet he had never thought of her in that light until he had seen her at Christmas.

Did that make him as shallow and foolish and blind as the majority of men? Apparently so, for he should have offered for her long ago, before she attracted such swarms of suitors . . .

With a sinking heart he remembered abruptly that he *had*

offered for her before, and she had gotten hysterical at the mere mention of marrying him. Not that she did not care for him—at Christmas she had made it quite clear that she held him in affection . . . as a brother.

Well, it was a start. At least she did not hold him in disgust. He would just have to make a concerted effort to work on those feelings and deepen them into the kind of love necessary between a man and wife.

But suppose Joanna accepted one of her other suitors before he himself even had an opportunity to win her affections? Before he had a chance to woo her properly? Before he managed to get her to think of him as something other than a substitute brother? Blast his sister for encouraging all those Bartholomew babies to run tame around Colthurst Hall!

Nicholas gradually became aware that he was just sitting on his horse in the rain, several miles from home, accomplishing nothing except to get wet. Turning his mount in the direction of the stables, he began mentally composing a very irate letter to his sister, telling her in detail just exactly what he considered to be the deficiencies of each of Joanna's suitors.

"It ain't goin' ter be enough, yer grace," Billy said, surveying the mountains of baggage being strapped onto Aunt Theo's traveling coach.

"They need only enough clothes to last them two days until they reach the London modistes," Darius replied with a chuckle.

"That weren't what I was referrin' to," the boy replied rather gloomily. "Capt'n Goldsborough is a fine man, and I don't want you ter think I'm criticizing him, 'cause I ain't. But he ain't been around Miss Dorie enough to be up on all her tricks. I'm thinkin' that someone what knows her oughter be goin' along t' Lunnon for t' keep a watchful eye over her."

Looking down at the boy, who though small for his age had such a way with horses that he had been made an under-groom on his twelfth birthday, Darius asked politely, "And might that someone be you?"

Billy heaved a mighty sigh. "I s'pose it'll have ter be me. Ain't no one else near as good as me at ferretin' out Miss Dorie's secret plans, and now that you learned me to keep me clapper shut about what I knows, I reckon I'll have t' make the sacrifice."

There was much truth in the boy's statement: he knew more about what was happening on the estate than anyone else, and he did have almost as much rapport with Dorie as he did with the horses. Besides, the boy was a hard worker and deserved to have a vacation in London.

"It is indeed noble of you to offer your services this way," Darius replied, "especially since it means you will be missing the entire foaling season. But there is much merit in your suggestion, and I shall willingly avail myself of your assistance. There is only one thing I feel I must insist on. Please take this money along in case you have an emergency."

Billy gave him a dubious look, as if doubting he had actually heard correctly. Then he pinched himself on the arm and immediately yelped. "Just checking," he said with a sheepish smile. "Though fer a minute I must be dreamin'." With no more hesitation, he pocketed the proffered money and dashed off to the stables to fetch his things, which Darius suspected had already been packed and ready for some time.

While the carriage was being loaded under the watchful eye of Miss Hepden, Elizabeth was having a late breakfast with her aunt and the two young ladies, who were busily engaged at the other end of the table in whispering to each other.

"They do make a lovely pair, do they not?" Aunt Theo commented. "I am so glad Joanna is not blond, since her black hair sets off Dorie's fairness to perfection. I could only wish that my daughter were not so . . . so *robust.*"

"I should not worry about that if I were you. Dorie will need a very strong man, and I have noticed that such men have a very low tolerance for feminine weaknesses."

Aunt Theo looked at her dubiously, and Elizabeth acted quickly to forestall a tediously long recitation of all the strong men Aunt Theo had ever met during her many years in the *ton* who had preferred clinging vines to capable women.

"Now, do not forget that Darius insists you use Colthurst House for Dorie and Joanna's coming-out ball. Kelso will come to London in time to supervise all the arrangements, so you will have nothing to do on that score."

"Oh, dear," Aunt Theo replied, and Elizabeth immediately realized to her deep regret that she had only succeeded in replacing one worry with another. "I do wish you could be there at my side. Could you not consider coming to London just for a week or so? You would not wish to miss out completely on Dorie's triumph, would you? We have reserved a very auspicious date quite early in the Season, so you would only be . . ." She began to count on her fingers.

"Only six months along," Elizabeth said.

"Oh . . . well, perhaps you will not be showing too much, assuming you do not intend to continue producing babies at double the normal speed."

"When the time comes, we shall see what Darius has to say. He has rather strict ideas about what a St. John may and may not do, you know."

"But a *duchess* may do anything she pleases," her aunt replied in a voice that brooked no arguments.

"But the mother of a future St. John may not," Elizabeth countered in just as decided a tone.

"But you are so robust, I am sure sitting around at a dance will not fatigue you unduly."

"After, of course, two days of driving in a carriage, followed, of course, by two days of driving in a carriage—"

"Well, if that is your attitude, I am sure you will never persuade your husband to let you attend the ball."

"I shall see how I am feeling at the time, and that is all I can promise you, and," she added quickly, when her aunt began to look mulish, "there is no point in saying you are having spasms at the mere thought of coping alone, because Darius is more than likely to throw a bucket of cold water in your face and then claim that is what he was used to doing in Spain."

"Really, my dear, I do not know why you put up with such a barbarous man."

Elizabeth smiled to herself. Really, that *barbarous* man was a daily delight in so many ways.

"And keep in mind that Darius has no excuses to avoid the ball himself. I shall be most put out if he fails to put in an appearance. Why, everyone might choose to stay away in droves, and then where would we be? But no one would think of turning down an invitation to a ball given by a *duke.*"

"Even if the said duke is a barbarous man?" Elizabeth could not resist teasing her aunt.

Ignoring her interruption, Aunt Theo continued, "And as long as Darius must travel to London anyway, it will not be that much extra work for him to bring you along also."

With maddening slowness they inched their way, one step at a time, up the stairs of Colthurst House. Alexander tugged at his collar, which was in truth strangling him, no matter what his Uncle Willard might say about its being no tighter than that worn by all the other men present.

"Stop fidgeting," his Aunt Matilda ordered.

The first month in London had not been as unbearable as Alexander had expected. His uncle had not only supervised his wardrobe, but had also procured for him memberships in various clubs, taken him to Manton's, and had even been persuaded to introduce him to Gentleman Jackson.

To all Alexander's pleas, however, that the acquiring of a little town bronze was thus quite adequately taken care of, his uncle had turned a deaf ear. Despite all his efforts, Alexander had been unable to talk his way out of attending this, the Season's premier ball—the one social event it was imperative to attend, according to his aunt—overshadowed only by the opening night at Almack's, which treat was still to come.

He was plotting when and how he would be able to sneak away early when they finally reached the top of the stairs and their names were announced, although the din was already so great, he doubted anyone could hear a word the majordomo was saying.

"Lord Glengarry, Mr. and Mrs. Willard Craigmont."

The Duke of Colthurst, who seemed a reasonable sort of chap, shook hands with them and introduced them to his ward, a tiny black-haired young lady who looked as if one harsh word would send her fleeing to her room.

Then they were passed on down the line, and a rather stout lady in turban and feathers cooed, "Dear Matilda," before embracing his aunt. "I am so delighted you could come," she added.

"My dearest Theophila, nothing could have kept me away. But I wish to make known to you my nephew, Alexander Lord Glengarry. He has come down from Scotland to spend the Season with us."

Alexander did not need any prompting to play his part. Yes, he was delighted to be in London; no, there was no city quite like it; yes, it did far surpass anything Edinburgh had to offer. His real opinion of London and the English he wisely kept to himself.

"And I would like to make my daughter known to you. Dorie, my dear, this is my dear friend Mrs. Craigmont and her nephew, Lord Glengarry."

The blond-headed miss in a buttercup-yellow dress turned from the guest she had been speaking with and looked straight into Alexander's eyes. The air around her virtually crackled with latent energy, and with that one glance she walked directly into his heart. Then she smiled, and without in the least bit understanding how such a thing had happened to him, the eternal bachelor, he knew himself to be utterly lost.

"I was surprised to see you here at the ball, my dear," Lady Letitia said to Elizabeth. "I would have thought Darius would have insisted you stay safely tucked away at Colthurst Hall."

Elizabeth smiled serenely. "He was, in fact, adamantly opposed to the whole idea, but I finally persuaded him that I really needed to come to London to consult with the renowned Dr. Quigley. Now, unfortunately, Darius is determined to hold me to my fib, and he has arranged an appointment with the aforementioned accoucheur for the day after tomorrow. But it has been worth it to observe Dorie's and Joanna's triumph. Be warned, however, that despite my assurances that I am really feeling quite fit, at the stroke of midnight Darius intends to whisk me away to my room. How he expects me to sleep with all the music and noise, I do not know. They make a lovely couple, do they not?" she said, abruptly changing the subject.

"To whom are you referring, my dear?"

"My brother and the young lady he persists in referring to as his self-appointed little sister, Miss Joanna Pettigrew. They are both deeply in love, but each thinks the other is completely indifferent."

"Yes, I noticed the strong attraction between them the first time I saw them together."

"Now, if only we could find a suitable husband for Dorie," Elizabeth said with a sigh.

"Actually, my dear, since I last wrote you, I have found the man I think will be perfect for her."

Turning to Lady Letitia, Elizabeth could not hide her relief. "Do tell me about him."

"He is the son of a dear friend of mine who married a wild Scottish Highlander. He—the son, that is—has a degree from the University of Edinburgh, and although he is not the least bit bookish, he is well able to hold his own in intelligent conversation. Besides being well-built, handsome, and utterly charming, he can outshoot, outride, outfence, outwrestle, outdance, outeverything any man he has ever met. When he marries Dorie, he will doubtless drag her all over the Highlands, taking her climbing, hiking, hunting, fishing, golfing, and who knows what all. From what his mother tells me, he is as bored with conventional society as Dorie is, and I think they will deal very nicely with each other."

"It does indeed sound as if they are perfectly matched. But tell me, if you do not mind revealing your professional secrets, how do you intend to arrange for them to meet each other?"

"Oh, they have already met. He is here this evening. In fact, they are dancing together at this very moment."

Elizabeth turned to look. "The Scottish baron?"

Lady Letitia nodded. "Lord Glengarry. His mother was Dorothea Beaumont before she married his father and removed to Edinburgh."

"But . . . but, he is nothing like you described. Twice during the course of this one dance I have seen him tread on her toes, which does not speak well for his agility, and as for holding his own in intelligent conversation, so far he has given me the impression that he is a total lack-wit. If he can put two words together in a sentence, it is more than I have noticed. Are you sure his mother is not exaggerating his qualities slightly—or even greatly?"

"He came to tea with me last week, and he is exactly as I have described him." Lady Letitia smiled. "I have observed this evening that it is only when he is around Dorie that words fail him and he is suddenly afflicted with two left feet. I suspect that any matchmaking efforts on my part would be superfluous."

"Oh, dear, this is terrible," Elizabeth said ruefully.

"Terrible? In what way?"

"Darius is dragging me back to Wiltshire at the end of the week, and I would dearly love to stay and observe both pairs of lovers. You must promise me, dear Lady Letitia, that you will write me long, long letters and tell me every detail of the courtships."

It was the afternoon of the next day before Joanna woke up, and she would have slept for another hour or two had not Dorie come bouncing in to see if she was awake.

"You are not really sleeping, because your eyes are too tightly scrunched up, so you may as well stop pretending."

"Really, Dorie," Joanna said without opening her eyes, "it should be obvious even to you that if I am pretending to be asleep, it must mean I do not wish to wake up yet."

"How can you be such a grouch this morning? We were each an absolute *succès fou* last night, you must admit. We did not sit out a single dance, except for the waltzes, which is the most aggravating thing.''

Bowing to the inevitable, Joanna opened her eyes and pushed herself up in bed. ''And I noticed you even tried to dance one of the waltzes, except that Nicholas stopped you before you got too far out onto the floor.''

Dorie grinned. ''Well, I warned everyone that it is my intention to scandalize the *ton* so that I will be sent home in great disgrace. But last night was fun in its own way, so perhaps I shall behave myself a little while first. But if I become bored, I still intend to do whatever it takes to liven things up.''

''Did you not feel the slightest partiality to any of your partners?''

''Actually, the only man who stands out in my mind was a singular disaster—a redheaded giant from Scotland, who seemed determined to dance on my feet instead of his own.''

''The only Scotsman I remember is Lord Glengarry, and I found him to be quite a good dancer. Surely you cannot mean him?''

''Yes, I believe that was the man—dressed in conservative clothes, clumsy, no conversation at all—in short, the most boring man present.''

''No, no, you must be mistaken. That description does not at all fit the man I danced with. Perhaps there were two overly large Scotsmen with red hair?''

''I would not know about that, but Mama has sent word that we have gentlemen callers below and that we are to present ourselves in the Chinese room as soon as possible. Perhaps he will be one of them, and we can discover if he has a twin brother.''

''Oh,'' Joanna cried, throwing back the bedclothes. ''Why did you wait so long to tell me we have visitors?'' Climbing out of bed, she tugged on the bell rope to summon Miss Hepden.

Dorie shrugged. ''Why should it matter to me if various and assorted young men have come to call? I have no interest in sitting indoors on such a beautiful day. I would rather go for a long walk or a gallop in the park, which is, of course, another of the pleasures forbidden to us during the Season. And *you* surely cannot have an interest in any of these ever-so-proper young men, because you are already in love with Nicholas. So let them sip tea with Mama until their back teeth float away, I could not care less."

Joanna splashed water on her face and felt a little revived. Hurriedly she began searching through her wardrobe for her new lavender dress.

Dorie suddenly laughed out loud. "I have just thought of the most marvelous plan. If you wish to attract Nicholas's attention, you need only make him jealous by flirting with other men."

"Really, Dorie, I wish you would give up all this scheming. I have told you over and over that I do not have any real expectations of winning Nicholas's affections. I have decided that I shall spend my life as a companion to some old lady."

Dorie grabbed her arm and spun her around, then shoved her face up to within inches of the mirror over her dressing table. "Take a good look at what is reflected in your mirror. Yours is *not* the face of a dried-up spinster who reads aloud to old ladies and takes their disgusting little pugs for walks in the park. Yours is a face that inspires men to write poetry, even to fight duels over."

Fortunately for Joanna, Miss Hepden appeared just then and chased Dorie back to her own room with orders for her to start her own toilette.

While the older woman combed out her tangled curls, Joanna stared at her reflection in the mirror and thought about what Dorie had said.

Her face did have a sort of appeal, though it held no measure of classical beauty. And as Dorie had pointed out, each of their dance cards had been filled very early in the evening. And the ball had not been a repeat of the dances Joanna had attended in Brussels, when the young men had scarcely noticed that they were dancing with her. Last night her partners had focused all their attention on her, and their glances had never drifted off to admire some other beauty.

So she should by rights have enjoyed herself immensely.

That she hadn't was all Nicholas's fault. Whereas in Brussels he had been the only one to converse with her, last night he had spoken to everyone except her. Not once during the course of the evening—not during dinner or the dance afterward—had he addressed a single remark to her. Nor had he ever looked her directly in the eye. His attention, in fact, had obviously been elsewhere, and she rather suspected that he had been watching for Belinda, who was apparently not yet come to London, since the footman had brought her invitation back, reporting that the knockers were not yet up on the Dillons's front door.

No, Nicholas had definitely singled her, Joanna, out—not as someone he especially cared about, but as someone he wanted to avoid having anything to do with. It was obvious to her that he still blamed her for almost trapping him into marriage.

Oh, if only she could leave London and Nicholas behind and return to Colthurst Hall when Elizabeth did! But the duke had already spent so much money on her wardrobe, and Elizabeth was counting on her to deflect Dorie from following a course leading to ruin, and Nicholas was determined to find her a husband—all in all, too many people would become upset if Joanna even suggested going back to Wiltshire.

And Joanna was too much a coward to face their combined ire.

9

The first person Nicholas saw when he entered his aunt's drawing room was the ubiquitous Scotsman. Did that blasted man have nowhere else to go? For the last sennight Glengarry had arrived with the first of the morning callers, planted himself firmly beside Joanna, and resisted all of her other suitors' efforts to dislodge him.

Even while Nicholas watched, Joanna looked up at the wretched man and began speaking in an animated way. What did she find in that dour, unsmiling Scot that caused her to be so free with her own smiles?

The man was persistent, Nicholas had to give him credit for that. No matter what evening festivities Nicholas had escorted his two charges to, the man had appeared, claimed his two dances with Joanna, and spent the rest of the evening standing around near her like a lovesick calf.

As much as it pained Nicholas to admit it, the time had come when he needed to find out exactly what the other man's intentions were. If he was trifling with Joanna's affections, Nicholas would challenge him to a duel and take the greatest pleasure in running his sword through the other man's gizzard.

On the other hand, he realized that it would be infinitely worse if the Scotsman's intentions were honorable, because it was quite obvious to Nicholas that Joanna had a decided partiality for the taciturn baron. If Glengarry put his luck to the test and offered for her, doubtless Joanna would accept, and then where would he be?

Where indeed? He knew precisely where. In a hell of his own making.

But on the other hand, where would he be if he refused to allow Joanna to marry the man she loved? Deuce take it, but this was the very devil of a coil.

Well, there was nothing for it but to speak to the man. No matter how distasteful the task, it could not be delayed much longer, because people were already beginning to talk. The Scotsman was so obvious in his pursuit of Joanna, bets would soon be laid in the clubs as to his probable success, and Nicholas would be powerless to do anything to prevent that.

By the time Aunt Theophila rose to her feet and indicated that visiting hours were at an end, Nicholas had exhausted his meager supply of patience. Following the Scotsman out of the house, he quickly caught up with him.

"A word with you, Glengarry, if you've the time."

The man halted his steps and turned toward Nicholas, and the look of abject misery on his face was pathetic enough that even Nicholas could not remain totally unsympathetic.

"The time has come when you need to state your intentions."

The man nodded glumly. "Of course. They are honorable. I wish to marry her, the sooner the better."

It was as bad as Nicholas had feared. Heartsick at the possibility that he was very close to losing Joanna forever, he began walking slowly down the street, the Scotsman automatically falling in beside him.

"Since I stand more or less as her guardian," Nicholas said when they had covered half a block or so, "I feel it is my duty to inquire as to your prospects."

To Nicholas's chagrin, the Scotsman's prospects were faultless—a large estate in the Highlands free of mortgage, ample funds inherited from his mother's side of the family, now prudently invested in government consols, an old and respected title, impeccable lineage.

There was no way Nicholas could possibly refuse to let such a man make Joanna an offer. It was, in fact, a real feather in her cap that she, an orphan with no dowry and no powerful relatives, had managed to attract such an eligible *parti*.

Nicholas now felt as glum as Glengarry looked. What was especially galling was the knowledge that the *ton* would consider it a much better match than if she were to marry Nicholas. There was, of course, the remote possibility that Joanna would turn down the offer. Women were illogical creatures, as he had learned to his chagrin, and one could gamble away a dozen fortunes trying to predict which way they would jump.

"Joanna has been encouraging me, but I fear it is hopeless," Glengarry muttered.

The last of Nicholas's hopes died a quick death. Joanna was actually encouraging the other man's suit. But wait. Why . . . ?

"Why do you say 'hopeless'? It seems to me your chances of winning her consent are excellent."

"Because the moment I look at her, my heart starts pounding in my chest, I become as breathless as if I had run twenty miles, and worst of all, my tongue cleaves to the roof of my mouth and I cannot utter a word. She is so beautiful, but it is more than that. The first time I saw her, I knew she was the woman I wanted to spend the rest of my life with."

Whereas Nicholas had not recognized the depth of his own love until months after he met Joanna. Granted, she had been a rather forlorn little waif when he had first made her acquaintance, but still, he should have been more astute.

"You are her cousin," Glengarry continued, "so you are undoubtedly too accustomed to her looks to recognize what a potent effect they can have on a man."

Nicholas started to explain that he was not actually Joanna's cousin when the truth suddenly hit him. Too embarrassed to admit to the other man that they had been talking the whole time at cross-purposes, he instead tested his new understanding of the situation by asking, "So you actually wish to marry my cousin Dorie?"

Glengarry nodded. "But how can I ever offer for Miss Donnithorne when I am unable even to say good afternoon to her without stammering? Or to dance with her without stumbling over my own feet?"

To Nicholas it seemed as if the sun had suddenly come out. The whole day was somehow brighter, and the Scotsman was with those few words magically transformed from a surly lout into a truly admirable chap.

"Well," Nicholas said quite cheerfully, clapping Lord Glengarry on the back, "you may count on my wholehearted support. But I feel it only honorable to warn you that Dorie will make you a wretched wife. She is good with children, but in all other ways she is quite an unnatural female. If you have any ideas that she will sit complacently at home by the fire and allow you to go off hunting or fishing, then I must rid you now of those false notions."

For a moment the other man's step faltered, but then he resumed walking. "It doesn't matter. I am willing to give up any of my activities to marry Miss Donnithorne."

"Give up? I said nothing about giving up hunting and fishing. What I was trying to say is that Dorie will insist that you take her with you. In fact, she will more than likely be leading the way. Her current stated ambition is to sail around the world, and knowing my cousin, I rather think you will be hard pressed to keep up with her."

"At last you give me hope that I may succeed," Glengarry said, his face also brightening.

"Your biggest problem, I am afraid, is that Dorie has long ago decided that men, with very few exceptions, are boring. But take heart. You have only to persuade her that if she marries you she will be escaping London drawing rooms forever, and she will likely fall into your lap like a ripe plum."

"I want a word with you, Nick!"

Nicholas moaned and tried to bury his head under his pillow. "It is not at all proper for a young lady to be in a man's bedroom, Dorie, not even when the man is her cousin."

"A pox on propriety!"

His cousin's words stabbed through his head like a knife, causing Nicholas to regret every drop of the truly superb brandy he had imbibed the night before, when he and Glengarry had futilely attempted to drown their frustrations. He should, he knew, remonstrate with Dorie for using such vulgar language, but it was too early in the morning for him to summon the necessary energy to pursue what he knew was a hopeless cause.

"I am sick to death of your constantly throwing that wretched Scotsman in my path. He is the last man on earth I would ever consider marrying, so you might as well give it up and tell him to leave me alone."

Dorie apparently thought it was necessary to speak especially loudly so that he would be able to hear her over the pounding inside his skull—she was now virtually shrieking.

"I am hereby serving notice that if you continue to inform him of all my plans in advance so that he can 'happen' to meet us when we are shopping or walking in the park or going to the theater, then I shall be forced to do something drastic!"

As if screaming in his ear would not be considered already drastic enough! "You have never even gotten to know the real baron. 'Tis not Glengarry's fault that every time he gets anywhere near you he becomes tongue-tied and clumsy and—"

"Bah! Do you honestly think I would marry someone who is afraid of me? Who cringes and cowers abjectly at my feet?"

No matter what the condition of his head, Nicholas could not allow such slander of the long-suffering and much-put-upon man who had become his best friend in London. Rolling out of bed, he grabbed his cousin's arm and shook her. "Glengarry is not a coward, and he is not the least bit intimidated by you. The poor man is in *love* with you, you wretched girl, which is a fate I would not wish on my worst enemy."

Surveying him up and down, Dorie remarked, "I always wondered what men wore in bed."

With horror, Nicholas realized that his legs were exposed from the knees to his bare toes, and he quickly dropped Dorie's arm and retreated to the bed, where he pulled the covers up to his neck, properly, albeit belatedly, concealing every inch of his nightshirt.

"You are an abominable brat."

"And you are turning into a more persistent and peskier matchmaker than . . . than even *Lady Letitia*!"

Just when Nicholas thought things could not get any worse, someone tapped on the half-opened door and Joanna stepped timidly into his room. It was too much for a man to face the morning after, and Nicholas promptly slid farther down, pulling the blankets all the way up over his head.

Someone—Dorie, more than likely, because at least Joanna had a healthy sense of proper decorum—tugged at the covers and tried to wrest them away from his face, but Nicholas was stronger than she was. That was about all he could be thankful for.

Then Joanna spoke in dulcet tones, which soothed rather than aggravated his jangled nerves. "Dorie, I think it would be best to come away now. Nicholas is not looking quite well, and it would be kinder to save your quarrel with him until he is feeling more the thing."

Just the sound of her voice eased his pain—how much more comforting it would be in his present wretched condition to feel her hand stroking his forehead! He groaned at the thought, and Joanna immediately intensified her efforts to remove Dorie from his room, finally succeeding only by invoking the name of Miss Hepden.

What an angel Joanna was! What a paragon of all the feminine virtues! She deserved someone finer than himself—someone with no faults or flaws—someone who never indulged in brandy to excess . . . someone who never bickered childishly with a girl cousin . . . someone who could be civil even before breakfast . . .

And if such a pattern card of respectability came along, Nicholas admitted to himself, he would not hesitate to call the man out or start scurrilous rumors about him or in some way besmirch his reputation—whatever it took to destroy the man in Joanna's eyes.

Generosity of spirit was another virtue he, Nicholas, seemed to be lacking, because there was no way he intended to do the honorable thing and stand aside to allow Joanna to wed another. One way or another, he would *make* her fall in love with him.

Fortunately, she was not yet showing signs of partiality for any other man.

Unfortunately, despite his best efforts, to date she still looked upon him as a brother.

Almack's—the holiest of all holies—the ultimate goal of all the matchmaking mothers determined to marry off their silly, flighty daughters. And without doubt the most boring place in London, Dorie concluded, staring around glumly. No matter how much the other young ladies were thrilled to be here, she herself, given the choice, would much prefer to be back in the stables throwing dice with Billy and eating hot meat pies purchased from a street vendor. Unfortunately, her relatives refused to give her a choice.

Here in these assembly rooms, she was not only forced to subsist on stale cakes and weak lemonade, but she was positively hemmed in by propriety, her every action cribbed by the patronesses' archaic rules. As if that were not bad enough, Nicholas had planted himself firmly on the chair beside her to ensure that she did not take it into her head to enliven the evening by breaking one of those selfsame stuffy rules.

It was enough to drive even the most patient person to violence, and she herself had never been known for her forbearance, which was about to be put to an additional test, because bearing down on them was Sally Jersey, and tagging along behind her was Lord Glengarry, who could always be counted upon to make the most boring situation deteriorate from vexatious to intolerable.

"Miss Donnithorne, I notice you are not dancing," Lady Jersey said coyly.

Of course not, you twit, Dorie thought to herself. Because you and your cronies have a stupid rule that forbids young ladies to waltz without first gaining your permission. Mutinously—and quite rudely—Dorie kept her mouth shut.

After waiting only a few seconds for the response that

should have been forthcoming, but which was not, Lady Jersey continued, "May I present to you Lord Glengarry, who I am sure will make you an admirable partner for this waltz?"

Dorie scowled, and it was obvious from Lady Jersey's supercilious smirk that she already knew full well Dorie had no desire whatsoever to dance with Lord Glengarry-of-the-two-left-feet. Well, Nicholas might be able to keep her from waltzing without permission, but he was about to discover that it was not in his power to *make* her waltz if she had her mind set against it, which she did.

"We thank you for your interest, Lady Jersey," Nicholas said quite properly, "and I am sure my cousin will be delighted to waltz with Lord Glengarry." Then without warning Nicholas jabbed his thumb into a particularly sensitive spot on Dorie's back which caused her to yelp and leap to her feet. "See how eager she is?"

Mentally vowing to get revenge on her despicable cousin, Dorie mutely allowed herself to be led out onto the dance floor.

The gods, who had been so generous with him at birth, giving him far more than his share of good looks, charm, wit, strength, intelligence, and courage, without, Alexander realized full well, burdening him with a single flaw or blemish that might somehow hamper his carefree progress through life, now seemed to regret their openhanded generosity. Of a certainty, some higher power must have loaded the dice against him, perhaps in an effort to teach him humility, or merely to toy with his heart before breaking it?

To be sure, his hand was now resting on the delightfully trim waist of his beloved, and she was waltzing gracefully in his arms, but he could not in all honesty say that either of them was deriving any enjoyment from the dance. Would that he could cast aside all considerations of propriety and pull her the rest of the way into his arms and kiss her thoroughly. Maybe that was exactly what he needed to do in order to regain his confidence and poise?

Since that course of action was forbidden him as a gentleman, however, he frantically tried to remember the suggestions Miss Pettigrew had offered him as suitable topics of conversation, but his mind was blank as a slate, wiped clean by one glance into the enchanting blue eyes of his ladylove, eyes that were no less enticing even though at this moment they were icy with disdain. In desperation he finally blurted out, ''That is a lovely gown you are wearing, Miss Donnithorne.''

As a conversational gambit, it lacked style, wit, and originality, but it still might have achieved a modest level of success had he not at that precise moment trodden on the hem of the aforementioned gown. The horrible sound of a flounce being ripped was like the death knell to all his hopes.

Completely forgetting that he was still holding her waist, he tried to back away from her with the object of preventing further accidents, but he succeeded only in bumping into the couple behind him, whereupon an inadvertent elbow in his back thrust him forward again, causing him to crash against Miss Donnithorne. By now completely off-balance, he was in danger not only of falling to the floor but also of dragging her—or even worse, her gown—down with him.

Somehow, no thanks to his clumsy efforts to help, she managed to keep them both on their feet and to prevent any further damage to her dress. She proved herself to be, in fact, surprisingly strong and agile for a female.

''Let go of me, you great lumbering beast,'' she hissed once he was steady on his feet, and no sooner did he release her than with one last disdainful look she turned and stalked from the floor, of necessity holding her skirts up slightly so that she would not trip on the dangling flounce.

There was a titter nearby, and Alexander was well aware that he was the cynosure of all the other dancers—an object of ridicule, ignominiously abandoned by his partner. None of it mattered one whit to him, however. The only one whose opinion he cared about was Miss Donnithorne, and once again he had failed to attain even a small measure of her regard.

Thoroughly disconsolate, he retreated to the sidelines with

the intention of seeking out Miss Pettigrew, who never failed to find a word of encouragement for him in his pursuit of her friend and companion—a pursuit that with every passing day only seemed all the more hopeless.

Joanna was not unaware of the fiasco recently enacted on another part of the dance floor. Indeed, it would be amazing if anyone in the entire room had missed observing it. When her partner returned her to her aunt's side, she was therefore not at all surprised to discover Lord Glengarry waiting for her. He looked quite sheepish, and reminded her forcibly of little Lord Edward after he had accidentally spilled his milk.

Unfortunately, this time she could not think of a single thing to say to Lord Glengarry to lift his spirits.

"That bad, is it?" he asked.

"She will forgive . . . might forget . . . could possibly . . ." The false words of encouragement stuck in Joanna's throat. "Yes, I am afraid I must agree that everything seems to be getting worse rather than better," she finally admitted.

"Would that I could drown my troubles in brandy, but not only is there nothing here to drink except weak orgeat, which I would have to drink by the gallon, but also Nicholas and I tried that last night, and all I got for my effort was a thick head. I suppose Nicholas was likewise feeling the worse for wear this morning," he stated more than asked.

"Nicholas was trying to drown his troubles last night? What troubles?"

Looking excruciatingly guilty and obviously aware that he had revealed more than he should have, Lord Glengarry became almost as tongue-tied as he was when he was around Dorie. After stammering a bit, he quickly and without actually answering Joanna's question excused himself to claim his partner for the next dance.

It did not matter that he refused to divulge the truth. Joanna knew very well what the problem was that was driving Nicholas to drink. Dorie was half of it, and she herself was the other half. Nicholas would not be able to return to his beloved home in Somerset until she and Dorie were safely married off.

Her partner for the next dance appeared and led her out to join a set that was forming, but Joanna went through her steps automatically, not making any effort to converse with the boy, a young, rather stout lad from Dorset who looked as if he would be more at home behind a plow than at a London assembly.

Nicholas's problem, she realized with a twinge of guilt, was that although Dorie had at least one viable candidate for her hand, Joanna had deliberately and firmly resisted singling out any one of her suitors for special attention, lest she nurture false hopes in some innocent man's breast.

She had thought, of course, that she could somehow kindle the warmer emotions in Nicholas—that she could cause him to fall in love with her. Never had she even for a moment considered how this might make Nicholas feel. "Trapped" was the only word for it, she now conceded. If she did not find a husband by the end of the Season, how could she expect him not to feel honor-bound to offer for her yet again?

This conclusion was now so obvious to her, she was appalled by her earlier naiveté. No, not naiveté, by her wishful thinking, which had blinded her to reality. She had sworn never to marry anyone except Nicholas, without realizing that because of her position—lacking money and family as she did—she was essentially forcing Nicholas to marry her.

By the time the dance was over, her mind was made up. She would put aside her futile dreams and marry whomever Nicholas recommended to her. Given his vehement reaction to her aunt and uncle, she could at least rely on Nicholas to pick out a husband who would be kind to her—someone she could respect even if she could not love him.

She checked her dance card and saw that Nicholas was down for the next dance, a waltz, and she was grateful that she could follow through on her new resolution at once, without having time for cowardly second thoughts.

With deep pain in her heart she watched him make his way across the crowded floor to where she was sitting. He was, to her way of thinking, quite the most handsome man in the room. But not the right man for her, no matter how she might wish it.

Bowing, he extended his hand, and laying her own on his, she allowed him to lead her out. The music started, Nicholas placed his hand firmly on her waist, and she almost burst into tears.

By biting the inside of her cheek, she managed not to disgrace herself beyond redemption, but it was a few moments before she could trust herself enough to speak.

"I have been wishing to discuss my suitors with you," she said. At her words, a fleeting expression crossed his face, but it was gone so fast, she could not identify it. Was it guilt? Or relief? "I am hoping you can advise me."

He smiled down at her, but his smile was patently false and covered up . . . what?

"Whom are you considering seriously?"

"Perhaps Lord Guybon?"

"Out of the question," Nicholas replied quickly. "He will never marry where there is not a fortune, no matter how serious he appears to be."

"Well, Mr. Lomax-Ogden is certainly not in need of a wife to fatten his coffers."

Again Nicholas shook his head. "He has stated quite openly in the clubs that he will settle for nothing less than an earl's daughter."

"I see. Well, then would Sir Rivington be acceptable?"

"Only if you wish to observe for yourself how quickly a man can gamble away every shilling that comes into his hands. All the Rivingtons are afflicted with that curse."

"Perhaps Mr. Cantrell, then? He seems to be a moderate man. I have never seen him gamble, nor heard him talk of any wagers he has made."

"He spends all his ready on . . ." Nicholas paused, then continued bluntly, "on his mistress."

"Oh," Joanna said, hoping she would not disgrace herself by blushing. She cast around in her mind for another possible suitor, but the only one she could think of was the Reverend Mr. Fitzwalter, whose only flaw was that he was a prosy bore. Well, a lifetime of listening to long-winded, tedious sermons was a small price to pay for Nicholas's happiness. "Then I suppose it will have to be the Reverend Mr. Fitzwalter."

Nicholas looked down at Joanna in dismay. That prosy bore? Surely she could not prefer such a conceited, pompous, self-important, egotistical bag of wind as Fitzwalter?

Frantically Nicholas searched for something to say that would render Fitzwalter clearly ineligible as a prospective bridegroom. But the man was as meticulous in his habits as he was offensive in his vapidity. On the other hand, the fact that the clergyman had never had an original idea in his life was hardly a reason to rule him out as a possible husband for Joanna.

A bullet through the chest might well make him less than a perfect candidate, Nicholas thought with bloodthirsty relish. Fortunately, it need not come to that, because just in time he remembered a fatal flaw, not in Fitzwalter's character, but in his family.

"Well," he said looking down into Joanna's trusting eyes, "the only thing you might wish to consider is that his mother, who would be your mother-in-law, reminds me very much of your own aunt." And that, he thought, watching Joanna's expression change to one of horror, quite nicely puts paid to the reverend's matrimonial hopes.

"But you need not fret yourself," he continued smoothly when she failed to suggest another candidate for his approval. "The Season is yet in its infancy, and there is still ample opportunity for you to attach the proper young man."

Unfortunately, when he thought about it, the weeks seemed to be flying by at an impossible speed, probably because he was making no progress with Joanna. Therefore he should perhaps, before his time ran out, make an effort to court her more intensively—make it quite obvious to her that she had caught his interest.

Before he could open his campaign with a suitably flowery compliment, however, his attention was caught by some late arrivals, who gained admittance only minutes before the doors were closed for the evening. Three people only, a man and wife and their fair daughter, but at the sight of them smiling and nodding to acquaintances, Nicholas was filled with righteous indignation, which soon resolveld itself into wrath.

The Dillons had apparently decided London offered more than Paris. For a moment Nicholas caught Belinda's eye, and to his utter amazement, she smiled at him. Did the stupid chit not even have enough conscience to feel properly guilty for what she had done?

Well, if she was imagining that he was willing to overlook her deliberate abandonment of Joanna—to consider it as being of no more importance than the accidental misplacement of a shawl or handkerchief—then Belinda was dead wrong. And so he would not hesitate to inform her.

And he had no intention of mincing his words. It was about time someone pricked her bubble of self-importance, of *amour propre*. Yes, those were the precise words to describe Belinda—she was so filled with love for herself, she could offer none to any other person.

For a few moments Joanna had felt hope. After all, why would Nicholas be so quick to disparage her other suitors unless he himself were attracted to her? But she was chasing after a chimera—a mere illusion—and was once more giving in to the dangers of self-deception.

Because the moment Belinda had appeared in the doorway, looking exactly like a golden goddess, all Nicholas's attention had been riveted on her. Even now, Joanna could sense his eagerness to join the ever-enlarging throng of young men surrounding Belinda. Moreover, from the look on his face, he was feeling despair at the mere thought of being too late to enter his name on her dance card.

Generosity of spirit made Joanna say, "If you would not mind, I am growing a trifle fatigued and would prefer to sit out the rest of the dance beside your aunt."

Without displaying even the slightest pretense of reluctance, Nicholas hustled her off the floor and back to his Aunt Theo. As she had expected, he then quickly worked his way around the edge of the room to where Belinda was holding court.

Joanna wanted nothing more than to flee out into the night—to lose herself in London. But even if she could run away from Nicholas, she could never run fast enough to escape from her own heart, which was now surely breaking.

10

''Why, Captain Goldsborough, how delightful to see you again.'' The entrancing Miss Dillon allowed her dimples to appear, then frowned prettily and rapped Nicholas playfully on the arm with her fan. ''But you have been too, too naughty, dear boy, staying away from us all this time. Why, it is now three full days since we returned to London, and this is the first you have shown your face. I am tempted not to let you have the waltz that I saved especially for you.''

There was a chorus of protests from the other young men crowding around her, and each one began importuning her to give him the waltz instead, but she merely laughed, a gay, tinkling laugh, like little silver bells. ''No, no, my gallant captain must have his waltz, as a reward for the noble way he has served his country so bravely.''

Nicholas felt a deep revulsion at the thought of holding this heartless flirt in his arms and dancing with her, but he could not pass up such a perfect opportunity to tell her exactly where she stood in his estimation. Gritting his teeth to hold back the angry words that were welling up inside of him, he took the card she was holding out to him and scrawled his name beside the waltz, which was the next dance after the country dance now forming.

Laying her hand on his arm and giving it a most improper squeeze, Miss Dillon looked up at him and batted her eyelashes artlessly. ''Oh, I do adore strong, silent men. They have such an aura of mystery about them, which I find *most* attractive.''

Immediately the men gathered around her stiffened their

backs, shut their mouths, and attempted to look as if they, too, were strong, silent, mysterious men.

With a last merry laugh, Miss Dillon allowed herself to be led out by a young man dressed to the nines in bottle-green jacket, puce satin waistcoat, and canary-yellow knee breeches.

Nicholas retired to lean negligently against the wall, from which vantage point he watched the delectable Miss Dillon dancing so gracefully that she made the other young girls in her set look positively awkward and gauche in comparison.

The country dance dragged on interminably, and the waiting did not cool Nicholas's temper in the slightest. Eventually, however, it was his turn to lead Miss Dillon out onto the floor. The music started, they began to dance, and at last he was able to express the feelings he had been bottling up inside him since he had first heard that she had abandoned Joanna.

"You are looking especially beautiful this evening, Miss Dillon. You quite take the shine out of the other young ladies."

Even while preening herself at his compliments, she pretended a modesty he knew was as false as everything else about her.

"Oh, la, Mr. Goldsborough, you will turn my head with such flattery."

"It is indeed unfortunate," he continued, carefully keeping his voice low so that none of the other dancers might overhear him, "that behind your beautiful face and form you have such a cold, calculating heart and such a mean, petty spirit. Do you not find it amusing, O most beautiful Miss Dillon, how so few people have seen behind that mask you wear?"

She stiffened in his arms, and her mouth took on a pinched look, and for a moment she allowed the ugliness in her soul to show on her face.

"Tut, tut, Miss Dillon, you must not forget to smile. Remember, all eyes are watching you, and you must not disappoint—or disillusion—your faithful admirers."

Her lower lip began to quiver adorably, and tears pooled in her beautiful green eyes, causing them to sparkle like emeralds. "Oh," she said in a truly piteous voice, "how can you speak so to me? Is it perhaps jealousy, that I have been neglecting you to dance with so many others?"

"Bravo, Miss Dillon," he replied with a smile every bit as false as her tears. "Well done, really well done. I had no idea you could do bathos so beautifully. Has it required long hours of practice in front of your mirror?"

She smiled in return, and her face lit up as if the sun had peeped out from behind the clouds, but in a low voice, which no longer held the slightest resemblance to little silver bells, she said, "Why are you persecuting me this way? What have I done to cause you to harden your heart against me?"

"Why, you have done nothing to me—but then, I was never your friend, and it appears that you save your greatest treachery for your friends. It is only your closest friends, in fact, whom you callously abandon at the first hint of danger to your own skin."

For a moment she looked truly puzzled; then he saw comprehension dawn—but not the slightest evidence of guilt. If he had seen the least sign of shame or repentance for what she had done, he would have given up his plans for revenge and returned her to her mother's side.

"Oh, I understand now. Joanna is the one who has turned you against me. Really, sir," she said quite earnestly, "it amazes me that you should believe such an untrustworthy, flighty girl. I do not know what lies she has told you, or how she has twisted the facts to make it appear that she was blameless. I am sure, however, that she did not bother to inform you that my mother told her quite specifically that there was no need for her to go running off to see her brother."

Miss Dillon's callous attitude was beyond belief, thought Nicholas, as was her glib manner of excusing her own inexcusable behavior.

"Unfortunately, Joanna was too willful to listen," Belinda said, looking quite affronted. "Why, I myself reminded her that she must be sure to return in time to accompany us to Antwerp, but I might as well have been speaking to the moon for all the heed she paid my instructions. She was totally set on having her own way, no matter how inconvenient it might be for us.

"Really, Mr. Goldsborough, it must be apparent even to you that everything that happened in Brussels was all Joanna's own fault. And I must tell you frankly, I feel it is quite wicked of her to try to lay the blame at my feet. Pon rep, one would think the girl would have the decency, after all I have done for her, to show a little gratitude for my generosity, rather than spreading scurrilous lies about my character."

Miss Dillon honestly believed what she was saying, Nicholas realized with amazement. The spoiled beauty was so totally self-centered, she had no idea of the enormity of the offense she had committed. She was apparently incapable of considering anyone else's needs or desires—except, of course, if they chanced to affect herself. He was obviously wasting his time trying to bring her to a sense of shame for her actions.

"Do you know, Miss Dillon, as beautiful as you are, you remind me of an apple that appears perfectly delectable from the outside, but when one cuts into it, one discovers it is wormy and rotten to the core."

Still smiling sweetly, she hissed at him, "And you, Mr. Goldsborough, may go to perdition and take your precious Joanna with you."

"Why, I should be delighted to set out at once, Miss Dillon." With one last smile, Nicholas dropped his hands and walked away from her, abandoning her on the dance floor as ruthlessly as she had abandoned Joanna in Brussels.

There were gasps of astonishment around him; then someone tittered, and someone else snickered. Then the whispering started and increased in intensity until it could be heard even above the music. Nicholas did not pause, nor did he acknowledge the stares that were aimed in his direction. He merely smiled, that wonderfully enigmatic smile of a strong, silent, mysterious man.

Belinda had never in her life—never, *ever*—been put in such an embarrassing position. People were staring at her, which in itself was quite normal, but they were also making sport of her, which was totally unheard of. No one laughed at her—no one! She was the incomparable Miss Dillon; she was not an object of amusement!

"May I escort you to your seat, Miss Dillon?"

A suave voice sounded beside her, and Belinda turned to see a young man dressed in scarlet regimentals standing there. Vaguely she remembered meeting him in Brussels.

"Lieutenant Gryndle at your service. We danced together at the Craigmonts' ball in Brussels," he reminded her, and the kindness and admiration she could see in his eyes was a balm to her wounded spirit.

"Thank you, you are most gentlemanly," she replied, casting her eyes down modestly.

Offering her his arm, he acted as if escorting abandoned young ladies from the dance floor were an everyday occurrence, scarcely worthy of remark.

After complimenting her on her dress and asking her if it was from Paris, he began to discuss French fashion with her in a knowledgeable way. Not once did he question her about or even allude to her present embarrassing predicament, for which he earned her undying gratitude—and more important, she even decided it was only fair to reward him for his gallantry by removing another's name from her dance card and substituting his for the next waltz.

Lieutenant Gryndle, at least, was properly cognizant of the great honor she was thereby bestowing on him, and he was not slow to voice his humble gratitude for such preferential treatment.

Owing to his family's refusal to support his more extravagant habits, Lieutenant Peter Gryndle was presently residing in a miserably cramped room above a common tavern. He was also forced by a cruel and unjust fate, which had not seen fit to make him the heir to a fortune, to supplement his meager income as a half-pay officer by the judicious use of a deck of cleverly marked cards, which he had taken the liberty of removing from the pocket of a treacherous Spaniard. Now, however, if he played his cards right, he realized, concealing a grin of triumph at his own clever turn of phrase, he was about to correct that omission.

The lovely Miss Dillon, only offspring and sole heiress of a wealthy, doting father, had just been handed to him on a silver platter.

He did not, of course, have any illusions that her gratitude would last much beyond this evening. He would, therefore, have to make all haste in the next days to trap her in a compromising situation in order to force her hand.

Force her hand—oh, but he was being witty this evening. It was too bad he could not share the joke.

"You are smiling, Lieutenant Gryndle. Pray tell me what you find so amusing," his partner said with a practiced pout.

"Forgive me, Miss Dillon, but I have so long dreamed of having an opportunity to waltz with you that I confess I am bursting with joy now that the blessed moment has finally arrived. You are my ideal, my goddess, and I would be content merely to touch the hem of your gown. But that you have so graciously, so generously condescended to dance with me—I vow, I am so overcome, I can scarce speak."

She preened visibly at his fulsome compliments. Apparently she had an insatiable appetite for obsequious flattery, and he began to believe his task would be easier than he could ever have anticipated. Well, he was perfectly agreeable to feeding her as many honeyed phrases as she was willing to swallow.

"You go too far, Nick." Dorie scowled up at her cousin, who had just taken it upon himself to check her dance card for "undesirables." Despite her outraged protests, Nicholas had scratched out Lieutenant Gryndle's name.

It was not that Dorie especially wanted to dance with the lieutenant. She had, in fact, only been introduced to him this evening. But that Nicholas should be allowed to interfere in her life in such a heavy-handed way was clearly intolerable.

"The man is a cad and a bounder," he replied. "He may still meet the criteria of the patronesses and be allowed into Almack's, but he is hanging on to his place in society by the skin of his teeth, and there are already any number of high sticklers who are no longer willing to recognize him."

"In case you have not noticed, I am *not* a high stickler," Dorie retorted.

"I have noticed, and it is highly likely half of society has noticed. But in case it has never occurred to you, if you damage your reputation, you will also drag Joanna down with you and ruin her chances of finding a husband, and that I will never allow."

Dorie stared at her cousin mutinously and wondered what he would say if she told him Joanna might be better served if her reputation *was* ruined. Maybe then Nicholas would take a good look at what was right under his nose . . . but no, he probably would not. More than likely he would decide it was his duty to marry her off to some man who could not afford to be choosy, such as a widower with ten children, or to some eminently respectable man like the Reverend Fitzwalter, whose own reputation was so elevated it could survive even the ignominy of his marrying a woman whose reputation was somewhat tattered.

"In fact," Nicholas continued, "I shall give you a list of the men whom you are not to dance with or acknowledge in the slightest way."

Dorie smiled her most innocent smile. "Thank you, Nicholas. I am sure I will find such a list most convenient." She was not lying. Such a list would be quite handy—to let her know exactly whose acquaintance she *should* cultivate!

"I declare, I will be thankful when I get Prissy married off," Mrs. Esmerelda Cunningwood said for approximately the forty-fourth time that evening. "Then I shall never have to show my face in these hallowed portals again. I vow, Almack's becomes more impossibly tedious with each passing Season. I declare, Cousin, I do not know how you tolerate it year after year."

Keeping a deliberately bland expression on her face, Lady Letitia eyed her companion with barely disguised distaste. One could not, unfortunately, choose one's own relatives. But Lady Letitia was also more than grateful that Prissy was the last of her cousin's daughters. The woman had "vowed" and "declared" repeatedly that it was her intention to retire to Northumberland as soon as her youngest daughter was wedded, and Lady Letitia was more than eager to be quit of the woman forever. Relative or no relative, the woman was a crushing bore.

"I said, dear Cousin Letitia, that I do not know how you tolerate Almack's year after year," Mrs. Cunningwood prompted.

"I expect it is because I like watching the dances, Cousin Esmerelda. There is such a fascination in seeing the patterns shift in subtle ways, in observing the way partners come together, then break apart to dance with others."

Her cousin glanced over at her with a patronizing smile usually reserved for small children and senile older relatives, then began picking up her scarves and adjusting them around her shoulders in preparation for leaving. "Well, I am sure I would not wish you to be as bored as I have been this evening. I vow, I would not wish *such* a fate on anyone!" Then she cackled, amused, no doubt, by her own wit.

I must be sure, Lady Letitia thought, following her cousin toward the door, to marry dear little Prissy off to someone from the north, lest Esmerelda have the slightest excuse to come south again.

Then her thoughts turned to other, more interesting things, such as Dorie and Lord Glengarry, Miss Pettigrew and Nicholas, and that insufferable Miss Dillon and Lieutenant Gryndle. There was danger in that last pairing—should she drop a word of warning in Mrs. Dillon's ear?

She should . . . but she rather thought she wouldn't. Little Mary Dalrymple had become quite stuck on herself ever since she snared the rich Mr. Dillon, and she deserved to be taken down a peg or two. And it would serve her spoiled, self-centered daughter right if she got leg-shackled to such a ramshackle fellow as Gryndle. Moreover, it would be such a relief for his long-suffering family to have his hand in someone else's pocket for a change.

Dorie had just reached the bottom of the stairs when the front door opened and she heard Nicholas say something and

Alexander respond. Quick as a flash, she darted through the nearest open door. She was not, absolutely *not* going to be trapped once again into entertaining that fumbling, bumbling lack-wit from Scotland.

Unfortunately, in her haste to evade them, she picked the library, realizing too late that her pigheaded cousin and her unswerving suitor were not proceeding on up the stairs to pay a call on the female occupants of the house, but were coming into the library for a private conversation.

Forgive me, Cousin Beth, she thought to herself. I know I promised you I would refrain from deliberate eavesdropping, but this definitely qualifies as accidental. Ducking down, she crawled under a library table. She scrunched herself up into a ball, trying to make herself as small as possible, and hoped no one would spot her in the shadows.

There was the usual desultory conversation, brandy was offered and accepted, followed by the clink of bottle and glasses, and then someone—Nicholas, apparently—came and leaned against the table.

Boring, boring, boring, she thought, listening to them talk of the people they had seen at White's, the cards they had been dealt, the bluffs they had called. Then abruptly her interest was piqued.

"There is a cockfight Tuesday night. Allingham is putting his reds up against Morwell's grays. Are you interested?"

She could not quite hear Alexander's response, but she listened intently to her cousin's recital of the exact time and place where the competition would be held.

To her great relief—and more to the point, to the relief of her knees and back—the two men dallied only a short while longer before leaving the library with the declared intention of joining the ladies in the drawing room.

Waiting only until she was sure they were safely out of earshot, she crawled out from under the table and began to dance around the room. At last, at last, she was going to have a real adventure. And Nicholas would never discover what she was about until it was too late to stop her!

Nicholas was so easy to outwit, there was no real challenge

in it, Dorie thought. Having checked her dance card and Joanna's also, and having seen no undesirable names, he had yielded to her mother's request to partner her for a few hands of whist.

Unfortunately for his efforts, he had no way of knowing that the Mr. Brown, whose name was inscribed for the next waltz, was in actuality Lieutenant Gryndle, who had been only too happy to cooperate in playing a joke on her cousin. Joanna had already taken her place on the floor, and Dorie's other watchdog, the aggravating Lord Glengarry, had not yet put in an appearance, which meant that as long as Nicholas did not take it into his head to check on her in the next five minutes, she would have her dance with the handsome officer, who was even now approaching to claim her.

"Miss Donnithorne, I believe this is our dance," he said with mock formality.

"Why, Mr. Brown, I do believe you are right," Dorie replied, allowing him to lead her out.

She should have been born a man, she thought. With her aptitude for intrigue, she could have been a spy. But on the other hand, being female did not automatically preclude her from such activities. During the course of history there had been numerous examples of women ferreting out important secrets and changing the course of history. Perhaps she should give up her ambition to be an explorer?

While she was musing on the possibilities of a career in espionage and not paying strict attention to where they were dancing, the lieutenant waltzed her out onto a balcony. The fresh breeze brought her back to the present, and she became aware of her surroundings and Gryndle's treachery only seconds before he kissed her.

Instead of weakly slapping his face or struggling ineffectually against his superior strength, she did exactly what Billy, the groom, had instructed her to do under such circumstances. The technique was more effective than she had ever dreamed it could be.

The lieutenant gave a cry of heartrending anguish, his arms went completely slack, and she was easily able to step away from him. Without her support, he doubled over and his knees slowly buckled; then, sucking in his breath through clenched teeth, he toppled to the floor like a felled tree.

Feeling not the slightest pity for him, Dorie looked down where he lay moaning pathetically, then turned her back on him and reentered the ballroom.

She was quite proud of the way she had handled what could have been a compromising situation, and she felt thoroughly satisfied with her ability to take care of herself, no matter what Nicholas thought. Her cousin might consider it necessary to hedge her around with all kinds of restrictions—for her own protection, of course—but she had just proved him wrong. Joanna, to be sure, was as timid as a mouse and in need of masculine protection, but she, herself, could best any man.

Of course, she really should remember to thank Billy for his lesson in self-defense. Although then she would have to tell him exactly how and why she had needed to use it. On further thought, she had better not say a word to him, or indeed to anyone, not even to Joanna.

"Billy, there's a female here to see you."

Hanging up the tack he was cleaning, Billy followed the other groom out into the stables, where one of the upstairs maids was fidgeting impatiently, her skirts fastidiously lifted up off the ground, as if he did not keep the flagstones as scrupulously scrubbed down as any floor in the house itself.

"Mornin', Polly, what brings you out ter the stables?"

She bobbed a quick curtsy. "You told me I was to tell you if Miss Dorie did anything suspicious—anything at all, you said."

"That's what I said. The duke sent me along special to keep her out of mischief."

"Well, this looks like mischief to me, it surely does. I can't think of no other reason for a young lady like her to have a suit of boy's clothes hidden under her mattress. And it wasn't there yesterday when I changed the sheets, neither, and that I can swear to."

Thanking her for her help, Billy escorted her back to the

kitchen door, where they parted company. So, Miss Dorie had a suit of boy's clothes hidden under her bed . . . .

He could, of course, simply tell Nicholas, who would doubtless remove the offending items. But would that stop Dorie if she were determined on her course? More than likely not. It would just drive her to ground.

Well, he would put Joe to watching the back of the house during the day, and he himself would have to take a nap so he would be fresh enough to watch all night. He doubted even Dorie would be brazen enough to march out the front door dressed as a boy, but beyond that he could find little to be thankful for.

Miss Hepden finished brushing Joanna's hair and left for her own room, and Joanna climbed into bed and snuggled down. Sleep eluded her, however, and she finally decided to read for a while. Relighting the candle by her bed, she looked for the book she had been reading, but it was not where she had left it.

A quick perusal of the room also failed to turn it up. She had not returned it to the library, and the maids would not have touched it. The only thing Joanna could think of was that Dorie might have started reading it.

There was a faint light shining under the door connecting their two rooms, so Joanna tapped lightly, then without waiting for an answer opened the door and went in.

"Dorie, have you got the third volume of the novel by Jane Austen I was—?" Joanna stopped in dismay. There was a *boy* in Dorie's room!

"Oh, heavens!" Joanna said faintly, not sure what she should do. Then the "boy" turned around, and she saw it was Dorie. "Oh, gracious! Whatever are you—?"

Hurrying across the room, Dorie clamped her hand firmly over Joanna's mouth. "Shhhh! Don't wake the whole household!"

Joanna jerked her head away, but she obediently kept her voice lowered. "Just what do you think you are doing?" she hissed.

"I am going to have an adventure."

"You are clearly deranged! Nicholas will be furious if he discovers you have sneaked out of the house dressed as a boy."

"Then we shall have to make sure that Nicholas does not find out, won't we?"

"But, Dorie, it is after midnight already! Where on earth can you go at this hour? Do you have a secret assignation with a man?"

"Now it is you who are being ridiculous. You know my opinion of men. How can you even think I would do anything so foolish? If you must know, I am going to a cockfight."

"And you do not call that being foolish? Nicholas would definitely disapprove of such a thing."

"That is all you know. Nicholas himself is going to this cockfight, which is how I learned about it. And that paragon of boring virtue, Lord Glengarry, whom you are always trying to foist off onto me, will also be there. Obviously, if attending a cockfight is all right for them, then it is also acceptable for me."

"Dorie, you cannot do everything a man can do—"

"There you are wrong."

Even in the dim light Joanna could see the determination in Dorie's eyes, and her heart sank. It was obvious to her that nothing short of being chained to her bed would serve to deflect Dorie from her chosen course.

"I *can* do anything a man can do, and I *shall* do anything and everything that men are allowed to do."

"Why? At least tell me that before you go. Why are you so determined to follow such a dangerous course?"

"Dangerous? Say 'exciting,' and I will agree with you. I am going because anything is better than a future of sipping tea and listening to gossip and living a dull, insipid life."

"Please, Dorie, do reconsider." Joanna's eyes filled with tears, and she could not hold back a sob.

Dorie hugged her quickly; then, before Joanna could stop her, she broke away and darted noiselessly from the room, leaving Joanna in a quandary. Should she awaken Dorie's mother? A moment's reflection and Joanna realized a hysterical female would do nothing but worsen the situation.

She would have to find Nicholas and let him . . . But no, Dorie said he had gone to the cockfight. One of the servants? But who could be trusted to keep it secret? And who might know where the cockfight was being held? The footmen were unlikely candidates . . . but perhaps one of the grooms?

Yes, they might have heard about the cockfight, especially Billy, who had come with them from Colthurst Hall. And Billy, at least, could also be trusted to hold his tongue.

But she could hardly ring for a servant and say that she needed to speak to a groom—not at this hour of the night. Which meant she would have to go to the stables herself . . . alone . . . in the dark . . . and somehow wake up Billy. Oh, dear, she was not even precisely sure where he slept.

Quaking at the thought of what she was about to do, she dressed quickly in her plainest gown, wrapped her cloak around her, and tiptoed through the darkened house. She was almost to the bottom of the stairs when someone opened the front door and she heard familiar voices.

"Nicholas, oh, Nicholas, thank goodness you are come home!" Without stopping to think, Joanna flew across the short distance separating them and threw herself into his arms. Clinging to him, she felt her fear subside, only to be replaced by bittersweet longing.

For the moment, even her worries for Dorie were pushed aside—she wanted this man with an intensity that amazed her, and the pain of knowing she could never be his wife cut into her like a knife.

11

It should have been pure delight. Joanna was in his arms, where Nicholas had for so long dreamed of having her. Unfortunately, not only was Alexander standing only a few feet away observing them, but Joanna was also shaking all over, crying, and babbling something about Dorie, which rather spoiled any romantic illusions he might have had.

"Shhh, shhh, calm down." He soothed her as best he could, stroking her hair, rubbing her back . . . wishing he could simply kiss her until she rested quietly in his arms . . . or until she returned his passion. "Take a deep breath and then tell me what Dorie has done."

"Sh-she has dressed herself up like a boy—"

Beside him Alexander cursed under his breath.

"And she has gone off to a cockfight, and she said you and Lord Glengarry were going and if you could go, then it was all right for her to go because she can do anything a man can do."

"That wretched brat! There are some times when I think my cousin is not playing with a full deck, and the rest of the time I am positive of it."

With great regret Nicholas disentangled himself from Joanna's arms and held her slightly away from him. It had to be one of the hardest things he had ever done in his life, and he added it to the reckoning he had to settle with his cousin.

Kissing Joanna's hands when he wanted nothing so much as to kiss her lips, which were now trembling sweetly, he said in a calm voice, "Go back up to bed now, my dear. Glengarry and I will take care of Dorie."

Glengarry, in fact, was already around in the stables saddling a horse by the time Nicholas caught up with him. Glengarry was also about as angry as Nicholas had ever seen a man get.

Geoffrey Anderby, the Earl of Blackstone, listened to the assorted cheers and groans of the assembled crowd when the gray cock dealt the red a death blow. He was not especially interested in the birds, although that particular gray had just won him two hundred guineas.

No, the pretty bird he recognized on the other side of the cockpit showed promise of being much more profitable than the feathered variety.

It would appear that the lovely and hoydenish Miss Donnithorne, who would come into a considerable fortune when she arrived at the age of one-and-twenty, and whose family were quite protective of her, had managed to slip her leash, at least for a short period of time.

Previously he had not felt it worth his while to attempt to fight his way past the ranks of her defenders . . . but if the young lady herself could be persuaded to cooperate? The possibilities that would then open up were numerous. He could compromise her reputation and thereby force her family to give him her hand in marriage . . . or he could run off with her to Gretna Green . . . or perhaps easiest would be if he merely enticed her into a situation from which her family would pay to have her extricated.

Before he made up his mind, he would have to check with his sources in the City and see just how considerable a fortune she stood to inherit. But in the meantime he would make a start at cultivating her friendship. More than likely she had already been warned against him and others like him, but as willful as she was, that could easily work to his advantage.

With an inward smirk he began to ease his way through the crowd of yelling and cursing men.

How on earth was he going to persuade Dorie to leave this crowded, smoky, noisy hellhole? Too late Billy realized he should have had a long discussion with the duke about what to do in cases like this.

A man tried to shove his way between them in order to get a better view of the fighting roosters, but Billy was not about to let himself get separated from Dorie. He jammed his knuckles into the man's side, about where the kidneys should be, and the man staggered backward with a grunt of pain. Other men quickly surged forward to fill in the gap, their attention luckily on the fighting cocks instead of on Billy and Dorie.

Billy racked his brains trying to think of some plan to persuade the most stubborn female it had ever been his misfortune to encounter into acting in a reasonable manner for the first time in her life, but he was stymied by the explosive nature of their situation.

It would take only one man—one man realizing that Dorie was a girl—and the crowd could easily become a mob. The lighting was dim, and all the men were fully occupied watching the fighting roosters. That was all that had saved Dorie from discovery so far, but luck could not be counted on to favor them forever.

And he knew very well that if he revealed his presence, she would immediately, without stopping to think, begin to argue, to berate him, to tell him just what she thought of him for being such a sneak as to follow her.

And with the first word out of her mouth, she would reveal to everyone around her that she was a young, gently bred female.

On the other hand, if he waited, someone might bump into her and feel a woman's curves where they were not supposed to be, or knock off her hat and see a woman's hair tumble down, or simply notice the line of her neck, which was too elegant to be a boy's.

Someone abruptly shoved him aside and grabbed Dorie from behind, one arm around her waist pinning both her arms, and the other hand firmly clamped over her mouth. Just as Billy was about to repeat his kidney jab plus a few other special blows, he recognized the man efficiently removing Dorie from the scene as the redheaded Scottish baron, Lord Glengarry, who was always hanging around the Donnithorne household, trying unsuccessfully, or so the maids reported, to court Miss Dorie.

At the moment there was nothing unsuccessful or especially loverlike about the way Glengarry was managing to drag her backward through the crowd. His size was great enough, and the expression on his face sufficiently ferocious, that no one protested when he elbowed them aside.

Forcing his way through the crowd with considerably more difficulty, Billy soon joined Nicholas, who was standing near the door. Reinforcements would probably not be needed, however. Glengarry appeared to have the situation well under control.

Billy emerged into the cool night air in time to see the baron toss Dorie up onto a large horse, which he then mounted also. From the way she was struggling to get down, it was obvious she was still spitting mad, but Glengarry was able to control both her and the horse, and seconds later the beast, which Billy recognized as coming from his own stable, was trotting down the street, its hooves striking sparks off the cobblestones.

Dorie finally ceased to struggle. It was pointless, because Glengarry had his arm locked around her waist, again efficiently trapping both her arms at the elbows, so she could do little more than wiggle . . . which she had lost all interest in doing once she realized what, or rather whom, she was wiggling against.

Unfortunately, Glengarry had her pulled back so tightly against him, she was virtually sitting on his lap, and the way he was holding her, she could feel every movement of the muscles in his legs. It was quite different from waltzing with a man, and she rather suspected it more nearly resembled making love.

The idea had unexpected appeal. There was nothing foppish or weak about the arm that was holding her, nor was there anything the least bit soft about the chest pressing against her back, and despite her normal contempt for the baron, she felt an unexpected and totally new response deep inside her.

The only thing soft about him, in fact, was the words he was speaking, which were in Gaelic, and which sounded to her uncomprehending ears rather like a lover's honeyed phrases.

She strongly suspected they were curses rather than endearments, and she wished she had the Gaelic, so she could answer him in kind. Somehow, compared to the fluency with which his words were now pouring over her, everything she could think of to say in English sounded rather weak and trite, so she held her tongue.

Which made it all the more unfair when Glengarry, reining in the horse in front of her mother's house and dismounting, finally spoke in English. "If you say one word, I swear I shall beat you."

Immediately indignant, she retorted, "So beat me. But I am still going to point out that it will be better by far if we enter from the stable side of the house, since I have a key to that door, and we shall thus not have to wake any of the servants."

He reached up and pulled her down off the horse, and for a moment she was in his arms—for too long a moment. He stood there holding her pressed up against him, and it was much worse than if he had beaten her.

She tried to resist—tried to remind herself that this was a man with no conversation, no wit, that this was a man who could not walk across a dance floor without stumbling—but there was nothing either weak or clumsy about him tonight. Slowly he tilted her chin up and lowered his head until she could see nothing but his face above her, his features shadowed in the moonlight, his expression inscrutable.

Spellbound, she waited for him to kiss her, which she knew he was going to do. Bemused, she realized she was going to let him, and the only protest she uttered, in fact, was a soft sigh, which did nothing to deter the man.

Before she could disgrace herself completely, however, the silence of the night was broken by the sound of another horse rapidly approaching. Startled, she pulled her head away far enough that she could look around her captor and see the newcomers. Even in the poor light she recognized her cousin Nicholas, and the boy hanging on behind him was Billy. At the sight of them, all thoughts of meek compliance went out of Dorie's head.

Until now, there had been something almost romantic about the way the baron had found her and carried her off on his horse into the night. It had, in fact, reminded her of the tales of gentlemen highwaymen, and Glengarry himself had seemed almost like a hero in one of Mrs. Radcliffe's novels.

But discovering her cousin and a groom were involved in this expedition to drag her home reduced this evening's adventure to the level of men once again deciding for a woman what she should and should not be allowed to do. And Glengarry, she realized, was nothing more nor less than a tiresome spoilsport.

"Unhand me at once," she said, "or I shall scream so loudly the neighbors will think they are all about to be murdered in their beds."

"It is not ended between us," he replied, his voice low and his words for her ears only.

"There is nothing between us to end," she retorted, deeply ashamed of the way she had almost given in to him, but proud that at least now, when everything was over, there was not the slightest hint of feminine weakness in her voice.

Nicholas was bone-tired. Billy had taken the horses back to the stables, Dorie had been sent off to bed—recalcitrant to the end—Alexander had drunk a much-needed glass of brandy with him and then departed for his own lodgings, and now at long last, undoubtedly a good hour before the milkmaids would begin to deliver their wares, Nicholas wearily climbed the stairs to his own bed.

But the night's adventures were not yet over. Someone else was waiting for him in the corridor outside his room. A dear little someone, an enchanting someone, who appeared not to realize how tempting she looked gazing up at him so trustingly—how enticing she was with her adorable little toes peeking out from under the bottom of her robe.

Oh, Joanna, Joanna, you should be safe in your bed with your door firmly bolted against men like me, who are too tired to play the gentleman, he thought. Do you not know that fatigue weakens a man? Makes him more susceptible? More vulnerable?

"I wanted to ask you," she whispered, and her soft voice promised him a haven from all the cares of the world, "if you found Dorie in time? She was not hurt in any way, was she? I could not sleep without knowing, but her door is locked, and she would not answer when I knocked and called to her."

Nicholas shuddered with the effort it took him not to pick Joanna up in his arms and carry her off to his bed. He was so tired, all he wanted to do was wrap himself around her and go to sleep, but in the end he was a gentleman, although the pain of restraint cut deep.

His voice was harsh with bitterness when he finally answered. "No, she is all right. No one had discovered her identity."

Tiredly he leaned against the door to his room, shutting his eyes to close out the vision standing before him. Gradually all his noble resolve melted away. Whatever the price he would be called upon to pay, he was going to hold his love in his arms again before this long night was over, even if only for a few minutes.

"Joanna, I love you—I need you," he whispered, extending his hand toward her.

There was no answer, and his arms remained empty. When he finally and with great reluctance opened his eyes, the corridor was deserted. The question that haunted him and kept him tossing in his lonely bed for an endless time before sleep claimed him was: Had she slipped away from him before he confessed his love . . . or after?

The room was overcrowded, the heat was intense, the same faces swirled around her in frenzied motion, the same voices uttered the same vacuous remarks, and her partner was a provincial hick striving unsuccessfully to make it appear that he possessed a modicum of town bronze. Dorie had such a strong sensation of being trapped by inanity—hemmed in by fatuousness, stifled by trivialities—that she could hardly finish the dance without screaming.

Such feelings were quite familiar to her, however, occurring more and more frequently of late, and she had, of necessity, devised her own stratagem for coping. After her success at defying Nicholas by dancing with Lieutenant Gryndle, she had adopted the habit of entering a fictitious name on her dance card, thereby giving herself a few minutes of privacy in the middle of the evening.

At the present moment she had about reached the end of her patience, so it was fortunate that her next partner was the mythical Mr. Stuart, named for the deposed kings, and conversely, it was equally *un*fortunate that she could not fill her entire dance card with the names of men long dead. They would, undoubtedly, make more entertaining partners than the ones who were her normal lot.

Timing was everything in maintaining the illusion of a fictitious dancing partner, she had discovered. Returned to her mother's side by one man, she waited until the dance floor was partially filled; then, availing herself of the fleeting opportunity when her mother's head was momentarily turned, she quickly slipped away to whatever bolt-hole she had earlier searched out. This evening she was indeed fortunate, because the ballroom was on the ground floor of a house some few miles outside of London, and the French doors led out onto an open terrace.

Apparently few were brave enough this evening to risk the dangers of the night air, and Dorie found herself completely, blessedly alone. She drank in the cool air, as refreshing after the stuffy atmosphere in the ballroom as a glass of cool spring water on an August afternoon.

"Slipped your leash, have you?"

The mocking words came out of the shadows behind her. It would appear that she was not quite as alone as she had thought.

Excitement already beginning to race through her veins, she turned to face the stranger, careful to keep all trace of emotion off her face. The voice had held a note of challenge, and if they were to engage in a duel of wits, it would not do to give any advantage to the man, whoever he might be.

The infamous Earl of Blackstone strolled close enough that she could recognize him even though they had never been introduced. The *proscribed* Earl of Blackstone, she should have said, since his name headed the list of men she was forbidden to associate with.

Dorie studied the earl carefully, curious to know how he had gained his reputation as a man too dangerous for respectable women to associate with. He was younger than she had anticipated, and his features were handsome but not startlingly so. His light brown hair and less-than-imposing stature did not fit the image of the devil incarnate . . . but yes, in his eyes she could see the secret of his attraction.

They were world-weary eyes, filled with a lazy boredom that was an automatic challenge to a woman. Are you the one woman in the world who can interest me? they seemed to ask. Who can stimulate my jaded senses? The one woman who can excite me? Provoke me? Rouse the sleeping beast in me?

Dorie fought back the urge to ask him how long he had needed to practice in front of a mirror before he was able to achieve such an effect, which obviously was more difficult than learning to tie his cravat in the most intricate style.

"Alas," he said, "I fear she has already been warned against me, for the lady answereth not."

So deeply meaningful was the look he gave her, it was all Dorie could do not to giggle. Really, if this was the most dangerous rake London could produce, it was a wonder any woman was tempted to stray. But she must not laugh in the man's face, or he might take offense and leave her, and he was at least amusing, even if she could not quite take him seriously.

"I do not believe we have been properly introduced, my lord," she replied with mock seriousness. Or even improperly introduced, she wanted to add. It was, in fact, highly unlikely that anyone with the least shred of decency would dream of introducing a hardened rake to a young lady in her first Season, more was the pity.

"But if you call me 'my lord,' you must have some idea who I am," he replied.

"But of course. You are the infamous Lord Blackstone, nicknamed by some Lord Blackheart."

He actually preened, as if she had given him a great compliment. Really, the man was too droll.

"Indeed, my lord," she said, barely able to maintain the note of seriousness this melodrama called for, "your name heads my list of men I am forbidden to talk to, so what are we to do? I fear we may be at an impasse."

"If we cannot speak with one another, then there is nothing left for us but dancing in silence," he said with a longing in his voice that was apparently supposed to sound romantic, but which made him sound more like a second-rate actor fresh from the provinces.

"But I am afraid that my dance card is already filled for this evening, and my cousin keeps such close watch over me, he would tear me from your arms, were we to try such a thing." There, that should be dramatic enough for such a posturing performer.

"Four days from now, on the night of the full moon, there is to be a masquerade at Vauxhall Gardens," he said, truly catching her interest for the first time. "We shall dance with each other there, with no one to guess our identities or forbid us our pleasures."

Although dancing with him was not particularly alluring, the idea of attending a masquerade was positively breathtaking. To wear a disguise, to escape for an entire evening from her watchdogs—it would be the most exciting thing she had ever done!

On the other hand, there might be a few trifling problems. For one thing, it was immediately obvious to her that Nicholas would become irrational at the mere mention of a masquerade, which meant she would have to sneak away.

"Oh, how enchanting that sounds," she said, playing to the hilt her role of a simpering miss being tempted into naughtiness. "But I greatly fear that my cousin will be unwilling to escort me to such a havey-cavey affair." Would the infamous earl take the hint? she wondered. Would he go so far as to actually propose an illicit assignation?

He stepped closer, and instinctively she stepped back, then caught herself. It would never do to act too coy, or he might lose interest, and then she would end up at the Seftons' soiree instead of at Vauxhall Gardens.

"I can arrange everything," he said in such dramatic tones that she almost felt called upon to applaud. "At eleven o'clock I shall be waiting in a carriage around the corner from your house. Do not fail me. But hark, someone comes." Dramatically he vaulted over the low stone parapet, leaving her alone.

She could not believe he had actually said "hark," and she was smiling when she turned to see who else had decided to take a turn in the fresh air.

To her dismay, it was Glengarry, the other of her two self-appointed guardians. She had still not forgiven him for dragging her away from the cockfight, and she was not about to allow him to keep her from attending the masquerade. The question was, how much had he seen? If he even suspected she was again up to some kind of mischief, her chances of success would plummet.

The best defense was a good offense, or so she had heard. "Are you following me, my lord?"

He bowed formally, then said, "This is our dance, and not finding you inside, I sought you out here. Forgive me if I have offended you."

After the posturing of the earl, the baron's quiet dignity should have been a relief, but it only made Dorie feel guilty that she was planning to deceive him—that is to say, that she was planning to deceive her cousin. This man standing here had no rights over her—no rights at all, because she had given him none—so it was no business of his how she behaved or where she went or whom she went with.

He stepped closer to her, his eyes shadowed, his expression inscrutable. Somehow she could not think he ever practiced in front of a mirror.

Reaching out with one hand, he ran his fingers lightly down her cheek, then touched her lips with his thumb. She felt an intense longing to move forward one more step, which was all it would take for her to be in his arms—arms that had held her so strongly once before.

"There is much I would tell you," he said. "Much that is in my heart."

Suddenly remembering Blackstone hiding behind the low wall, undoubtedly listening with amusement to everything they were saying, she jerked away from the Scotsman's touch. The guilt she had felt earlier now overwhelmed her. She could not—she absolutely could not allow him to speak to her in such an intimate manner when they had an unseen audience.

No! As much as she disliked Glengarry, she could not allow him to appear foolish before another man, especially not a posturing codfish like Blackstone.

"Leave me," she said curtly. "I do not wish to dance. I wish to be alone."

For a moment she feared—hoped?—he would pick her up in his arms and carry her away as ruthlessly as he had the night of the cockfight, but after a long moment when the issue stood in doubt, he turned on his heel and walked away without a backward glance.

She put her hand up to her face where he had touched it, and found her cheek was wet. She was crying. She never cried, not since her father had died. Why did she now feel as if she had suffered another great loss?

Wiping her face with the back of her hand, she stiffened her spine, expecting at any moment to hear the wicked earl's scoffing voice. But the night was quiet around her—no mocking words broke the stillness, no rustling sounds of anyone moving. Turning, she leaned over the balustrade and peered all around. No one crouched in the darkness. Blackstone was gone.

Which meant she had deliberately offended Glengarry and sent him away from her side, and all to no purpose.

Joanna had been ready to go to the soiree for a good half-hour, and even Aunt Theo, who'd had to return to her room three times to retrieve items she had forgotten, now appeared to have herself entirely collected. Only Dorie had yet to put in her appearance, and Nicholas could scarcely curb his impatience.

He had not been sleeping well the last few nights, and he knew his temper had become ragged. Even acknowledging that it was not entirely his cousin's tardiness that was aggravating him did little to help. He still snapped at Dorie when she finally descended the stairs to where they were all waiting.

Without deigning to reply, she elevated her chin at a haughty angle and moved past him. He was about to follow when something about her appearance jarred him. Grabbing her by the arm, he swung her around until she faced him. Then with the other hand he jerked away the shawl that was tied demurely around her shoulders.

It would appear, Dorie thought smugly, that her alterations to the neckline of her evening dress were sufficient for her purpose. Joanna was staring at her in speechless horror, her mother was loudly having palpitations and calling for the support of the footman and butler. And Nicholas? He was neither speechless nor hysterical. He looked, in fact, as if he were about to strike her for the first time in her life.

Picking up her shawl from where it had fallen, he wrapped it back around her. "You have five minutes to go upstairs and change into a decent gown," he commanded in a voice that brooked no argument.

Undaunted, Dorie rocked back on her heels and returned glare for glare. "And if I refuse?"

"You are not appearing in public in that gown," Nicholas said, his voice rising.

"I happen to like this gown. If you are objecting to the décolletage, then I must point out that many women wear dresses cut this low in front."

Her mother gave a loud shriek at her words, and even Joanna began trying to remonstrate, but her voice was much too timid to be heard over Nicholas's bellow.

"That dress doesn't even have a front. If it were cut any lower, it would be to your waist! There is no point in arguing, because I refuse to allow you to go out in public looking like a kept woman!"

"Why not, since I am a kept woman!" Dorie yelled back with equal volume. "I am kept bored! Well, as far as I am concerned, I either wear this dress or I am not going to that blasted soiree!"

Instantly Nicholas became calm, though he still looked as if it would take next to nothing to start him yelling again. "Very well, if that is your attitude, you may stay home tonight, and perhaps you will find your own company fascinating enough to suit you."

"But . . . but . . ." She started to protest, but he cut her off.

"No, we have waited long enough. You have made your decision, now live with the consequences." Swiftly he herded the other two women out the door. "I wish you a pleasant evening," he said before closing the door.

Mindful of the footman and butler still watching, Dorie was careful to continue her performance as a spoiled, willful brat—at least until she reached the safety of her own room. Then she quickly bolted the door and began to change her clothes.

She would have to write a note for Nicholas, of course. What was the point in flouting his authority if he wasn't even aware that she was doing it?

She smiled to herself. Perhaps Glengarry would again . . . But no, he seemed to be avoiding her ever since she had banished him from the terrace four evenings ago.

Shrugging, she found a sheet of blank paper. Well, if that oversized Scotsman thought he could capture her interest by playing least-in-sight, he hadn't a hope in the world.

"I say he should have beat her," Davey, the second footman, was saying when Billy entered the servants' hall. "A good thrashing is what that girl needs to straighten her out."

"Or a good loving," Polly replied, winking at the footman.

"Who needs a beating?" Billy asked with idle curiosity.

"Miss Dorie, that's who," Davey replied. "You should have seen what she did to her dress. Cut it down in front so low it was a proper scandal, then thought she could sneak out without anyone being the wiser. But Mr. Goldsborough wasn't born yesterday. Before anyone else even suspicioned she was trying something smoky, he twitched off her shawl quick as a cat can wink. Lord, I thought his eyes would pop out of his head. I only got a glimpse of her myself, but it was enough to make you blush."

"You, Davey? Give over," Polly said.

"Never mind all this," Billy said quickly. "Where is Miss Dorie now?"

"Why, she's up in her room, 'cause she flat out refused to change her dress," the footman answered absently, his mind and attention obviously preoccupied by his female companion. "You know, Polly, you'd look mighty sweet in a gown like that." For his audacity he was rewarded with a giggle and a playful slap, obviously designed more to encourage than to discourage.

Of course Miss Dorie was in her room, Billy thought, taking the back stairs two at a time. When pigs fly.

The door to her room was closed, and no one responded to his knock. A quick look inside confirmed his worst suspicions. The offending dress lay in a heap on the floor, but the owner of the dress had once again flown the coop. Why had he ever suggested to the duke that he be sent along to London to watch over such a troublesome young lady?

12

Halfway down the main stairs, Billy saw the large front door soundlessly closing. Oh, aye, Mr. Goldsborough was a knowing one. Ha! He had fallen for Miss Dorie's playacting without a suspicion.

Emerging from the house, Billy glanced quickly each way, and to the left at the end of the block he spotted a shadowy figure in a cloak turning down the side street. Running at full tilt, he reached the corner in time to see Miss Dorie, or so he assumed it must be, climbing into a closed carriage pulled by a team of horses.

Without wasting a second, the coachman cracked his whip, and the horses lunged forward, but by luck—good or ill, only time would tell—Billy managed to catch hold of the back of the coach and swing himself up and wiggle his way into the boot.

Women, he decided as he was jostled roughly back and forth, were more trouble than they were worth. After this "vacation" in London, he was going to stick with horses, which never did anything worse than bite or kick or throw you off their backs.

The carriage seemed to be driving on forever into the night, and when Billy finally pulled back the leather flap enough to peek out, he was disheartened by their surroundings. A glance at the moon was enough to tell him they were heading north, and the houses were already beginning to thin out.

Surely the wretched girl could not be eloping? Miss Dorie might be willful, but she was not at all stupid, even he would have to admit to that.

Well, the way the coachman was springing the horses, they

would be reaching their goal soon, or they would need to stop for a fresh team. Either way, Billy would be able to discover what Miss Dorie was up to . . . or what skulduggery she had gotten herself mixed up in.

"Really, Nicholas," his aunt admonished him, "if you were so worried about leaving Dorie home alone, you could have come back by yourself to check on her. There was no need to drag Joanna and me away. You are letting my wretched daughter spoil everyone's enjoyment this evening. I, for one, am quite ready to let the girl sit in her room until she is willing to be more amenable."

There should have been two of him, Nicholas thought wryly, sprinting up the stairs. That was the only way he would be able to please everybody—one of him to stay at the Seftons' and watch over Joanna, and the other to check up on Dorie, who was not going to be pleased, no matter what he did.

Or better than two of him, he could solve his problems by simply wringing his cousin's neck, he decided upon finding her room empty. The mutilated dress lay on the floor where Dorie had dropped it in her obvious haste to leave, but she had at least taken the time to pen him a note.

" 'Dearest Nicholas,' " he read out loud, " 'I have gone to the masquerade at Vauxhall Gardens. If you are reading this, then it means you are once again acting like my jailer, and you therefore deserve to spend the rest of the night worrying. If you are showing me any trust, then you will never know about my adventure this evening because I will destroy this note when I return. Your loving cousin, Dorie.' "

Jailer? Trust? Why should he trust someone who was going to such lengths to deceive him? Enraged as much by her total lack of logic as by her actions, he crumpled the note in his fist. "The devil take all females," he muttered. "What have I done to deserve such punishment, that I have two of them on my hands?"

A gasp from the doorway drew his attention. Joanna was

standing there staring at him, her eyes filled with deep hurt, caused, he knew, by his unthinking remark.

Before he could say another word, she turned and fled from him. He wanted to follow, to find her, to explain he had not meant he wanted to be rid of her.

But Dorie was in danger. Wretched child that she was, he could not take time for Joanna until his cousin was safely back under his protection. On the other hand, if he did not beat Dorie before this night was over, then he would qualify as a saint, and unfortunately for her, he was not feeling particularly kind or noble at the moment.

The coach slowed abruptly, turned sharply, and before it even came to a complete stop, Billy had rolled out of the boot and slipped to the ground. It was as bad as could be. They were indeed in the courtyard of a busy posting house, and while he watched, the door to the carriage opened and a man descended—Blackstone, the infamous earl.

Billy not only recognized him but also remembered all the stories he had heard through the servants' grapevine of the lord's meanness and cruelty. Handsome he might be, but if Blackstone had any ounce of decency or kindness in him, he kept it well hidden.

The coachman who climbed awkwardly down from the driver's seat was broad and squat, and as nasty a character as Billy had ever laid eyes on. He turned and looked directly at Billy, who immediately put a vacant look on his face, which was usually all a boy had to do to keep an adult from noticing him.

"You, there," the coachman snarled at him. "Fetch out a new team for his lordship and be quick about it."

Billy tugged at his forelock, feigning a subservient manner and in the process neatly hiding his face. Luckily the coachman did not wait to see if his orders were carried out, but followed his master into the inn.

Quick as a wink, Billy scooted around to the other side of the carriage, where he could not be seen from the inn, and opened the door. "Miss Dorie," he whispered into the dim interior. "Miss Dorie, it's me, Billy. I've come to rescue you."

There was no response, and his groping hands found an arm dangling down to the floor—a limp arm, which did not react when he tugged on it. "Miss Dorie," he called urgently again, even knowing it would do no good. His fingers touched her face, but her eyes were shut.

Drugged! The wicked earl had drugged her.

For a moment Billy wanted to sit down where he was and curse his own lack of inches. If only he were as big as the Scottish lord, he could simply throw her over his shoulder and carry her away. Although if he were as big as Lord Glengarry, he wouldn't have to sneak away. If he had the Scottish lord's breadth of shoulders, he could challenge the earl to a duel and slice his head off.

Well, since that opportunity was not likely to come his way, the only thing left that he could actually do was send for the brawny Scotsman, who would make quick work of the wicked earl.

Quickly scooting out of the carriage, Billy dashed to the stables and ordered the requested team. Then he accosted a stableboy near to his own age.

"You've got ter take a message to Lunnon for me," Billy said. "It's a matter of life and death."

The boy looked at him as if he had taken leave of his senses. "Not on your life, guv. Baxter would skin me alive if I shirked my duties to go larking off to London."

Standing up straight as he could, Billy said, "You would not be 'larking off,' as you put it. I work in the Duke of Colthurst's stable, but the evil earl who is wettin' his whistle inside the Green Man has abducted my mistress and is carrying her off to Scotland. It is up to me to stop him, so I will pay you to take a message to Lord Glengarry in London and tell him what has happened."

"Duke? Earl? Lord? Someone should wash your mouth out for telling such fibs." The lad tried to shove past him, but Billy caught his arm.

"Just look in the coach, that's all I ask. He's drugged her, that's what he's done."

Faced with an unconscious lady, the boy, who admitted to the name of Tommy, agreed that there might be truth in what Billy was telling him. Upon being shown a gold guinea, he allowed as how whipping or no whipping, it was clearly imperative for him to carry a message to the Scottish lord waiting in London.

"You sure you can find his lodgings? He is staying with the Craigmonts in Berkeley Square."

"You think I'm dumb? 'Course I can find it. I knows my way around London better'n you, I'll wager."

By the time the earl reemerged from the taproom of the Green Man, Billy was safely back inside the boot, this time with an old horse blanket to help cushion his ride.

It would be a long night, he realized when the horses set off again at a gallop, and he could only hope Lord Glengarry would catch up with them before they had gone too far.

The sky was becoming lighter in the east and Vauxhall Gardens was almost emptied of pleasure-seekers when Nicholas finally gave up his attempt to find his cousin, who was doubtless even now sleeping soundly in her own bed. Signaling a hack, he gave the driver instructions, then wearily climbed inside.

He was definitely going to beat her—drag her out of her bed, turn her over his knee, and whack her bottom until she cried for mercy.

The coach hit a bump and threw him sideways.

Bread and water for a week. That might help her see the folly of her ways. And he would threaten to discharge any domestic who contravened his orders and tried to smuggle any other food up to her. No, no threats. He would just fire one or two servants, and after that the rest would fall into line.

The coachman yelled something obnoxious at the driver of a lorry.

And the most diabolical punishment of all, he would set her to hemming a dozen sheets. With her abhorrence of all forms of needlework, that would be the punishment that would break her—that would cow her into a semblance of obedience for the rest of the Season.

He amused himself for the rest of the ride by imagining the ways she would try to soften his heart, how she would doubtless try to enlist Joanna to intercede for her . . .

Joanna . . . he had forgotten what he had said . . . his wretched tongue again . . . first he would beat Dorie . . . then he would explain to Joanna . . . make her forgive him . . .

He slid into a light doze, which was troubled by dreams of Dorie eluding, taunting him, dancing away, always out of reach, and then somehow it was Joanna he was chasing, but she was fleeing from him, her eyes wide with fear, and no matter how he struggled to run after her, he could not catch up.

The sun was hovering on the horizon and there was no village or posting house in view when the coachman abruptly reined in the horses, the door to the carriage was thrown open, and as Billy peeked through a hole in the side of the boot, the wicked earl dragged Miss Dorie out. She was awake, but her face was as white as a sheet, and she seemed dazed, as if not fully aware of where she was.

Afraid of what evil deed the man might intend to do in this out-of-the-way place, Billy prepared to leap out. There was little he could do against two men, especially when one of them sported a brace of pistols, but he meant to try his best. Looking around, he spotted a large stick he could use as a club.

Before he made his move, however, the reason for the unscheduled stop was apparent: after only a brief moan Dorie became violently ill.

Blackstone tried to keep his polished Hessians out of the way, but it was obvious she could not stand without support, so he was forced to hold her arms, cursing her all the time until the attack stopped.

"Water," she croaked out. "Give me something to drink—water, wine, anything. I am so thirsty."

"I have some very lovely wine," the earl said with a cruel laugh. "But as you have doubtless realized, it is drugged. Still and all, you may have as much of it as you wish."

"No, no." She tried to shake her head, but the movement only triggered another attack of violent spasms.

"You may have water if you prefer, my love," Blackstone said in a gloating voice, "although I do not drink it myself. But keep in mind that if you make the slightest effort to escape or try to enlist the aid of anyone to help you, I shall pour the whole bottle of wine down your throat. The choice is up to you."

For a long moment she seemed to be debating in her mind. Billy tried to will her to make the right decision: Don't drink the wine, Miss Dorie! It doesn't matter what you have to promise him—just don't let him drug you again. I can't help you escape if you're unconscious.

Screwing up his face, he thought about it as hard as he could, and finally was rewarded by hearing Miss Dorie say, "I promise I'll not try to escape."

"And you won't try to persuade someone to carry a message for you?"

"I promise," she repeated wearily, and finally the earl appeared satisfied. She was too weak to walk, however, and in the end he was forced to carry her the few steps back to the carriage.

Joanna was waiting in the hallway, and as soon as he saw her face, Nicholas knew Dorie was not sleeping safely in her own bed. Joanna looked the same way she had when he had found her in Brussels. Her cheeks were pale, her eyes appeared bruised, and the fear emanating from her was almost palpable.

If it were possible, Nicholas became even more angry with his cousin for what she was putting Joanna through.

"You did not find her?" she asked in a low voice.

"No," he said softly. Wanting only to comfort her—and perhaps needing some of her comfort also—Nicholas took a step toward Joanna. If he could just hold her in his arms for a few minutes . . .

But she backed away, eyeing him with distrust—or fear? Was she afraid of him? Because of some careless words he had said in a moment of anger? Did she truly believe he considered her a burden to take care of?

Her actions hurt him more than he had believed possible, and he had to turn away for a moment to hide his weakness from her.

"What shall you do?" Joanna asked. "How shall you find her?"

He could not admit that he had not the slightest idea where to begin. Joanna appeared to think he could do anything, and he would not allow himself to disappoint her—to disillusion her.

Forcing his tired brain to function, he said firmly, "First of all, we must keep the news of her disappearance from spreading all over town. We shall tell everyone that Dorie is sick—'broken out in spots' might be most effective in discouraging would-be visitors—and we can pretend she is merely keeping to her room. We must, of course, enlist the aid of some of the servants, but as few as possible, and only those we know for sure can keep their tongues quiet. And under no circumstances do we dare let my aunt know."

"But Dorie is her daughter—"

"And my aunt couldn't keep a secret if her life—or in this case, her daughter's reputation—depended on it. We shall have to tell Miss Hepden, of course, and that way she can be the one to bring Dorie trays of food in her room. And I know a doctor who will help us. He served with our regiment in Spain until he was wounded in the arm. If need be, he can issue an order that Dorie's illness is not serious but that it is highly contagious, requiring her room to be quarantined."

"Keeping her disappearance a secret is all very well," Joanna pointed out quite unnecessarily, "but none of this will help us actually *find* Dorie, and that is the most important thing."

Putting on a show of confidence, Nicholas said, "Glengarry and I will find her, never fear. And we can let Billy in on the secret too. He is more familiar with Dorie's tricks than the rest of us, so he may have some ideas of where she might have gone."

Tears welled up in Joanna's eyes, and once again Nicholas had to restrain himself from taking her in his arms. "But it has been hours—anything might have happened to her. Oh, dear, it is all my fault."

Covering her face with her hands, she began to sob, and Nicholas balled his hands into fists, fighting the impulse to take her into his arms. If only she would allow him to hold her—to comfort her if nothing else.

"It is not your fault. That is nonsense."

"I tried and tried to tell her that adventures are not always fun—that they can be dangerous. I tried to make her understand how horrible it is when one is all alone—with no money, no friends, no one to turn to . . ."

Her voice broke, and Nicholas was unable to control himself any longer. Wrapping his arms around her, he held her close. To his relief, she did not try to resist—to pull away—but actually clung to him while she cried.

"It is not your fault," he repeated. "We have all tried to make Dorie pay attention, but she has always been an obstinate child who had to learn everything by her own experience. It was never enough to tell her that roses have thorns—she had to prick her own fingers before she believed. So you must not blame yourself. It is not anyone's fault."

Except maybe the man, whoever he was. There had to be a man involved in this escapade somehow. Dorie had said in her note that she would be home before dawn, and from the tone of her words, she had meant to be. So someone had to have prevented her. But who? And how? And where?

The why was not that hard to figure out. Dorie would come into a considerable inheritance on her twenty-first birthday. Not really an astounding amount, but definitely enough to interest a gazetted fortune-hunter.

"If you wish to assign blame, I probably deserve the lion's share," Nicholas said ruefully.

Joanna lifted her head from his chest and looked up at him. "You?"

"Yes, me. I foolishly gave her a list of men she was to avoid. I should have realized what a challenge that would be for her."

"But surely she would not . . ."

"Surely she would. She has undoubtedly made an assignation with one of the men on that list, so all we have to do is determine which one." Putting his arm around Joanna's shoulders, he started leading her toward the back of the house. "So now we must begin. You will please go up and wake Miss Hepden, and I shall go around to the stables and rouse Billy. Let us meet in the library to discuss our plans, so that by the time the rest of the servants are awake, we shall have our conspiracy well organized."

"Good morning, my lord."

Alexander opened one eye and glared balefully at his valet, who had pulled back the draperies, letting in the early-morning sunshine, and who was now cheerfully sorting through Alexander's wardrobe.

"Might I suggest your new blue superfine jacket? With perhaps the rose waistcoat?"

May the saints deliver him from fools and English valets, thought Alexander, wishing he could close his ears as easily as his eyes. He had not slept well, which made the "ministrations" of Duxell all the harder to endure.

Having dressed himself for all of his twenty-six years—or at least since he was a very small lad—Alexander had objected when his uncle had insisted upon providing him with a properly trained valet. His objections had, of course, been overruled. Uncle Willard was determined to have everything precisely correct for his nephew's visit to London.

Uncle Willard rose punctually at eight every morning, no matter what the circumstances, ergo all proper gentlemen should rise at eight, even if the gentleman in question had only fallen into bed at five. Despite Alexander's efforts when he first arrived in London, the servants had all—man, woman, and boy—relentlessly forced him to adjust his schedule to the one prevailing in the Craigmont household.

"Mr. Craigmont has suggested you might wish to accompany him to Lock's this morning, as he is thinking of purchasing a new hat." The valet continued to chatter, even though Alexander remained mute. It was deliberate, Alexander knew, and unfortunately also effective.

Unable to go back to sleep, Alexander finally dragged himself out of bed and allowed the valet to shave him and dress him. Descending to the breakfast room, he found his uncle before him. Laying down his newspaper, his uncle made a great show of taking out his pocket watch and looking at it. Then, with firmly compressed lips, he snapped it shut and returned it to his waistcoat pocket, in effect telling Alexander without words that he was a *bad boy* for being all of ten minutes late.

Such a to-do over nothing, Alexander thought, suppressing a smile. He could sympathize with Miss Donnithorne, who, according to Nicholas, was still struggling against the rules and restrictions young ladies had to adhere to.

But he could not feel too much pity for her, since it was she who had invaded his dreams and disturbed his sleep. Dragging her away from the cockfight had cured him of being tongue-tied in her presence. Whether or not he had also gotten over being clumsy, he could not determine, since she had point-blank refused to dance with him after that night.

Morosely he stirred his cup of tea and stared down at the plate of boring English food the footman had put before him. She was also destroying his appetite. A few more weeks of not sleeping and not eating, and he would be as puny as an Englishman.

There was a loud commotion in the hallway, such a total departure from the normal routine that his uncle spilled half his tea on his paper. Then suddenly the door to the breakfast room was thrown open and a small boy of twelve or thirteen years burst into the room, followed by the butler and two footmen.

Yelling at the top of his lungs, the boy raced madly around the room with the servants in hot pursuit. Then, rolling his eyes wildly, the child grabbed Alexander's arm and hung on like a barnacle.

The servants were vociferous but ineffectual in their attempts to remove the lad, until finally Uncle Willard, who looked positively apoplectic at this blatant disruption of his precious schedule, bellowed out, "What is the meaning of this outrage?"

The room instantly became quiet, and Hickins, the butler, began to explain. "Please excuse us, sir, but the boy here was told quite specifically he would have to wait until after his lordship had breakfasted before he could be granted an audience with his lordship, if it please you, sir. But he, as you can see, sir . . ." the butler continued explaining in an apologetic voice, but Alexander had ceased to listen.

There was only one member of the peerage in the room, which meant that the boy, whoever he was and wherever he had come from, had come to see him, Alexander.

"You wanted to see me?" he inquired in a low voice.

"If you are Lord Glengarry, then I has been trying since the middle of the night to get word to you, but they wouldn't let me into the house, no matter how I banged on the door. Said I was to cease my racket, else they'd call the constable and have me thrown in jail."

The butler threw the boy a darkling look, but continued talking rapidly to Alexander's uncle, explaining how everything was the boy's fault—none of the servants were guilty of the slightest breach of etiquette.

"Then, this morning, they finally was willing to let me in, but first the valet said I had to wait until you were properly dressed, and then the butler said not until after you had eaten—I tell you, m'lord, I think it proper foolish to waste so much time when every minutes counts. I'm 'bout ready to say the devil take the lot of you—if you don't want to hear my message, then I'll just keep mum."

Grabbing the boy by the arm, Alexander convinced him with one fierce scowl that even thinking about refusing to deliver the message was a dangerous piece of folly.

"He said his name was Billy, m'lord, and he gave me half a crown and said I was to find you and tell you that the Earl of Blackstone was abducting Miss Dorie and carrying her off to Scotland. I work at the Green Man in Barnet, and at first I thought he was trying to tip me the double, but he showed me the lady in the lord's carriage—drugged, she was—and told me I was to hurry and fetch you. Well, I tried, m'lord.'' He glared accusingly around the room, which had now grown amazingly quiet. ''I hurried as best I could, but some people here just *wouldn't listen.*''

The butler now made the fatal mistake of trying to excuse himself to Alexander, who for the first time since his arrival in London allowed his Highland heritage to surface. With the same wild, bloodcurdling yell his ancestors had used when they charged naked into battle against the encroaching English, he grabbed the butler by the throat and hoisted him off the ground.

The man's eyes bulged out, and he seemed for the first time properly aware of his own culpability.

''Do you know what we do in the Highlands with traitors who aid and abet the enemy?'' Alexander spoke in a low voice, which held a wealth of scorn.

Unfortunately, the butler was doomed to remain in ignorance, because at that moment the door opened again, this time to admit Alexander's aunt.

''What is all this commotion about?'' she asked. Clearly annoyed at seeing Alexander holding the butler several inches off the ground, she said, ''For heaven's sake, Alexander, put the poor man down this instant. Can't you see he is turning blue?''

She sounded so much like his mother, who used to scold him in just the same way, that Alexander obeyed. The butler staggered backward, into the arms of the two footmen. ''Boo!'' Alexander barked out, and the three servants turned tail and ran from the room.

He delayed only long enough to explain to his aunt that the woman he loved had been abducted, that he was going in pursuit, that no, he was not taking along his valet or any other English servant, and that no, he was not going to waste time packing all his London clothes, and no, he would not be returning to England after he rescued his love.

''Unless,'' he added in his most threatening voice, ''one word of this event leaks out and the slightest hint of scandal attaches itself to Miss Donnithorne's name, in which case I will return and take a Highlander's revenge against everyone not related to me *by blood.*''

He was glaring directly at his uncle when he spoke, and for once his uncle had nothing to say about the proper way for a London gentleman to act.

With one last kiss for his aunt and one last curse for his uncle's servants, Alexander hurried out to the stables. He was just finishing hitching his team to his phaeton when his aunt appeared, dragging behind her the portmanteau he had brought from Scotland with him.

"I cannot think you will wish to be without a change of linen for the whole journey," she said. "So I have packed some of your clothes for you. And I put in your uncle's pair of dueling pistols. I doubt he will ever challenge anyone to meet him at dawn, whereas you may find them useful. And I shall speak to the servants myself, so you need have no worries about gossip."

Smiling down at her, he gave her another hug. "You are so like my mother, I cannot think how you married such a stuffy old man."

"Well," she said with a twinkle in her eye, "he was not an old man when I married him."

"But stuffy?"

"Let us say a bit set in his ways even then," she replied. "Oh, my dear, I do hope you find the girl in time—before that wretched villain forces her to marry him."

"It matters little. I shall marry her in the end, even if I have to make her a widow first. That being the case, you may do me an additional favor if you would, and send the announcement to the paper so as to forestall any gossip." He did some rapid calculations of distances and times, then said, "Arrange to have it appear the day after tomorrow." Quickly he told her what the wording should be. "Even if I am delayed a day or two, it will not matter, because no one in London is likely to discover the discrepancy."

But it did matter, and Blackstone would pay for Miss Donnithorne's pain—for every minute she suffered grief or anguish, the wicked earl would pay double, even triple. With his life, if necessary, Alexander vowed. The English lord would come to rue the day he had dared trifle with a Scotsman's chosen lady.

13

Joanna had been right, Dorie was forced to admit. Being abducted was not the least bit comfortable. Too weak from the drugs to sit up for long, she was again lying down across the forward seat, facing the wicked earl, who was sprawled opposite her, looking perfectly at ease. She shut her eyes, not only because she was tired of seeing the satisfaction on Blackstone's face but also because it was easier to control her nausea that way.

Nicholas had also been right—there were certain men it was better for young ladies to avoid. Not because they were exciting, but because they were heartless, despicable, dishonorable, and . . . dangerous.

How could she have been so stupid? Why had she not been able to see behind Blackstone's conceit to his wickedness? Why had she been so eager to deceive her cousin that she had not been wary of being duped herself?

The only answer she could think of was that she was an idiot, a fool, a witless wonder—

"Your cousin does not appear to be coming after you." Blackstone virtually purred with satisfaction. "Can it be that you have written him a note directing his attentions toward Vauxhall Gardens? Do you suppose, my little turtledove, that he wasted all those hours of darkness trying to discover which dominoed and masked lady might be you?"

Was she so easy to read? Were her actions so easy to predict? How could Blackstone have anticipated that she would do something so rash as leaving a note?

The answer to that question did nothing to bolster her low spirits. Apparently he had taken her measure when she had immediately, without the slightest demur, fallen in with his suggestion to attend the masquerade. He had not only seen that she was a fool, but a gullible fool—someone it would be child's play to manipulate.

"Assuming you did leave word of *your* intentions, that will mean it should take your cousin six or seven hours to realize *my* intentions are quite different, which will serve to put him a good six or seven hours behind us. I misdoubt he will be able to make up those hours easily, assuming he is even clever enough to discover the truth. But then, why would it even occur to him that I had abducted you? No one but the two of us even knows we have ever met."

Dorie's head still hurt, but the nausea was passing, and now she was beginning to feel hungry. She also had the most childish urge to whine and stamp her foot and demand he release her. But into her mind came the image of a very large Scotsman. Oh, if only he would—

As if he had read her mind, Blackstone continued taunting her in his nasty, silky-smooth voice. "There is, of course, your other watchdog, that hulking Scotsman who had been following you around like a tame puppy. He was quick enough to remove you from the cockfight."

Dorie stifled a groan—did this man know the full extent of her folly?

"But then, I have noted he has been conspicuous in his absence from your side for the last few days. Have you perhaps been so adamant in refusing to have anything to do with him that he has decided to let you sulk awhile before he resumes his unproductive courtship? He would have been better served to have taken a page out of my book and simply carried you off whether you were willing or not."

Dorie missed her large Scotsman so much she wanted to cry. Why had she thought she was invincible? More to the point, why had she thought life was all a game in which everyone followed the same rules?

"I'm hungry," she said crossly. "The least you can do is feed me. Or do you plan to starve me into submission?"

"I have no need to starve you," Blackstone replied. "And when I decide it is time for you to submit, then you will.

You see, my sweet Dorinda, I am not only more clever than you, but far, far stronger, and I will not balk at causing you pain. I have never had any compunctions about using my strength against those who are weaker than I."

Dorie carefully kept all emotion off her face, but she had come up with an idea—a delaying tactic, no more, and of marginal effectiveness, but nevertheless a small thing she could do to circumvent the earl's plans.

She would dawdle over her meal, drag out every bite, and for every minute she delayed their journey, Nicholas would be one minute closer to catching up with them.

How many minutes would it take to equal six hours? a discouraging voice in the back of her head asked, but she ignored it, the same way she ignored Blackstone's gloating at his own cleverness. She held her tongue until the coach finally turned into the courtyard of another inn and lurched to a stop.

"There is no need for you to get out, my pet."

Forgetting her meek act, Dorie sat bolt upright and glared at the earl. "You promised to feed me. Are you going back on your word? If so, you are even more detestable than I thought!"

"I fear you may be right, my precious. I am truly despicable. But though I have been called Blackheart by some, I am not so black-hearted as to starve you. On the other hand," he continued smoothly, "you may forget all your plans to delay us—not that a few minutes' delay will matter in the long run. But I am a prudent man, and I never take unnecessary risks. Therefore, you will wait in the coach and I will bring your food out to you, and then as we continue on our way to Gretna Green, we shall share a comfortable repast in the privacy of our own carriage."

"This is not my own carriage," Dorie was stung into objecting.

"But what is mine is yours, and more important, what is yours will soon be mine—legally mine. Not only your fortune, which I discovered is more than adequate to my immediate needs, but also your delectable body."

His eyes traveled the length of her, and she felt her skin

crawl. He laughed and she knew he noted her blushes. Reaching out, he stroked her cheek with one hand, and when she jerked her head away from his touch, he laughed again, then stepped down from the coach.

For the first time in her life, she understood how a woman could choose death over dishonor. Not that she was contemplating killing herself. On the other hand, would she hesitate if the opportunity arose to kill Blackstone? If she had a foil in her hand, would she be able to run him through?

Through and *through*, she decided. Henceforth she would, in fact, be on the alert for any opportunity to overpower him, disable him, maim him—

"Psst, Miss Dorie!"

Her ears must be deceiving her—it sounded like Billy.

"Quick, get out. We must escape while they are both in the inn!"

It *was* Billy—she was not alone! She was so happy to see the boy, she wanted to hug him.

"Miss Dorie, can you understand what I am saying? Oh, blast, she's still drugged."

"No, I am awake. But however did you get here?"

"There is no time to explain—they may be back any minute. Come quick."

"I'm not sure how fast I can move. My legs don't seem to want to work very well."

"If you can just get out of the carriage by yourself, then you can lean on me the rest of the way."

Spurred on by thoughts of what the wicked earl might do to Billy if they were caught, Dorie managed to pull herself up by the straps and move the few feet to the door, but before she could make good her escape, a hand caught her from behind and jerked her back down onto the seat.

"So, your word of honor is worthless," Blackstone gloated.

"It is worth every bit as much as your word," Dorie retorted, hoping that Billy had escaped notice. "Perhaps it has not yet occurred to you that you will never be able to trust me—that even after we are married I shall never submit to you."

The earl did not bother to answer. He smirked in a way that made Dorie wish she had one of her cousin's foils—she could run this blackguard through the heart and rid the world of the most evil person she had ever encountered.

As if he could read her murderous thoughts, the earl laughed out loud. The coachman's voice could be heard outside the coach directing the hostlers to look lively and get the new team hitched up, 'cause his lordship was not one to tolerate unnecessary delays.

The horses stamped restlessly, rattling their bits, as if eager to carry her to a "fate worse than death." Then the carriage swayed as the coachman clambered up and took his place on the box.

Well, in the novels she and Joanna had giggled over, the hero always managed to ride to the rescue in the nick of time, killing the villain and saving the heroine, who was usually a total ninny to have gotten herself into such a predicament in the first place. Who would ever have thought that she, Dorie the adventursome, Dorie the intrepid, would be playing the role of mindless ninny.

"They were out of lemonade for the ladies, so you have a choice between drinking ale or going thirsty. Or, of course, there is always the wine if you prefer."

His smile was so nastily gloating, she knew he was lying about the inn being out of nonintoxicating beverages. Well, she had no intention of going thirsty, even if she had to drink something as vile as ale.

She had eaten most of one sandwich before she realized he had also drugged the ale. As the now-familiar lassitude crept over her and her limbs became too heavy to move, she wished she could at least know if Billy was all right—and more important, if he was able to follow.

Her last thought before darkness overtook her was of Glengarry, and it was less a thought than an emotion—a desperate, intense longing to feel his strong arms around her once again, protecting her, loving her.

The knocking bespoke a high degree of desperation, but Hickins did not let the violence being enacted against the great front door interfere with his stately progress across the marbled hallway. Decorum was the main thing, especially after that horrible contretemps this morning, when Lord Glengarry had dared chastise him for what had been, after all, merely the proper performance of his duty.

Opening the door, the butler stared impassively at the man standing there. Young Mr. Goldsborough, one of Glengarry's more moderate friends, appeared to be remarkably distraught today.

"Is Glengarry awake? I must speak to him this instant."

The young man rudely tried to push his way into the house, but Hickins blocked his advance. From now on he was determined to follow his orders to the letter, and his orders were that no one was to know where Glengarry had gone.

"He has already left the house."

"Where can I find him, then?"

"I'm sure I cannot say."

"He left no message? No word as to what his plans might be?"

I was told to follow my orders, the butler thought with satisfaction, and those orders were to lie outright if necessary. "No, he did not let anyone know where he was off to."

After a few more fruitless questions and uninformative answers, Hickins was finally able to shut the door and return to his other duties. Knowing full well that his employer's nephew would have wished him to tell Mr. Goldsborough all about the stableboy's message and the abduction, the butler could not entirely suppress his urge to gloat. Despite his smaller stature, in the end he had bested that barbarous Scotsman, and moreover, he had done it while strictly following a direct order.

The trail was not hard to follow, thanks to Billy. At each posting house a stableboy would approach Alexander, ask him if he was Lord Glengarry, and then tell him how many hours ahead the other coach was. It was a discouraging number of hours.

Blackstone had obviously driven all through the night, which had given him a head start of nine hours. On the other hand, Alexander was driving a much lighter vehicle, so he was able, barring accidents, to travel much faster. Still and all, even though he had now pared down that lead considerably, with the distance remaining to be covered only two hundred and fifty miles, his success depended upon Blackstone stopping for the night while he himself continued in pursuit. He could only be thankful there would be a full moon tonight—assuming that the sky did not cloud over.

The other question that preyed on his mind was: could he stay awake for another twenty-five hours or so, or would he himself need to stop for sleep?

The earl, unfortunately, had the advantage of traveling with a coachman, so if they were pressed, the two of them could alternate driving and sleeping. On the other hand, there was a good chance Blackstone might think himself safe enough to risk halting for the night. After all, unless he had noticed and identified Billy, why should he anticipate pursuit?

After a frustrating day spent scouring London for any trace of Dorie, Billy, or Glengarry, Nicholas finally thought of checking the coach road north out of the city. At the first posting house he found the information he sought in the form of a small postboy named Tommy, who was more than happy to spill his budget.

"And then his lordship brought me back here and left me and continued on alone. That was about nine-thirty this morning."

Nicholas mentally calculated the hours that had elapsed—Blackstone had passed through Barnet around twelve-thirty, so Glengarry was about nine hours behind them. And he, Nicholas, was about ten hours behind Glengarry. There was clearly no point in proceeding—he could not hope to catch up with either the pursued or the pursuer.

Before the Italian tenor finished his first piece, Joanna had realized social events were not really enjoyable without Dorie beside her. Sitting alone—somehow Aunt Theo did not count—Joanna had felt exposed, as if everyone attending the Ridgefords' musicale were staring right at her rather than listening to the music. And it had also seemed as if everyone were whispering about Dorie—as if every laugh were someone scoffing at the falsehood Joanna had been telling to explain Dorie's absence.

Unnerved, Joanna had finally given in to her fears and during the intermission had mumbled an excuse to Aunt Theo and then found herself a seat behind a pair of potted palms, where she was safely hidden from the pring eyes of the curious.

"Miss Donnithorne is not with you this evening?"

Disheartened that someone else had decided to make use of the potted palms, Joanna started to utter her oft-repeated lie about Dorie being ill, when she recognized the woman now calmly seated beside her. Her companion in hiding was the formidable Lady Letitia.

Something about the older woman's eyes made it impossible for Joanna to speak falsely. "No, she is not," she answered simply. It was the truth—just not all the truth.

"The rumor floating around this evening is that she is covered with spots . . ."

Wordlessly Joanna nodded, praying Lady Letitia would change the subject.

"Strange . . . I remember quite well when she had the measles and the chickenpox as a child." This time there was a glint of humor in her eyes. Unfortunately, she was only making Joanna feel like a little bird about to be pounced on by a large and very hungry cat.

When Lady Letitia did pounce, however, it was in a totally different direction from what Joanna had expected.

"He loves you, you know."

Without thinking, Joanna squeaked out, "Nicholas?" in a suddenly breathless little voice. Then, realizing what she had said, she profoundly wished she could sink through the floor.

"Of course Nicholas. He is a dear boy, and I have known him since he was breeched, but like all men, he is sometimes a little obtuse and needs to be nudged before he will come up to scratch."

But now Joanna could feel herself turning red as a beet,

and there was no way she could answer Lady Letitia or even meet the other woman's eyes.

"I am quite adept at that, you know—at giving men little nudges."

Horrified, Joanna raised her eyes from her lap and stared at Lady Letitia. "Oh, no, you must not!"

"Do not try to convince me that you are not in love with him. I am not yet so far into my dotage that I cannot read the expression in your eyes when you look at him."

There was kindness in Lady Letitia's eyes, Joanna realized with a shock. The most formidable, intimidating, thoroughly terrifying lady in London was actually smiling as kindly as if she were Joanna's grandmother.

Relaxing slightly in her chair, Joanna tentatively decided to accept the friendship the other woman was offering. "Yes, I do love him, but too much to force him into a marriage not of his own choosing. He loves someone else, I am afraid, and thinks of me solely as a nuisance he cannot wait to be rid of." She was forced to blink her eyes rapidly, but she managed to hold back the tears at the thought of Nicholas wedded to another.

"If you are referring to the incomparable Miss Dillon, then it will surprise me very much if we do not read of her engagement in the *Gazette* before the week is out—and Nicholas's name will not be linked with hers, of that you may be sure."

"He will be so disappointed." With the best of intentions, Joanna could not quite feel the proper degree of sympathy for Nicholas. In fact, with Belinda out of his reach, might he not . . . ? She hardly dared allow herself the thought.

"I must disagree," Lady Letitia corrected. "Contrary to your beliefs, I would say that Nicholas has not spared a thought for the fair Belinda since he deliberately abandoned her in the middle of the dance floor at Almack's."

"He did what? Oh, he could not have done such an ungentlemanly thing!"

"I rather suspect he was punishing her for running away like a coward and leaving you alone in Belgium."

"You know about Brussels?" Joanna felt herself go numb

with horror—the whole tale would soon be around town, and Nicholas would again feel honor-bound to marry her.

The singing stopped and the applause began. Then after a short pause the tenor was replaced by a soprano.

Lady Letitia patted Joanna's hand. "My dear, there is so much I know, you would be positively amazed were I to tell you the least part of it. But I do not pass on stories without good reason, and I will keep your secret to the grave. I only wish to point out that Nicholas feels very protectively toward you, which is quite a good indication that his feelings are already deeply involved."

"No," Joanna corrected dolefully, "it merely means he thinks of me as a little sister. He has promised, you see, that he will be like a brother to me."

"Well, I certainly hope you were not taken in by such a bag of moonshine. Men are dear creatures, but that altruistic they are not. They do *not* go around adopting 'little sisters' who are of a marriageable age. Of course, men are quite good at self-deception, and they may *delude* themselves into believing that their thoughts are purely platonic, but no, it will not wash. A man simply does not exert himself to any great degree for a woman unless he is in love with her."

"In love? With me?"

Lady Letitia continued with scarcely a pause. "In your case, my dear, I think the only solution is to do something designed to jar Nicholas out of his complacency—something that will make him realize just how much he loves you."

Joanna sighed. "Well, that is the problem, you see. As much as I might wish to do something wild, I am not in the least like Dorie. I could never run off . . ." Suddenly aware that she had revealed too much, she stopped in mid-sentence. "Oh, dear," was all she could say—which mild words did not exactly express her emotions at the moment.

"It is all right. Alexander is a stubborn Highlander and an excellent whip. He will catch up with them in time, especially if Dorie manages to delay Blackstone along the way, and she is very ingenious, you know."

Joanna's mouth hung open. "How could . . . ? Who did . . . ? How had . . . ?"

Chuckling, Lady Letitia reached over with one finger and pushed Joanna's chin up. "I told you, did I not, that I know almost everything. But you needn't fret yourself about Dorie. Instead, you must concentrate all your energies on bringing Nicholas up to scratch."

"Dorie wanted to arrange for me to be abducted so that Nicholas could rescue me, but I have not the courage for such adventures. I am not really a very brave person, you know."

"I expect right now that Dorie is discovering for herself the drawbacks inherent in being abducted. But you wrong yourself when you say you are not brave. I have heard very nice things about you from some of the surgeons in charge of the wounded in Belgium. 'Cowardly' was not the word they used to describe you."

"But you see, they did not truly know. I merely *acted* brave, but inside I was terrified."

"I think, my child, that you do not properly understand what being brave means. It certainly does not mean feeling no fear. Rather, it means doing what you know has to be done *in spite of* being afraid. Do you think all our English soldiers held firm in the face of the French cavalry charges because they were too stupid to know they might be killed? No, the English squares held because the English foot soldiers knew that Corsican monster had to be stopped before he again gobbled up half the continent.

"And you, my child, were very brave to help bandage up wounds and comfort the dying. You should be proud of your courage instead of calling yourself a coward."

There was much for Joanna to think about in what Lady Letitia said. Was that all being brave meant—doing what had to be done, no matter how much one might wish to avoid facing what was unpleasant or scary?

Belinda had refused even to look at the wounded soldiers, and then Belinda had run away in panic, thinking the French were about to invade the city. Did that mean Belinda was the coward rather than Joanna?

"Now, then, my dear," Lady Letitia interrupted Joanna's thoughts, "if we might turn our attention back to your problem with Nicholas. My plans, I think, you will find a great deal more comfortable than Dorie's."

It was dark again when Dorie awoke from her drug-induced slumber, but she continued to feign sleep. Perhaps when they halted the next time, she and Billy would have another chance to escape. Although what they would do once they were free, she had no idea.

She had not a shilling with her, and dressed as she was for a masquerade at Vauxhall Gardens, the good citizens of Lancashire and Westmorland would likely take her for a member of the muslin company. If she claimed to be an abducted heiress, Blackstone had only to counter with the assertion that she was his mistress, and there was no doubt who would be believed.

But still, to try to escape, even if the attempt were unsuccessful in the end, was bound to cause a delay.

Unfortunately, once again luck was against her. When they pulled into the courtyard of the posting inn, no sooner did Blackstone climb out of the carriage than his coachman climbed in, settled himself on the opposite seat, linked his hands across his fat stomach, and began to snore.

Which left Dorie, as the night progressed, with nothing to do except cudgel her brains for another way to delay their progress.

Lying in bed late that night, Joanna was forced to conclude that Lady Letitia had been wrong to think her brave. If she were brave, she would have agreed to the plan Lady Letitia had proposed. It was actually quite a reasonable plan, and had much to recommend it.

All she had to do, in fact, was travel on her own from London to Edinburgh, there to accept a position as companion to Alexander's mother, Lady Glengarry, a woman Joanna had never met. Lady Letitia, however, was a good friend of Lady Glengarry's and had assured Joanna that the lady would be a most kind and understanding person to work for.

To be sure, such a course of action might show Nicholas that she was no longer in need of brotherly protection . . .

except that she could not bring herself to take such a radical step. The mere thought of traveling for hours—days—in a carriage with total strangers was appalling.

Added to that was the fact that she would have to cope with procuring meals along the way, fighting off the advances of whatever cads and bounders lurked around posting inns, just waiting to take advantage of young girls traveling alone . . .

No, it was not to be thought of. At least Joanna could not think of it without feeling again the old panic, which meant she was in truth a coward, no matter what Lady Letitia might say to the contrary.

"And I say, if we do not stop soon so that I might have a bath, and if you do not procure some fresh clothes for me, then by the time we reach Gretna Green I shall be quite the most repellent bride ever married over the anvil. In fact"—here Dorie wrinkled up her nose in distaste—"I would appreciate it if you, too, would condescend to fresh up your person. You are beginning to reek."

Blackstone stared at her for long moments, his face wiped clean of expression, and Dorie concentrated on projecting an image of feminine indignation.

"That is indeed blunt speaking, my sweet," the earl finally replied. "I begin to suspect that I shall find more satisfaction in our marriage than I had anticipated. I do hate mealymouthed females."

He had not actually agreed to stop, but perhaps if she acted as if he had? "But I warn you," she said firmly, "that I have no intention of wearing some maid's cast-off gown. You can send that miserable servant of yours around to the shops to purchase something suitable."

Holding his hands palm-up, Blackstone replied, "But, my dear, you overestimate my resources. Had I not been fortunate in the nag I picked at Newmarket, I would not even now have the wherewithal to pay for teams of horses on this journey. But I am afraid my winnings do not extend to the purchase of dresses and bonnets for ladies."

Dorie uttered a very unladylike oath she had overheard

in the stables, and Blackstone laughed. "My sweet, I am in complete charity with you, but alas and alack, I am not plump enough in the pocket to do as you request. Regrettably, we must push onward, ever onward."

"Here," Dorie said in disgust, pulling a gold ring set with a blue sapphire off her finger. Holding it out to him, she said, "This should cover the cost of several dresses and bonnets."

Taking it from her hand, he held it up to the better light near the window and regarded it appraisingly, then tucked it into the pocket of his waistcoat.

Dorie wanted to ask him if his acceptance of the ring meant they would be stopping, but she realized just in time that any further questions on her part would be interpreted by Blackstone as a sign of weakness. So she settled back in her corner of the carriage and studiously ignored the earl . . . all the while hoping the light was dim enough that he could not see how the pulse was pounding in her throat.

Her acting ability was also needed when they arrived at the Two Lions in Penrith. To her great relief, the earl helped her alight from the carriage, then gave the landlord orders that they would need a room and hot water for two baths. If she let the earl see how overjoyed she was, he might even yet change his mind and decide to push onward—which meant Nicholas could not possibly catch up with them in time.

So she contented herself with hissing angrily at the earl that if he thought she would agree to sharing a room with him before they were married, then he was about to witness a bout of feminine hysterics that would be talked about here in Penrith for years to come.

Gallantly offering her his arm as if he were in truth a gentleman, Blackstone laughingly agreed to her demand. "But be warned, my pet, that *after* we are married, nothing will keep me out of your bedroom."

The earl was regrettably prompt about disposing of her sapphire ring and procuring her a new dress and a change of linen. Dawdle though she might, Dorie was unable to delay their journey longer than an hour and three-quarters.

She wished there were some way she could determine if Nicholas had even yet discovered which way they had gone. With a sigh, she admitted to herself that owing to her stupidity in sending Nicholas off on a wild-goose chase to Vauxhall Gardens, even a full day's delay might avail her nothing.

But on the other hand, she did feel immensely better now that she was clean again, so from that standpoint the stopover was successful.

Hearing the key turn in the lock, she rushed to open the door, determined to cajole Blackstone into allowing her to partake of a light nuncheon before they set their journey forward. Instead, Dorie found herself face-to-face with Billy.

His arm was twisted behind his back, held in the firm grip of the earl's coachman. Behind the pair of them stood Blackstone himself, not a trace remaining of his earlier amiability.

"My servant informs me that he saw this very same stable lad at the Green Man in Barnet. Would you care to explain how he has managed to match our speed for more than two hundred and eighty miles?"

14

The news at the Two Lions in Penrith was better than Alexander could possibly have hoped for. Blackstone had evidently grown so confident he was not being pursued that he had chosen to remain in the town for more than two hours and was now on the road only half an hour ahead. Barring a carriage accident, Alexander could foresee no problem in stopping the earl before he managed to carry Miss Donnithorne across the River Sark.

The unforeseen is precisely that, however—unforeseen. Having arranged for a quick change of teams, Alexander was about to set forth on the last thirty miles of the journey when he was delayed by a miserably unhappy stableboy.

"If you please, your lordship, I knows you're in a powerful hurry, but I got to tell you what they done to Billy. That earl—Blackstone, the one what's abducting the young lady—he discovered Billy'd been hiding in the boot, and he sent for the magistrate and brought charges against Billy for being a stowaway. Billy'd already told me the whole story, 'bout everything what happened, and if it'd've been me, I'd've told the world what the earl was doing, but I reckon Billy kept mum so's to protect the lady's reputation."

It was an unfortunate turn of events, but Billy would have to stay locked up for a few hours, Alexander decided. As soon as Miss Donnithorne was safe, they could return together for Billy, but until then—

"Oh, m'lord, please, Sir George is a hard one, and he says he'll have the truth out of Billy before the sun is over the yardarm."

Round-eyed, the boy stared up at him, and Alexander knew

he was well and truly caught. And he was also reasonably sure this was exactly what Blackstone had had in mind when he'd called for the magistrate.

Alexander's decision to waste precious minutes seeking out the magistrate was not reached easily. Of the two people needing his help, Miss Donnithorne was his primary concern. He could not begin to feel as much anxiety for a groom he barely knew as he did for the love of his life.

On the other hand, his fair lady had willfully set her foot on this course—receiving more than she had bargained for, no doubt—all for the sake of adventure. Billy, however, had gotten himself involved not out of a love of mischief, but out of a desire to protect his mistress, and were it not for Billy's help thus far, Alexander might even yet be in London—totally ignorant of what was going forth.

No matter how he looked at it, Alexander could not allow Miss Donnithorne's thoughtless, foolhardy actions to injure Billy, which meant Alexander would first have to rescue the boy, even if it meant he did not catch up to the other carriage before it crossed the river into Scotland.

After ascertaining the directions to Sir George's residence, a former merchant's house just this side of the White Ox, Alexander was soon pounding on the door, determined to minimize the delay as much as possible.

Sir George, he was told, was occupied at the moment—could he come back in a few hours?

Sir George, Alexander told the servant, would do well to remember what his ancestors had learned from hard experience, namely, that raiders from across the border were not put off by polite requests.

Forcing his way into the house, he easily followed the sounds of a child's cries to the back of the house, where Sir George was employing the time-honored method of extracting the "truth" from reluctant victims.

Or rather, he was attempting to do so. Apparently Billy was quite lacking in the proper submissive spirit, and Sir George was berating his two menservants for not managing to catch the boy and hold him fast.

Moments later the whip was in Alexander's hand, the

servants had taken to their heels, and Sir George was the one cowering on his knees. "But his lordship swore an oath that the boy was lying! Surely you don't expect me to disbelieve the word of a peer of the realm? He is an earl, after all—"

"I expect you to when the earl is infamous—despised throughout the length and breadth of England. Or haven't you heard of the man nicknamed Lord Blackheart?"

"No, no." The magistrate clutched the hem of Alexander's coat. "I hadn't heard—we live so far out of the way here—"

"Then perhaps, living so close to the border, you have heard the name Glengarry?" Alexander said in a menacing voice. "Or are you so isolated that my name also means nothing to you?" Although Alexander could not rightfully claim that he had done anything to make his name notorious, his father had had a violent temper when he was in his cups, and his grandfather had been a regular old tartar whom no one dared to cross.

Sir George turned even whiter if that were possible. "Oh, please, my lord, I had no idea—"

"That's a bunch of poppycock," Billy piped up, sauntering over to stand beside Alexander. "I told you and told you that the earl was a bad one and that Lord Glengarry was comin' and he would be fearful angry. So that means you're lyin' to his lordship, and you told me yourself, liars has got to be whipped."

It was obvious the magistrate had not had his hands on the boy long enough to break his spirit, but Alexander carefully kept the grin off his face. Let the man have a taste of his own medicine for a few more minutes.

"No, no, please, I beg you!" The man bent even lower, transferring his attentions from Alexander's coat to his boots. "It was an honest mistake, my lord, an honest mistake."

Alexander threw the whip on the floor, but the other man made no effort to pick it up and defend himself. "I have no time today to deal with sniveling cowards like you, but be warned—if you continue to fulfill the duties of your office without compassion, I shall hear of it, and I shall return."

Leaving the man sobbing on the floor, Alexander strode

out of the house with Billy. Not surprisingly, no one made any effort to stop them.

"Did he hurt you badly?" he asked the boy, who winced when he climbed up into the carriage.

"Didn't manage to lay a hand on me," Billy said with a cocky grin. "Though I can't say I was sorry to see you charge through that door. And I can't say I'm sorry to be sitting in the carriage instead of tucked up in the boot. I like to got bruises on top of my bruises." With those words he began to burrow into the hamper of food beside him on the seat, and before they had breasted the first steep hill leading out of Penrith, he had consumed two thick sandwiches, three boiled eggs, and half a roast chicken.

"A word with you, Goldsborough."

Recognizing the voice of Lieutenant Thomas Walrond, who had served in his old regiment, Nicholas paused on the steps of White's and waited for his friend to catch up with him. "But how is this, Walrond? You are not in uniform."

The smile that lit up the younger man's face was truly infectious, and despite his worries for Dorie, Nicholas began to smile too.

"Sold out just yesterday. M'great-uncle finally came through. Always said he would leave everything to me, but you never know with old bachelors. Might have married his housekeeper in his dotage and fathered a brat of his own."

"So you have come into a fortune?"

Walrond looked sheepish. "Well, as to that, 'fortune' is a bit of an exaggeration. But I'm now the sole owner of Fair Winds. 'Tis only a medium-sized estate in Hertfordshire, but it's been in the family for generations. M'uncle kept it well maintained and free and clear of mortgage, and he left me the blunt to run it properly with enough over that m'wife won't be needing to pinch pennies."

"Wife? Am I to wish you happy, then?"

"Don't know." The color rose in Walrond's face. "That is, haven't asked her yet. That's what I was wanting to talk to you about."

Nicholas knew what his friend was going to say before he even said it, and with a sinking heart Nicholas wished he'd chosen to go to Brooks's today instead of White's. As futile as it would be in the long run, at this point he would welcome even a day's postponement of the inevitable.

"Wasn't quite sure what was proper in this case, since her brother is dead and she don't have any other relatives, but you seem to be acting in the capacity of guardian."

"You wish to make Miss Pettigrew an offer?"

"If you've no objections."

Nicholas had many objections—starting with the fact that he wanted to marry Miss Pettigrew himself—but none of his objections were valid. If he had deliberately set out to pick the ideal husband for Joanna, it would have been someone exactly like Walrond, who was kind, brave, even-tempered, hardworking, sober, and industrious. Unfortunately, even Walrond's relatives were all highly thought-of.

The only thing Walrond had lacked until now was sufficient assets to support a wife, and that deficiency had apparently been corrected by an uncle, who could not have died at a more inauspicious time, at least as far as Nicholas was concerned.

"I have no objections," he said finally.

"When would be a good time to call on her?" Walrond asked. "Tomorrow morning, perhaps?"

There was no need to rush these things, Nicholas thought. May of eighteen-sixty-three would be soon enough. "Yes, that would be fine," he said. "About eleven o'clock?"

"Wonderful." Walrond clapped Nicholas on the shoulder. "But come, you must let me buy you a drink—not that I'm at all sure she'll have me, but at least I know she don't hold me in aversion."

Nicholas immediately declined. He was not in the mood to wish his friend luck. He was more in the mood to take a leaf out of Blackstone's book and carry Joanna off to Scotland before she could even hear Walrond's offer.

Dorie stared out the window of the coach as they came

into Longtown, which lay on the River Esk, the last place they would be changing horses before the border. A desperate plan had come to her since Blackstone had wickedly and maliciously had Billy arrested.

The drugged wine was still reposing in a hamper on the floor. Surely even in Scotland no one could be married if she were unconscious . . . could she? It was now or never, she realized when Blackstone stepped down out of the coach to arrange for a new team.

Snatching up the bottle, she eyed it with distaste. All she had to do was drink enough of the nasty stuff to pass out . . . but how much was enough? Suppose she drank too much and killed herself?

But suppose—here she began to smile—just suppose she didn't drink any of it? Suppose she just persuaded Blackstone that she had?

Looking around, she realized immediately that if she poured it out onto the ground outside, either he or the coachman might see it and realize what she had done. On the other hand, the squabs were a dark velvet, so stained and worn that the original color was not easily apparent.

Quickly tucking the neck of the bottle down the crack between the back and the seat, she tilted it until a sufficient quantity of wine had gurgled out. Then, replacing the cork, she returned the bottle to its place in the hamper. Mere seconds later, Blackstone was climbing back in and slamming the door behind him. The carriage immediately lurched forward.

The odor of wine was overpowering—something she had not considered. For a moment she felt panic. If he were to discover too soon what she had done, she had no doubt but that he would stick his finger down her throat. Fortunately, when he returned, it was obvious that Blackstone had imbibed deeply of whatever brew the landlord offered, because his breath was almost as strong-smelling as the seat beside her.

"Well, my dear, do you not wish to look out and admire the River Esk? It is not, unfortunately, the border, but we have less than four miles to go, and then we shall be in

Scotland. Are you savoring your last few minutes of freedom? I advise you to do so, because once we are married, I shall keep you on a short leash, and you will soon learn to obey me, no matter what I order you to do."

Dorie did not respond. She allowed her eyes to droop down, but he did not appear to notice. She could hardly call his attention to it, although . . . Gradually she slumped over sideways on the seat.

"What the devil?" Blackstone no longer sounded complacent. Shaking her roughly by the shoulder, he demanded, "What the deuce have you done, you wretched brat?"

Doing her best to make it appear that she was exerting a great effort, Dorie slowly opened her eyes. "I . . . drank the . . . wine . . . Can't get married if I'm . . ." Then, as if her eyelids were too heavy to keep open, she allowed them to shut, and made her breathing as slow and even as possible.

Really, Lord Blackstone's curses and oaths were rather unimaginative. Billy had used much more colorful expressions the time one of the horses had trodden on his foot.

The hardest part was when they arrived in Gretna Green and she had to continue to lie there motionless. Doing nothing was not one of her special talents. Not only that, but she had one arm twisted under her in such a way that it had gone to sleep, which meant it was going to hurt like the devil when she finally moved.

After about half an hour she heard the coachman cry out for his master to come see something. Moments later the door to the carriage was jerked open. All her instincts screamed at her to leap up and run for her life, but her only real hope lay in continuing her charade. She was concentrating on remaining quiet when a man's hand boldly grabbed her breast. Automatically and without thinking, she swung her arm and felt immense satisfaction when her fist connected with the owner of the hand.

Her satisfaction was as nothing compared to Blackstone's. "So, all this time you have been shamming. I suspected at once when my coachman showed me the coach was 'bleeding' red wine. It was a clever trick, but it has availed you nothing. Whether you are willing or not, the time has now come for us to say our vows."

"On the contrary, I refuse to leave this coach," Dorie hissed. "You will have to drag me bodily before the vicar—I shall never go willingly. How do you think that will look?"

"With enough money, which I have, thanks to the donation of your ring, people can be persuaded to overlook anything, my sweet," Blackstone replied quickly, looking as if he would derive a great deal of enjoyment out of laying his hands on her again.

With a scowl, Dorie pushed past him and left the vehicle under her own power. Looking around, she was not impressed with what she saw. Gretna Green was a rather small village with nothing to lend it distinction. It would really have been quite insignificant and easily overlooked by a traveler coming upon it, were it not for its reputation as the site of hundreds of clandestine marriages.

Well, you could lead a horse to water, but you couldn't make it drink. And Blackstone could carry her all the way to Scotland, but he could not make her say, "I do." Nothing and nobody was going to make her utter a single word, she decided. Resolutely she clamped her jaws shut.

"There's his carriage! In front of the King's Head!" Billy was bouncing up and down on the seat with excitement.

Leaving Billy in charge of the horses, Alexander stormed into the inn, checking quickly in each room until he found the proper one. "Stop," he bellowed in a voice loud enough to shake the rafters. "She can't marry him—she's already married to me. She's my wife."

The man conducting the service did not blink an eye. Instead he turned to Miss Donnithorne and asked, "Is this true? Are you his wife?"

With great glee she grinned at Blackstone and said in a clear voice, "Yes, I am married to Lord Glengarry. He is my husband." Then she childishly stuck her tongue out at the earl.

"That's that, then," said the stranger. Turning to Alexander, he said, "That'll be five pounds, if you please."

"I'll take care of the fee in a moment," Alexander replied. "But first I have to deal with my Lord Blackheart."

"Since it appears that you have won the prize, I shall bow out gracefully," Blackstone said suavely. "I see no need to duel with you now that you have won."

"Dueling is reserved for honorable men," Alexander said in a low voice. "For curs like you, a thrashing is more appropriate."

Abruptly the earl bolted for the door, throwing a chair on the floor behind him, which action succeeded in delaying Alexander a few precious seconds. Never having seen a bout of fisticuffs, Dorie ran after the two men. Emerging into the sunshine, she was disappointed to see the two of them running madly round and round the earl's carriage.

Blackstone was bellowing for Pigot, his coachman, and the growing crowd of spectators was cheering and placing bets as to whether Scotland or England would win the footrace.

In the end, the earl got away. Waiting until Pigot was in place with the horses ready to bolt, Blackstone managed to achieve just enough lead that he was able to scramble into the carriage and hold the door shut despite the determined assault by Glengarry.

"He won't get far," Billy murmured beside Dorie. "While Glengarry was rescuing you, I loosened the pins what hold the wheels on the axles."

Dorie scarcely heard what he was saying. His other prey having escaped, Glengarry was now approaching her. She began to wish that Nicholas had been the one to come after her. The look on the Scotsman's face was . . . She couldn't figure out what his expression meant.

She felt the urge to turn and run the way Blackstone had, but she was made of sterner stuff than that coward. She would never run from any man. Stiffening her back and trying to keep her knees from trembling, she waited, hoping that she looked calmer than she felt.

That she was in for a lecture, she did not doubt. And she had to admit Glengarry had every reason to scold after what she had—

Without uttering a word, he scooped her up in his arms, to the delight of the crowd, which had hung around watching even after the earl had made his escape.

"What do you think you're doing?" she hissed. "Put me down this instant!"

Instead of putting her down, he carried her back into the King's Head. "I want the best room in the house for me and my wife," he said loudly.

Dorie had never been so mortified in her life. No, not mortified—angry! He had come to her rescue like a knight in shining armor, an image that had been only slightly tarnished when he had childishly chased Blackstone around the carriage, but now, to treat her as if she were a common doxy, as if, having been rescued, she had no choice but to be his mistress. It was the outside of enough!

There was nothing calm about her voice when she screeched at him, "Put me down! How dare you say I am your wife! You know perfectly well that was just a lie to stop Blackstone from forcing me to marry him!" She tried to wiggle out of Glengarry's arms, but he was holding her too firmly.

"Begging your pardon, m'lady," the landlord said, "but you just married this man not ten minutes ago."

Dorie ceased her struggling. "What do you mean, I just married him? Have your wits gone begging? Or are you trying to collect your fee without having performed the ceremony? Whatever you do, Glengarry, don't pay this man, for he is a crook and a robber."

"In Scotland," Glengarry explained, the laughter clear in his voice, "the only ceremony necessary is to say before witnesses that you are a man and a wife. I said you are my wife—you said I am your husband."

"That means you're buckled as tight as if the Archbishop of Canterbury himself had hitched the two of you together," the landlord said.

"This is the most ridiculous thing I have ever heard," Dorie said, sneaking a peek up at the man who was now—apparently—her husband. "And I suppose that to get a divorce, all you have to say is, 'I divorce you'?"

The landlord had the nerve—the gall—to laugh. "Why, no, m'lady. Divorce is nigh impossible in Scotland. And England recognizes Scottish marriages, no matter how hastily or inadvertently they are entered into."

"About the room?" Alexander said pleasantly.

The landlord led the way up the stairs and Alexander followed, still carrying Dorie, who was having trouble assimilating the knowledge that she was married for life to this . . . this . . . this *deceitful* man.

He had tricked her! He had pretended to come to her rescue, and then he had taken advantage of her ignorance of Scottish law. Well, if he thought she was going to become a meek, complacent wife, he was dead wrong.

Left alone at last, she began his education. "Put me down," she ordered.

He obeyed, although he did not actually release her. She should, really, order him to unhand her, but it was rather pleasant being in his arms.

"The first thing I want to know is, do you intend to take me back to London?"

"No," he replied promptly. "I intend to take you to my castle in the Highlands."

Dorie began to think he was not half bad. In fact, she was starting to feel quite in charity with him. "I have always wanted to sail around the world," she said in an argumentative voice.

"Well," he countered, "I already have a small boat and can teach you to sail on the loch by my castle. If you do not become seasick the first time out, we can buy a larger ketch and try sailing to the Western Isles."

She considered for a moment, knowing there were many other demands she should make before she accepted him as her husband, but standing so close to him, feeling his large hands on her waist, made it hard for her to think clearly.

"But I think, my love, that first I shall teach you something else—something much more exciting than sailing," he said.

He is going to kiss me, she thought, finally admitting to herself that she had been waiting for this moment ever since he had almost kissed her the night of the cockfight. Reaching up to touch his lips, she murmured, "I think you will find me a most apt pupil."

"On that score, I have never had the slightest doubt," he said. "And I think you will find me a very patient teacher."

Hours later she was forced to agree that sharing a bed with Alexander was the most exciting thing she had ever done in her life . . . and the most thoroughly satisfying. In fact, she was so content with her new husband, she doubted she would ever wish to be anywhere but at his side—a notion he thoroughly approved of when she told him.

The mood at the breakfast table was not exactly congenial, Joanna had to admit. Nicholas was acting as if he had a sore head, and she herself was too worried about Dorie to make any attempt at polite conversation.

Only Aunt Theo burst out laughing. "Oh, it serves her right! Listen to this . . ." She began reading aloud from the paper, " 'Married by special license, Lieutenant Peter Gryndle and Miss Belinda Dillon.' Oh, I would dearly love to know how that came about. Mrs. Dillon told me herself in the greatest confidence that an earl had already come up to scratch but that they were holding out for a marquess at the very least. You can rest assured that there is something quite havey-cavey about this. As if anyone would believe they have willingly settled for a mere half-pay officer."

Rustling the paper, she continued unabated. "You may count on it, the Dillons will try to gloss it over. More than likely they will claim it is a love match, but if they will take my advice, they will leave town until the talk dies down."

Suddenly her cheerful good humor deserted her. "Well, of all the nerve! Really, the *Gazette* is becoming quite irresponsible these days. Imagine, someone has inserted an announcement saying that Lord Glengarry married my daughter yesterday in Edinburgh. You would think they would check their facts before printing such a thing. I vow, I am tempted to sue them for libel. Nicholas," she said sharply, "you must go down to their offices this morning and force them to print a retraction."

"Well, I admit it was undoubtedly Gretna Green and not Edinburgh, but I hardly think you will wish to have that fact published far and wide."

"What are you saying? My daughter is upstairs in her room covered with spots."

"Your daughter is in Scotland, undoubtedly covered with—"

"Nicholas! There is no need to be crude!" Joanna stated before hurrying around the table to try to comfort Aunt Theo, who was, of course, having the hysterics.

"But, madam," Joanna said soothingly, "only consider, your new son-in-law is not a half-pay officer like Gryndle. Glengarry is a peer, and though he is only a baron, it is quite an old and very respected title, and his English relatives are also of the first stare." Her attempt to calm Aunt Theo was having little effect, but resolutely Joanna continued her efforts.

"And people will think you a regular slyboots, hiding the fact that Dorie has made what will doubtless be considered one of the premier matches of the Season."

"Oh, oh," Aunt Theo moaned, "I cannot bear the thought of all the gossip—all the idle speculation that is sure to result from this announcement. Oh, if only dearest Simon had not taken my darling Florie off to Italy. What an ungrateful daughter Dorie is! I have done everything a mother could do to cure her of her hoydenish ways! She shall be the death of me before I get her safely off my hands!"

Joanna immediately leapt on the last complaint. "Only consider, dear madam, that Dorie is now *already* off your hands—for good."

After a few more moans, which became less and less forceful, the older woman said petulantly, "I need to go up to my room. I am quite burnt to the socket with all this racketing around that we have been doing. I declare, I am too old to chaperone young girls, and I do not know why my kindness and generosity must be so *imposed* upon.''

Stricken to the core, Joanna sank back down onto her chair. Making no further effort to console the older woman, she watched in silence as the footman helped Aunt Theo totter from the room.

''My aunt spoke without thinking,'' Nicholas said. ''She is actually quite fond of you, and she dearly loves racketing around London.''

''Do not try to make me think that at this moment she does not wish me off her hands, for I shall not believe you.''

There was a long silence before Nicholas spoke again. ''Walrond has come into a large inheritance, and he has asked permission to speak to you. I have told him he may come at eleven this morning. I trust these arrangements meet with your approval?''

Joanna felt chilled to the marrow. It would seem that Nicholas had meant what he said when he had fervently wished he were not responsible for chaperoning two young females. Now that he had Dorie off his hands, he apparently could not wait to dispose of her also.

Rising to her feet, she said calmly, ''I shall be ready at eleven, then.''

Nicholas scowled up at her, and she knew what his expression betokened—he could not make it more obvious that he expected her to accept this offer, which was better than any penniless orphan such as herself had a right to expect.

15

"Well, am I to wish you happy?"

Joanna looked up from her packing to see Nicholas standing in the door to her room. "No, I told Mr. Walrond that we would not suit and that I have made other plans."

"Other plans?" Nicholas stepped forward into her room, which was not exactly the proper thing for a gentleman to do, but then, what did propriety matter after all the days she had spent traveling alone with him?

"Yes, Lady Letitia has found me a position as companion to Lady Glengarry—"

"Dorie? That's ridiculous! You cannot possibly want to subject yourself to her mad starts any longer."

"No, not Dorie—I am speaking of the dowager Lady Glengarry, Alexander's mother. She lives in Edinburgh, and I am—"

"You turned down a perfectly respectable offer from Walrond in order to run away to Scotland?"

Nicholas was sounding really angry now, but Joanna was not about to buckle under and blindly obey his dictatorial orders. Just how and when did he get it fixed in his mind that he had any right to pick out her husband?

"You make it sound as if I am eloping. Well, I am not as irresponsible as your cousin—I am not 'running away' to Scotland, as you put it. I am traveling on the mail, which is completely respectable, to take up a position as companion to an elderly lady who is also completely respectable. You can hardly expect me to continue forever as a charity case, living off your brother-in-law's generosity."

"You don't have to live off his charity—you can get married."

"To whom? Walrond? No, thank you. I am not the least bit attached to him."

"Or to me!"

There was dead silence in the room while they stared at each other.

"Why should I marry you?" she asked, praying that he would say because he loved her.

"Because I promised your brother—"

Turning back to her packing, she said firmly, "Botheration, are you harping on that again? Really, I wish you would play another tune. I absolve you from any commitment you feel you may have made to my brother."

"And I promised you I would be like another brother to you—"

Her voice shaking with rage at his obtuseness, she said, "And I find that I do not need a brother's protection any longer. I am a grown woman who is fully capable of taking charge of her own life. Find some other unfortunate girl to browbeat!"

"Browbeat? Browbeat! Here is thanks for you!" Turning on his heel, Nicholas stalked out of the room.

I am not going to cry, Joanna thought. I am *not* going to cry. I will be brave. Traveling the length of England by myself is a mere trifle. Why, I could go around the world by myself if I set my mind to it. I have the courage to do anything I have to do.

And if Lady Letitia is not correct in her suspicions, and if Nicholas does not love me, and if he does not follow me to Scotland, what then?

Then I shall be brave enough to make another life for myself, Joanna thought, doing her best to be resolute. After all, she had only to hide her secret fears until eight o'clock this evening, when she would board the mail. Once she was safely out of London, she could cry all the way to Scotland if she was of a mind to, provided she did it quietly enough that she did not bother the other passengers.

* * *

Charging into his aunt's bedroom, Nicholas said without preamble, "Aunt Theo, you must help me talk some sense into that witless girl."

His aunt was lying on her bed with a vinegar-soaked cloth over her eyes, while her maid scurried around the room folding items of clothing and packing them in an assortment of trunks, portmanteaux, and bandboxes.

"Oh, Nicholas, I pray, do not speak to me in such penetrating tones. My head is ready to split."

"Joanna has some cock-brained notion that she should go haring off to Edinburgh to be companion to some lady she has never even met."

"Really, Nicholas, I wish you would leave me in peace. My nerves are quite overset. You obviously have no idea how dreadful it has been for me to discover that my daughter, whom I thought was lying in her room virtually at death's door, is instead in the best of health, cavorting around Scotland with her new husband. Wretched child—I wash my hands of her!"

"I don't care about Dorie—I am talking about Joanna!"

"There, I *knew* it! If you had *cared* enough to *exert* yourself in the *slightest* to watch over your cousin and give her the benefit of your *advice*, Dorie would not have felt *obliged* to elope! After such *dereliction* of duty, I am surprised you even *dare* show your face to me. You should be *ashamed* of yourself."

"Women!" With a cry of frustration, Nicholas stalked out of the room, deriving only a little satisfaction from slamming the door behind him. Was he then the only sane and sensible person left in the entire household?

Passing Dorie's room, he heard sounds inside, and poking his head around the corner of the door, he discovered Miss Hepden busily packing his cousin's clothing. At the rate trunks were being filled, it would appear that he would soon be the only person in the house *period*.

"And I suppose you are also going to blame this whole debacle on me," he said.

Miss Hepden paused in her packing. "Why, no. Considering that Miss Dorie deliberately set out to ruin herself, I think we came off fairly well. Her grace will be very pleased with the marriage."

"I was talking about Joanna," Nicholas ground out. "She has some harebrained notion about becoming a companion."

"Well, that is really the only suitable occupation open to her. She does not have enough education to be a governess, although she is certainly not the least bit stupid and could, given time, easily make up any deficiencies. But on the other hand, as attractive as she is, if she were to be employed in any household containing a young man, she would be forced to spend all her time fighting off unwelcome advances."

"But she does not *need* to find employment. I have said I will take care of her as if she were my own sister."

Miss Hepden smiled at him strangely. With a shock, Nicholas realized she was looking at him pityingly. It was beyond bearing—any more attempts on his part to reason with females would doubtless result in his being carried off to Bedlam.

What he needed was brandy—no, he was not going to let a woman drive him to drink. He needed a clear head if he was going to salvage something from this mess.

The hackney rumbled and bumped through the streets of London on its way to the General Post Office in Lombard Street, where the mail coach waited to carry Joanna far, far away from the man she loved.

That Nicholas did not love her was now perfectly obvious. After a few empty protests this morning, which he had clearly made only out of politeness, he had dropped all attempts to change her mind. Indeed, he had gone about his business almost as if he had already forgotten her. She had thought he would at least see her off—say good-bye—but that was left to Miss Hepden, who would herself on the morrow be departing for Colthurst Hall.

"Remember, do not allow strange men to strike up conversations with you, no matter how polite they seem. They should be able to tell by your clothing that you are respectable, even though you have no maid traveling with you, but some men consider unescorted women to be their natural prey."

Joanna nodded. Miss Hepden had been repeating the same motherly instructions over and over for the last several hours.

"And it will be best if you avoid eating heavy, greasy food along the way, since it is sure to make you queasy."

Joanna did not bother to point out that if the trip across the English Channel from Antwerp to Harwich had not bothered her stomach, it was doubtful anything would.

"And I hope you will find time occasionally after you are settled in Scotland to drop a line to me." Miss Hepden's usual tone of brisk instruction was now softened.

Reaching out for the older woman's hand, Joanna clung to it momentarily, then without knowing which of them had initiated it, they were embracing each other.

"Oh, Miss Hepden, of course I shall write to you. You have been so kind to me, I do not think I will ever forget your generosity."

"And of all the ladies I have served, I think you are truly the most deserving to be called a lady—except for her grace, of course," she added as an afterthought, lest Joanna think she was being disloyal to the duchess.

Sitting back and surreptitiously wiping her eyes, which were becoming suspiciously damp, Joanna felt obliged to protest. "How can you say such a thing about me? I am only the daughter of a naval officer, and I have none of the accomplishments of a true lady."

"The world may consider it necessary for a lady to splash watercolors about on a page and assault the ears of her visitors with her caterwauling, but as for me, I think a kind and generous heart is the mark of a true lady, and in all my years in service, I must tell you that I have met very few 'ladies' who deserve that title. In fact, other than her grace, the only one who comes to mind is Lady Letitia."

"You know Lady Letitia? Oh, was it you who . . . ?" Realizing the question she had been about to ask was impertinent, Joanna stopped, but Miss Hepden understood what was being asked, and she answered easily.

"You are wondering if I am the one who told Lady Letitia about Miss Dorinda being abducted? Yes, I did, which means I deliberately disobeyed the strict injunctions for secrecy that Mr. Goldsborough laid down. But then, I am not in his employ, and her grace, who is my employer, gave me orders also, before we left Colthurst Hall, and her instructions were that I was to keep Lady Letitia informed of everything that went forward during our stay in London, so that she might keep Miss Dorinda under her watchful eye also. As old as she is, Lady Letitia is not the least bit senile, and she can see clearly many things that other people never notice."

Can she? Joanna wanted to ask. But Lady Letitia appears to have been wrong about Nicholas. Showing him that I no longer need him in the capacity of a brother was supposed to make him realize he would actually prefer being my husband . . . but instead he appears to have jumped at the chance to wash his hands of my affairs.

All too soon the hackney arrived at Lombard Street, where the scene that met Joanna's eyes was more a nightmare than a dream. Coaches were loading everywhere, amid what appeared to her to be utter confusion. How easy it would be, she realized, to climb into the wrong coach and wake up tomorrow in Exeter instead of on the way to Edinburgh.

It was all she could do to resist the almost overwhelming urge to hang on to Miss Hepden's hand the way a small child clings to its mother—but she was not five years old, and she must put such childish ways behind her.

Seemingly unperturbed by the chaos around them, Miss Hepden gave the jarvey instructions for dealing with Joanna's baggage, then pressed a small purse into Joanna's hand.

"Just a little bit extra I have saved up. You will not wish to be without money of your own."

"Oh, but Lady Glengarry's man of affairs has already given me enough money for the journey."

"Be that as it may, you will find it much more pleasant when beginning a new position if you do not have to be asking for an advance on your salary every time you need to buy a few hairpins or a new handkerchief." So saying, she folded Joanna's hand tightly around the small purse. "I shall feel much better knowing you are not penniless,'' she added.

And I would feel a lot better if I had never agreed to Lady Letitia's plan, thought Joanna. How much better it would be if everything were back to normal and Dorie and I were dressing for an evening's entertainment, with Nicholas waiting impatiently below, calling up to us to hurry.

But such thoughts only served to make it harder to control her tears, which she did not want Miss Hepden to see. In any event, in the long run it would be better to discard foolish hopes rather than to continue dreaming absurd dreams.

Despite her best efforts to be brave, when she was instructed to board the small coach, she hung back just for a moment. Then, gathering her courage around her like a cloak, she moved forward with the rest of the passengers, and when her turn came, she climbed up the steps and seated herself in the proper corner marked on her ticket.

Without feeling any great interest, Joanna inspected her traveling companions. Across from her sat a young cavalry officer and two women whose resemblance to each other made it obvious they were mother and daughter—or perhaps merely aunt and niece. On the same side as Joanna, there was an empty seat in the middle, and the far corner was occupied by a man who appeared to be a wealthy merchant.

Then the door was thrust open again and a man climbed past her legs and took the last remaining seat. Joanna stared at him in amazement. Nicholas? But—

He did not look at her or in any way acknowledge her presence. He sat staring straight ahead, his face a wooden mask that betrayed not the slightest emotion—but his very presence on the mail coach said all that Joanna needed to hear.

All urge to cry immediately left her—indeed, it was all she could do to avoid laughing out loud. It would appear that Lady Letitia was not such a bad judge of men after all.

The driver cracked his whip, and precisely at eight o'clock the carriage lurched forward, beginning the journey north that would end more than forty-two hours later in Edinburgh.

Nicholas realized full well that Joanna was doubtless enraged by what he had done. If he knew anything about women, she was even now preparing to give him the proper set-down for having the presumption to book a seat beside her on the mail. Coward that he was, he was afraid to look at her and see just how much trouble he had gotten himself into.

Since all he wanted was to ensure her safety, her attitude was unfair to the extreme, especially after all the trouble he had taken to procure the seat beside her. Everything had been booked by the time he realized he absolutely could not consider permitting Joanna to travel without an escort.

Consequently he had wasted the entire day making inquiries and tracking down the original passenger, a sweet little old lady who had bargained like an experienced horse trader until in the end he had been forced to pay her quadruple the cost of her ticket to compensate her for the delay in her plans. Women, bah!

Unable to withstand the suspense any longer, he finally sneaked a peak at his unwilling companion. In the dim light it appeared she was . . . smiling at him? That couldn't be right. He turned his head and stared down at her, and she responded by tucking her arm through his and laying her head down on his shoulder.

It would appear that his understanding of women was woefully deficient.

How could a woman who had twice turned down his proposal of marriage now cuddle up against him as cozily and snugly as if she were a new bride setting off on a honeymoon with a beloved husband?

If, like Dorie, Joanna was determined on a course of independence, then why wasn't she berating him the way Dorie would have done under similar circumstances? Why wasn't she chastising him for his interference? Bawling him out for his presumption?

By the time he joined the other passengers in the land of nod, he had not come to any conclusions—or rather, he had reached only one, which was that he had nothing at all to gain by sitting in a jouncing, bouncing mail coach all the way to Scotland, where he would then only have to turn around and retrace the miles all the way back to London.

* * *

Joanna awoke gradually from a lovely dream in which Nicholas had held her close while vowing eternal love and devotion. To her dismay, she discovered that she had not dreamed he was embracing her. Somehow during the night she had ended up virtually sitting on Nicholas's lap. Hoping none of the other passengers had noticed, she surreptitiously extracted herself from his arms and hurriedly tried to straighten her clothing.

She felt herself still blushing when the carriage turned sharply into the courtyard of an inn and came to a stop. Immediately the door was opened and the steps let down. Then the coachman bellowed that they had forty minutes to break their fast in Grantham before the coach set forth again, and that they had better be prompt and keep their wits about them because the mails waited for no one.

There was an immediate scramble of passengers, pushing and shoving to be the first through the dooor, and automatically Joanna shrank back into her corner. Nicholas also avoided the general rush, and when they were alone, she dared peek at him.

He was unshaven, the stubble on his face appearing golden in the early-morning sun, and his hair was tousled. Other than that, he looked much better than anyone had a right to look after sleeping all night on the road.

Knowing how much he hated conversation before breakfast, she postponed the myriad of questions that sprang to her mind, such as exactly why he was so determined to look after her even after she had made it clear—or at least she *thought* she had made it clear—that she no longer needed the protection of a brother.

They were definitely not the kind of questions one wished to discuss in front of total strangers, nor the kind of question one should bludgeon a man with when he was still groggy from sleep.

So she decided when he helped her down from the carriage and escorted her into the George, she would postpone satisfying her curiosity a little longer, until . . . oh, dear, there would probably not be an opportunity to be private with

Nicholas until they reached Edinburgh . . . and perhaps not even there, since she would then have to assume her role of companion.

Really, Lady Letitia's plan had a great many weaknesses, in spite of the fact that she had assured Joanna that every possible contingency had been allowed for.

"I want to hire a private parlor," Nicholas growled beside her—not addressing her, of course, but the landlord, who immediately beckoned a maid to lead them up the stairs.

"But we have only—" Hurrying after him, Joanna started to remind him of the shortness of their stopover, but then she realized it would probably not take any longer to eat in private than it would to share the communal board in the common room.

Meekly she followed Nicholas to the room, which was a bit on the smallish side, but clean. The maid left them at once to fetch their food and, at Nicholas's order, a basin of water and some towels.

Nicholas immediately sat down in the largest chair, stretched his legs out in front of him, and appeared to fall asleep again. It was all Joanna could do not to shake him awake and demand he explain why, if he did not love her, he was going to so much trouble—why he was putting himself out to such a degree when he could be home sleeping much more comfortably in his own bed.

Lady Letitia had said such concern was a sign that Nicholas's affections were engaged, and she did appear to know everything . . . but then, some of the things she knew were merely the result of having people like Miss Hepden confide secrets to her. Lady Letitia was not actually omniscient. She could not, in fact, actually know what thoughts were in Nicholas's head—or what emotions were in his heart.

There was a light scratching at the door, and Joanna opened it for the maid, who brought in hot rolls, boiled eggs, and, most welcome of all, a steaming pot of tea.

Despite the bubbles of excitement and nervousness tickling her insides, Joanna discovered she had a hearty appetite, and the smells of hot bread were quite enticing.

Having had previous experience traveling with Nicholas, she made no attempt at small talk. He ate like a soldier—quickly and efficiently—but she was only halfway done with her meal when the maid returned to inform them that the passengers were now boarding.

Before Joanna could move, Nicholas grasped her wrist, easily holding her in place. "We are not going any farther," he growled, his mood clearly not improved by the breakfast. "I'll be damned if I'm going all the way to Scotland and back."

The maid, who had started clearing the table, now paused in her labors to stare at them with open curiosity. "Has you changed your mind about eloping, then?"

"We are not eloping," Joanna said firmly, trying unsuccessfully to peel Nicholas's fingers away from her arm. "I am going to Edinburgh to take up a position as companion to an elderly lady. This gentleman is merely tagging along—to what purpose, I have no idea."

Nicholas ignored her words and her efforts to extract herself from his grasp. Instead he spoke directly to the maid. "Do you see anything wrong with me that would cause a lady to hold me in disgust?"

"You, sir? Oh, no, sir, you're a proper fine one. No girl would turn down the likes of you."

"Well, this chit has. Told me twice point-blank she wouldn't marry me."

"Nicholas!" Joanna started to protest, but he ignored her completely.

"The first time I compromised her, she got hysterical when I informed her we would have to get married. Then yesterday when I said she would do better to marry me instead of dashing off to Scotland, she as much as told me she'd rather fetch and carry for an old lady than warm my bed."

Joanna was beyond speech—that he had the effrontery to speak so to a perfect stranger! The maid, however, was not so handicapped. She batted her eyes at Nicholas and smiled in a way that indicated she would be not only willing but also eager to "warm his bed."

"Oh, indeed, sir, it is beyond understanding."

Reaching the end of her patience, Joanna said, "Leave us!" in such sharp tones that the maid quickly picked up her tray and backed out of the room.

With a slight tug on her wrist, Nicholas pulled Joanna down onto his lap. "What are you going to do?" she asked, her voice no longer firm, but surprisingly high and squeaky.

"I'm going to do what I should have done months ago when I realized I loved you," he replied. Then, wrapping both arms around her, he kissed her thoroughly, the touch of his lips against hers holding her more firmly in place than if he had chained their wrists together.

When he finally released her, she made no effort to move off his lap. "When?" she asked softly, nuzzling her face down against his neck.

"When what?" he replied, a great deal of masculine satisfaction in his voice and a great deal of comfort in his hands, which were now stroking her back and tangling themselves in her hair, which had somehow come loose from its pins.

"When did you realize you loved me?"

There was a pause. "Not until Christmas," he finally replied. "But I hope you will excuse me for being so slow to know my own heart."

"I forgive you," she murmured.

"Good. Now, please explain why, loving me as you do, you turned down both my offers of marriage."

She pulled back enough that she could see his face. "I don't remember saying I loved you."

He grinned down at her. Yes, there was definitely a great deal of smug, self-satisfied complacency in his smile. "You told me when you kissed me," he said simply, and she was unable to contradict him, especially when he kissed her again and again and again, and each time she could not refrain from kissing him back.

Curled up in his arms, her head resting on his shoulder, she persisted in trying to make him see the error of his ways. "I have no moncy," she began, "and no family and no accomplishments. And I am not really beautiful, so you must realize you could do much better than me if you are wishful of finding a wife."

"To me you are the most beautiful woman in the world," Nicholas replied with laughter in his voice.

"I am serious," she replied, beginning to play with a button on his waistcoat. "You are so handsome and so well-connected, you could easily have any woman you wished, and there are so many young ladies who are prettier and cleverer and richer and—"

"And if you tell me there is anyone who has a kinder, more loving heart than you, then your tongue will fall out for uttering such a lie."

"But—"

"And if you tell me that anyone else loves me as much as you do, then I think that will be an even bigger lie."

Joanna felt herself blushing again.

"Well?" he asked. "Do you tell me I am wrong?"

Mutely she shook her head against his chest.

"Then will you do me the honor of marrying me? I must warn you that if you say no a third time, I shall probably sink into a decline, and then people will label you a heartless flirt."

"I only refused the first time because you made it so clear that you did not really *wish* to marry me."

"I was blind. You must allow for the fact that I am a mere male and therefore not as clear-sighted as you are. Do you forgive me?"

"Yes," she said, still feeling a wee bit bashful to be sitting on his lap—but quite unwilling to move an inch away from him.

"And will you marry me?"

"I would have accepted your second proposal with alacrity if you had only said you loved me, or even if you had said you were somewhat fond of me, or even if you had said you had grown used to having me around, or even—"

He interrupted her by kissing her—so thoroughly that when he finally finished she was too breathless to speak.

"Now," he said firmly, "without any more roundaboutations, answer my question. Will you marry me?"

She started to reply, but with a smile he clamped his hand over her mouth. "No, allowing you to talk has proved too risky. Simply nod your head if you agree to marry me."

She nodded her head.

"And we shall be married in St. George's by special license as soon as we return to London. Nod if you agree."

She shook her head.

"What? You cannot possibly prefer eloping to Scotland?"

Shaking her head, she began to chuckle—or at least it would have been a chuckle if he had not been holding his hand over her mouth.

"Then what? Why? Oh, the devil, I suppose I cannot expect to keep you mute the rest of our lives." Removing his hand, he said with resignation, "So tell me all your objections, and I shall attempt to counter each and every one."

"I have only one," she said meekly.

"And that is?"

"Except for the dress I am wearing, every stitch of clothing I own is on its way to Scotland, and I refuse to be married in a gown I have been sleeping in."

"If that is all," he said with a lazy smile that tickled her insides and made her toes curl, "then you will be happy to know that I am acquainted with a modiste who can supply gowns of any size at a moment's notice."